PAWNS OF SALISTYA

THE QUEENDOM SERIES

H J BOGUE

Dear Melody Lane Little Library Reader,
This book has teleported from the Fyriane
archives and landed at Melody Lane, Reno, Nevada.
As the Goddess wills it, fate has placed this
in your hands. Welcome to Fyriane.

First published by Busybird Publishing 2024

ISBN:
Paperback: 978-1-923216-20-4
Ebook: 978-1-923216-21-1

Cover image: Joshua Griffin

Cover design: Joshua Griffin

Layout and typesetting: Busybird Publishing

Busybird Publishing
2/118 Para Road
Montmorency, Victoria
Australia 3094
www.busybird.com.au

This book is dedicated to the paths they don't tell you about. The part where you hit a fork in the road, where you're conditioned to believe there are only a couple of options.

But they don't tell you about the other paths. The ones you carve out for yourself.

I hope you walk down that newly created path, fiercely, with your head held high.

THE QUEENDOM SERIES

Queendom of Salistya (Sah-list-ee-ya)

Amire (A-meer)
A member of Valare's Sol – Mazyr's twin sister.

Bastra (Bas-tra)
Slaviya's Second.

Dwyla (Dwy-lah)
Heir to the Salistyan throne – Valare and Slaviya's sister.

Mazyr (Ma-zeer)
A member of Valare's Sol – Amire's twin brother.

Meredith (Mer-e-dith)
A member of Valare's Sol – Valare's best friend and maid in Arlom.

Rynelle (Rye-nell)
A member of Valare's Sol – an attendant in Arlom.

Slaviya (Sla-vee-ya)
Queen of Salistya – Valare and Dwyla's sister.

Varqel (Var-quel)
Head trainer and army general in the Solista Isles – father figure to Valare.

Kingdom of Arlom (Ar-lom)

Eliasson (Ee-lee-a-son)
King of Arlom – Valare's husband and Tarn's brother.

Fyrel (Fuh-relle)
Eliasson's Second.

Tarn (Tar-n)
Heir to the Arlom throne – Eliasson's brother.

Valare (Va-lair)
Queen of Arlom, formerly the heir to the Salistyan throne – Eliasson's wife and sister to Dwyla and Slaviya.

Queendom of Nyarelle (Nyah-rell)

Lyzia (Lyz-ee-ah)
Affiliated to Salistya via marriage to Varqel – head healer of the Solista Isles.

Qynthia (Kwin-thee-ah)
Queen of Nyarelle.

Ramone (Rah-moan)
Qynthia's Second.

Kingdom of Marlyst (Mar-list)

Orlandia (Or-lan-di-ah)
Xylan's Second – Xylan's twin sister.

Xylan (Zai-lan)
King of Marlyst – Orlandia's twin brother.

Other Terms

Areeya (Ah–ree–ya)
Wystia's mother.

Fyriane (Fire–ee–ahn)
The continent housing the Kingdoms and Queendoms.

Kryol (Kree–yowl)
Merlot's father.

Merlot (Mer–low)
A God recognised by Marlyst and Nyarelle.

Ophiscair (Off–is–care) Prophecy
The name of the prophecy the Solistan religion is based on.

Solista Isles (Sol–is–ta Isles)
Under Salistyan rule, the Isles are the training grounds for
physical mages.

Strahn (Strah–n)
Wystia's sire.

Svaxlyn (Ss–vax–lin) Pact
An agreement made centuries ago between unknown characters
and Wystia and Merlot.

Thais (Tah–ees)
Merlot's mother.

Wystia (Wis–tee–ah)
A Goddess recognised by the Arlomans, Salistyans and Solistans.

Before you enter the Fyriane continent

*This book contains sexually explicit content,
crude language and themes of abasement
and emotional abuse i.e. gaslighting.*

It also contains mention of forced pregnancy off-page.

Enter at your own risk.

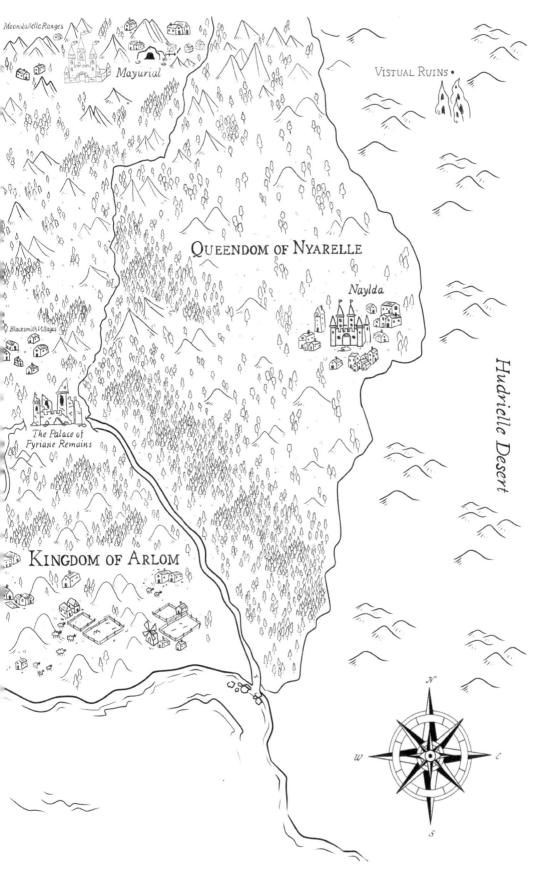

CHAPTER 1

'You're awfully quiet tonight, Valare. Do I need to be concerned?' Eliasson drawled as he directed his ocean-blue gaze straight to mine.

Feigning shock, I reached my left hand out to run teasingly down Eliasson's side, stopping at mid-thigh. 'You say this like I'm not a demure, introverted, compliant wife all the time, husband.'

'Because you're not,' Eliasson shot back, pushing my hand away. Despite his tone and actions, I didn't miss the way he momentarily softened at my touch. 'I can see that mind working and it can only mean you are devising a plan for Goddess knows what. I'm not in the mood, Valare. Do not push me tonight.'

Funny that, I also am not in the mood tonight.

I took a deep breath. 'Let's put my uncharacteristic nature this evening down to the approaching new moon and beautiful wine, shall we?'

Batting my eyelashes, I downed my glass of wine and held it out to be filled in the next instant. It paid off to spend time training the attendants in what I deemed a high priority service.

Eliasson threw me a sidewards glance but was unable to hide his amusement. With a shake of his head, he returned to his own meal without comment.

His judgement for my love of the fruit of the vine added to my already quiet mood. He wasn't wrong; my being quiet is cause for concern. Usually. But tonight, my mood had nothing to do with scheming and everything to do with a little thing called nostalgia.

In the year of my being married to the King of Arlom, I can count on one hand the number of times I had allowed myself to get lost in contemplation in his presence. I don't usually allow him the luxury of seeing any part of my mental armour cracking.

But this day would always be one that slightly revealed those cracks. Because on this day, two years ago, I received the decree ordering my marriage to King Eliasson Arlom.

With her decree, my sister, Queen Slaviya of the Queendom of Salistya, ripped my world and heart apart when she ordered me to take her place, stepping into my royal duties and marrying the King of Arlom. As only third in line to the Salistyan throne behind my parents and two older siblings, I had been expecting a peaceful life with minimal responsibilities. But things changed and my role irrevocably altered to be part of a union that ceased the never-ending fight for the highly coveted Solista Isles, which was under the Salistyan rule.

A deep yearning stirred in the core of my being as I thought of the Solista Isles. My home. My now forbidden love.

Shutting down my thoughts, I attempted to distract myself by looking around the intimate dining room in the Royal Quarters. After taking in the trademark blue walls of the Kingdom of Arlom, I turned attention to the attendants, half of those being my staff from the Solista Isles and the other half being Eliasson's. The former were obvious with their mossy green eyes and olive skin, while the Arloman staff had the well-known ocean-blue eyes and fair skin.

As I looked at my spouse sitting at the six-seater dining table finishing up his dinner, I thought for the millionth time that I really could've done far worse. Any girl would be lucky to call a lean, six-foot tall man with a heart-shaped youthful face their husband. On top of that, Eliasson had sun-kissed blonde hair which normally finished a little higher than his shoulders. Currently it was tied at the nape of his neck. Knowing this was my favourite hairstyle on him, I would place a hefty amount of gold that he'd done this on purpose, with the purpose being to send a very loud message of 'down to fuck' to me.

At the moment Eliasson finished his dinner, he pushed his chair slightly away from the table, and placed his hands on his lap. His blue eyes met mine, an unwavering, expectant look on his face – yeah, definitely down to fuck.

Who was I to say no?

'Dinner was lovely as always, my King. I will take my leave to prepare for the rest of our evening,' I purred. Not one to miss an opportunity to enjoy the small delights of the world, I finished the rest of my wine before standing and made my way behind Eliasson to the door to my private quarters.

Just before shutting the door, Eliasson said my name as a command, making me stop and turn around.

'Yes, Eliasson?'

'Wear something white. I want to relive our wedding night.' No room for argument. He didn't even bother turning around to face me. He wasn't kidding when he said he didn't want to be pushed tonight. I've rarely seen him this upset, but he'd been acting strange ever since he returned from a meeting earlier this evening.

In a perfect world I would reply with a snarky 'Sir, yes sir' and army salute. Instead, I settled for rolling my eyes as I stared at the back of his head. 'As you wish, husband.'

Closing the door, I let a huge breath out before rushing to freshen up, my bath having already been fixed for the night. Bless Meredith.

Making quick work of bathing myself, I hurried to the closet, not wanting to keep Eliasson waiting. Patience was not his strong suit. Not when he was in this kind of mood. I picked out a simple, yet sexy white silk slip with light lace detailing around the chest that fell to mid-thigh – sans bra and underwear. I aim to please.

Placing my long, dark hair in a bun on top of my head, I gave myself a once over in the mirror. With my Salistyan skin tone, white was a complementary colour on me. While in my younger years I had mossy green eyes, upon inheriting my magical gifts at the age of sixteen, my eyes had turned a sharp lime green colour. Having been the only known Salistyan (or Solistan, because there is a difference) to have this reaction, a lot of eyebrows had been raised in the Solistan community. Nevertheless, pairing my looks with my hourglass figure, generous breasts and behind, I was looking quite tasty in this outfit, if I did say so myself.

Making my way out of my room and across to the dining room, I knocked on the door to Eliasson's quarters.

'Come in.'

Before I could even close the door, Eliasson had me in his arms. He cupped my cheek and kissed me softly, a flash of approval glinting in his eyes when he caught sight of my attire.

'Does my clothing choice please you, husband?' I purred as I pulled away and spun slowly, calling upon my rigorous training in the art of seduction. My years on the Solista Isles had prepared me for every eventuality.

'You know it does, wife. Come here, I fancy making love to you tonight. Just like our wedding night last year.'

Ugh. Making love. If only he knew this wasn't my favourite approach to sex, yet it was the most powerful way of luring him into my façade of a devoted wife.

Sauntering past him and laying back on the bed, I leant up on my elbows, smirking. Beckoning him forward with a nod, I replied, 'As you wish, my King.'

Without missing a beat, he moved towards me. The clear passion in his eyes almost made me feel bad. Almost.

Unfortunately for King Eliasson I had had extensive training that allowed me to ensure his love for me, which was critical to fulfilling my mission. Unfortunately this mission involved him, but not in a way he would appreciate. Unfortunately for King Eliasson, I was sent to kill him.

CHAPTER 2

T he gentle, humid breeze was a welcome feeling over my bikini-clad body. I knew it must have come from the south-west because I would recognise that feeling of the Solista Isles, my chosen home, anywhere.

At the same moment, I reminded myself that I needed to stop dwelling on the past. It wasn't going to appease the constant homesickness I experienced. In fact, it only seemed to make it worse, building my irritation at the situation I was in.

Sighing, I returned to reading my book – my happy escape where reality doesn't matter, and where the political pawns and games aren't real. Ever since my marriage, these games had become my harsh reality. But, at least I could live vicariously through the political pawns in this book having interesting sex. I would happily have that as my reality over my recent 'making love' escapades with the sappiest king to have ever lived.

Before I drowned further in my frustration and self-pity, I sensed the physical presence of a five-foot-five woman approaching. Luckily for her, I was quite partial to her, otherwise this encounter would not end well. No one is allowed on my slice of ocean paradise unless I say so. A wedding gift from Eliasson, this is my oasis, and I came here for space.

Feet stopping just out of reach on my left, Meredith unceremoniously dropped her slim yet powerful build into the beach chair beside mine.

'Is it all organised for tonight?' I asked.

'Yes, Valare.'

'Thank the Goddess,' I said, releasing breath I wasn't aware I had been holding.

'It has been some time, Valare. The people are eager for your return.'

'I know, Mer, I know. I'm eager to return too. You know if I had it my way I would've never left.'

'I know that, Val. The Solistan people know that too. But, this is bigger than all of us.' Mer's tone notably softened.

'Bigger than all of us,' I muttered. 'Isn't that just the story of my fucking life? Ironic really considering I am a queen. How is it still bigger than me? I rule a kingdom, Mer. A quarter of the Fyriane continent. I am by birthright a Salistyan royal. I am tired of being a pawn in all of this mess. I was raised to fight, to use my magic gifted by the Goddess Wystia. Not use my body to 'make love' with a king who is too smitten to realise what is going on right under his nose.'

'You're not simply collateral damage in all of this, Valare, and you know it. Need I remind you of your tendency for these outbursts?

What you are like when the illusion of what you thought your life in the Solista Isles was going to be like enters your mind again? It's been two years, Val. You're a queen and have your part to play. Not to mention you're the most powerful mage alive. Instead of complaining, put your big queen boots on and start playing the game a little better, like we all are. Hell, I've had to learn how to be your fucking maid. And Mazyr is a cook for Goddess' sake.'

Even without looking, I felt her grimace.

'You know I love you,' she continued. 'But you have no idea the amount of shit I get from the Solistans back home. 'Meredith, lethally trained Solistan assassin and right-hand to the most powerful Salistyan, now acting as a maid to said powerful Salistyan, more commonly known as the Queen of Arlom.' We both have our crosses to bear here, girl. I've got over mine.'

I shot her a doubtful look, and she screwed up her nose, flicking her straight, shoulder-length brunette hair away from her face. 'Okay, mostly I've got over mine. The sooner you can get over yours, the sooner we can be done with the first move. Here's to hoping Slaviya will finally tell us what the next steps are. It's annoying being kept in the dark.'

The first move, how could I forget: kill the King of Arlom. It was the first of a series of predetermined power plays set into motion by my father years ago. At the time it didn't affect me as I was never supposed to be involved. Hell, I hadn't even known that there were ulterior motives at play. I was mindlessly living my best life on the Isles, blissfully unaware of the games behind the scenes. That all changed when my parents, the Queen and King of Salistya, and my brother, the heir to the throne, passed away in a shock accident. That was the point my life changed forever.

Their sudden deaths brought utter chaos to Salistya, followed by a swift coronation of my older sister, Slaviya Salistya. Since no crowned king or queen can wed another Dom's royal in order to keep the equilibrium between the Doms of Fyriane, her then impending nuptials to King Eliasson were brought to a quick end.

On the surface, the union was a political move to strengthen ties, as the Queendom of Salistya and Kingdom of Arlom had been left vulnerable in the face of the historically strong relationship between the Kingdom of Marlyst and Queendom of Nyarelle. The recent death of the Marlyst King had brought into question whether this relationship would be maintained with Qynthia Nyarelle, Nyarelle's Queen. The deaths of monarchs were a notoriously unstable time and had even been known to upend traditionally held relationships.

In the mix of changes as well was the attempt to at least share the Solista Isles between Arlom and Salistya despite the Queendom having refused to give up control of them for centuries. It had long been a source of contention, which made it all the more interesting that Slaviya had gone ahead with this. I couldn't help but wonder why she would continue with Father's plans. It was frustrating, though unsurprising, that she refused to reveal her intentions – sharing was not her strong suit. I just hoped that it would have nothing to do with our little sister, Dwyla, who was currently in the middle of her own Solistan training.

'It'll be interesting to see how the Arloman trainees are settling in,' I mused, following that train of thought.

Meredith quirked a brow in question.

'Think about it,' I explained. 'We were raised knowing that when we turned fourteen, we would move to the Isles and undergo the rigorous training of the Solistan forces. In some ways knowing that prepared us for those first two years of combat. But the Arlomans? Sure, they underwent their own, less extensive, training. But magic? It's been kept from them. No one outside of Salistya and the Solista Isles knows the secrets of the Isles and that they are the real reason Salistyan's are exceptional warriors.'

Meredith nodded, pondering. 'It's pretty wild to think that Salistya has been able to keep this secret under wraps. Goddess knows how they managed to do that. I don't really see the point of it.' A born Solistan, Mer, much like the other Solistans, struggled to understand why Salistya functioned the way it did, having never been to Salistya to experience it herself.

'Neither,' I agreed. 'Secrets always come out in the end, one way or another. I'd like to think Slaviya's push for mine and Eliasson's union was to right the wrongs of our ancestors, to give back the gift of magic that had been taken from Arlom. But that would be giving her too much credit. She doesn't think of anyone but herself.'

She hummed in agreement. 'I've checked on the training from time to time. There's a clear divide between the Arloman trainees and the Salistyan trainees. The Solistan-born trainees have been more welcoming towards the Arlomans, which is to be expected. We are a welcoming bunch, after all,' Meredith teased, knowing I'd always been envious of her Solistan heritage. Where Salistyans tended towards mistrust and secrecy, Solistans were more open and accepting of the other Doms.

'I hear what you're saying, though,' she continued. 'I remember when I received my magic. The new moon fell two days after my sixteenth birthday and the process was chaos. There were about twenty of us being herded like cattle, Solistan trainers teleporting in and out to take us to the Temple. I was equally scared and excited. Nothing can prepare you for that. But, at least I knew what was going to happen. But you're right, the Arlomans don't. The minute they landed on the Isles, their world would've turned upside down.'

I could only imagine the shock of the first Arloman trainees when, on the first new moon after their sixteenth birthday, the Goddess Wystia gifted the trainee her magic in the form of enhanced physical capabilities and an affinity to one or two elements. I didn't even know if they had been told that they would spend the next three years on the Solista Isles honing their magic, becoming acquainted with their heightened senses, supernatural strength, ability to physically control another and detect physical presences. Throw in an affinity and ability to work with fire, air, water or earth, and it would have been a shock to the system.

As time went on, the best and brightest who showed an affinity for two elements would be swiftly identified and trained elsewhere to become assassins for the royals – known as Sol – much like Meredith and myself. Normally when they graduated, they either enlisted in the army back in Savast, Salistya's capital, or stayed on the Solista Isles. All along knowing the royals had the right to order their move back to Salistya at any time, and that was only if their decision to stay was respected. Often, their decision was rejected, especially with women and unlucky men who favoured only one of the elements. They were sent straight to the breeding programs, ensuring the continuity of Salistya's army for the next generations. As a result, a lot of people didn't actually get a choice.

I had planned to stay back, marry the love of my life, embark on confidential missions, and live my life on the Solista Isles. I was one week from finishing my training when my parents and brother died. A year later, I was married to Eliasson in place of Slaviya.

And now here I am, the day after our first wedding anniversary. Looking back now, I could see how naïve I was to think being third in line meant I could essentially avoid any form of royal duties. But at least today had been turned into a holiday for Arlom, which meant I could spend the whole day by the ocean whilst Eliasson was away for the night on a hunting trip. Translation: I'm able to leave for the Isles as soon as the sun sets. Home sweet home.

'Copper for your thoughts?' Mer asked, interrupting my reverie. But then she hesitated, looking at me. 'Actually no, don't tell me if it's a continuation of your wallowing. I should be the one wallowing having to listen to your late-night antics last night after not getting laid in forever'.

Rolling my eyes, I retorted, 'Forever? Please. I know you and Eliasson's second-in-command got it on not four nights ago. From the way Mazyr was talking, your satisfaction level screamed a five-star rating.'

'That little gossipy shit,' Mer muttered, throwing her water bottle in the sand. 'I'm just doing my duty in creating strong connections with our allies.' She threw me a wink. 'And four days is forever, Val,' she added as an afterthought.

I burst out laughing. Trust a mage to say that. We were sensual by nature and had specific needs that required regular fulfillment. Because of these needs, it wasn't abnormal for a mage to have multiple partners.

'Now, now, Mer, don't be too upset with him. He was trying to make me feel better that one of our own was having a raunchy time. It may have just come at the cost of your privacy. But let's not forget the barracks on the Isles. There was no privacy there, nor any shame.'

'We were fourteen and had just found independence out of home, Val. Totally different,' Meredith shot back.

'Hmmm, perspective is a beautiful thing, isn't it?' I teased, before soberly continuing, 'Sex is sex, Mer. Whether you're male or female, whether you like doing it with a male or female. Hell, why not both? Either way, there's no need to be embarrassed or ashamed. It's a normal part of life, so good on you for having a good time and going after what you want. I shall live vicariously through you having settled down into my wise, married age.' I may or may not have attempted and failed to sound serious at the 'wise, married age' part.

Mer rolled her eyes. 'You're almost twenty-one, Val. Not sixty. Plus, we all know you have the capacity to get a little side bang occasionally.' Raising her voice before I could interrupt, Mer continued, 'And don't you even try lying to me. I know that half the reason you're going to the Isles tonight is to have a little rendezvous with lover boy, away from watchful eyes.'

Releasing a breath, I remained quiet. Not because I wanted silence to convey that she was right, but rather the current state of my sexual deprivation was so dire that the word rendezvous was enough to stir some serious emotions inside of me. In a certain region. Down below. Eliasson and his want to make love alone was just not cutting it for me.

'Speaking of rendezvous, though, I need to take my contraceptive remedy. Goddess forbid I'm with an Arlom heir.' I pulled a face.

Watching the sun slowly sink towards the horizon, I realised it was time to go. I had a home to visit. I stood up and reached my hand down to help Mer up. Our hands stayed intertwined as we walked up the beach back to the royal apartments.

Before we were in earshot of Arlomans inside, Meredith halted my movements. I raised an eyebrow in question.

'I know this time of year is difficult for you, Val. I want you to enjoy yourself on the Isles tonight, forget all your worries,' Meredith stated. A sincere look crossed her face for a split second before the face of a trained Solistan assassin took over.

'But when you come back, our Sol needs to plan how we will execute the first step,' she continued. 'It has been a year already and some Arlomans have been gifted their magic on the Isles. We can only hold off correspondence with their parents for so long. The secrets of the Isles can't be released, not until he's taken care of and the Kingdom of Arlom is under your reign. Your sister is becoming restless, and

13

we all know that avoiding the Queen of Salistya's outbursts, for lack of a better description, is in everyone's best interests. Including yours. Push comes to shove, despite their loyalty with Salistya and Slaviya as their official ruler, the Solistans have always seen you as their rightful heir. You have trained with us, laughed with us, and fought with us. It's time to play the game and avoid a conflict that would put the Isles in the middle. You owe them that and you know the time is upon us.'

I wished there was a way to get out of this mission. To reverse time and stay far away from it all. But there was no going back. Once a mission was assigned, no other Salistyan could touch the target. Once a mission was underway, there was no backing out of it. The price of interference or aborting a mission was death.

Turning to her, knowing my own face was that of a trained assassin, I said, 'I know, Mer. It will be done.'

She gazed intently at me, trying to see Goddess knows what. After a moment, apparently happy with what she saw, she nodded, kissed her three middle fingers, placed them on her chest and bowed as a sign of respect in the presence of royalty. But we both knew she wouldn't have bothered with that had there not been guards watching our every move. 'For the Goddess Wystia, and the Queendom of Salistya.'

Kissing my three middle fingers, I placed them to the middle of my brow, the third eye of Wystia. 'Protect our family,' I finished.

Meredith straightened her back. 'I'll see you in an hour, Val.'

Nodding, I resumed my path to the royal apartments as she went the other way, ignoring the guards surrounding the outskirts. I headed straight past the living area, up the stairs and into my sanctuary.

I loved my quarters. It was a place that I could call my own in this foreign kingdom. I had gone for a minimalist coastal aesthetic when decorating my space. A bed, a separate day bed, and bedside tables with ocean blue cushions and decorations, which made the light weathered-wood furnishings pop, filled the room. Of course, I had also insisted on some tropical indoor plants, to acknowledge my ties to the Isles. They help keep me grounded and connected to home. I loved laying in my bed, looking out the glass doors that led to my personal balcony. The natural light of the sun when it was setting landed perfectly in my room. It was one of the small yet magical moments in life that I soaked up as much as I could.

The only thing that rivalled my love for that sight was the closet next to the balcony. My wardrobe was filled to the brim with everything a girl could ever want. Sometimes it wasn't all bad being a royal. Granted, those times were highly infrequent, but they were there.

Walking past my bed, I stepped out onto the balcony to enjoy the sunset and the last of the south-westerly breeze. Butterflies swarmed in my stomach as I allowed in the excitement for my upcoming trip to the Isles. I would've loved to have gone first thing this morning once Eliasson had disentangled himself from his bed, but I had to restrain myself. Our marriage may have solidified a political union, but Eliasson didn't confuse lusting after me with trusting me completely. I always had guards on me, and knowing what I know, I guess I couldn't blame him, though it was highly inconvenient, frustrating, and annoying – the list went on.

It left me in a less than ideal situation; forcing myself to be out and about in Arlom's capital city, Amarald, so as not to raise any suspicions by disappearing from sight whenever I wanted. However, when night came, no suspicions were ever raised as I mostly had them to myself. From the minute I had stepped foot in the kingdom, Eliasson knew where I stood regarding night-time events, such as dinners and balls, namely that they were to be limited unless critical. The definition of critical had to be heavily negotiated, but I managed to get it to unavoidable Dom events, including visits and Forums with the royals of the other Doms.

It wasn't that I didn't enjoy being out and about at night – in the Solista Isles this was a very common way of living – but I needed to provide myself an opportunity to explore Arlom and return home frequently undetected. Also, sometimes a girl just needed some time to herself. For me, this time is needed every day. Some may say I was anti-social, but I called it self-care. And maybe I was a tad selective as to who I spent my time with outside of royal obligations, but people were exhausting.

With a final, longing glance as the sun disappeared for the day, I left the balcony and headed towards my bed. Mer had laid out a pair of casual high-waisted moss green culottes and a cropped t-shirt that fell just below my chest, revealing a sliver of my stomach. It was a strategic pairing by Mer. The Queendom of Salistya's royal colour was moss green, so it was always wise that, as the Queen of Arlom, I showed up to the Isles in an outfit reflecting my origins. Even knowing where the Solistan loyalties lay, it's wise to never assume I had unequivocal support as the most powerful mage in Fyriane. I may have despised my father and his hideous lessons growing up, but if there was one thing I took away from them, it was to not trust anyone. 'Everyone has their own motives,' he would say, 'spies are around every corner you turn, and when you think you can trust someone? That's when you can't.'

Now, I wouldn't say I didn't trust anyone, but I damn well made it difficult for others to earn it. If my own sister, my own blood, could fuck me over by taking me away from the love of my life and completely changing my life course, why wouldn't someone else try? So, my outfit was just another way of reaffirming my loyalties.

A voice interrupted my thoughts, becoming increasingly louder the closer it got to my door.

'Now, I don't want anyone disturbing us tonight. It will be a tradition for the Queen and I to have a girl's night on this holiday. Anyone who does disturb us is subject to the Queen's wrath. Do you hear me?' Silence reined before a confident, 'Good', ended what appeared to be a one-sided conversation held by Meredith.

A single knock was the only warning I had before Meredith hurried into the room holding two bottles of champagne and glasses. Clearly, she was ready for her party for one – I didn't envy future Meredith and her hangover. It's lucky that problem was strongly sitting in the 'her issue' category.

Shutting the door before any guards could see my clothing, Meredith not-so-gracefully plopped herself onto the daybed.

'So,' Meredith started, blinking innocently at me, 'Since you're getting your rocks off tonight, I'm hoping you left one of your fabulous books for me? You know, of the erotic kind. Guy chases girl, girl denies him, he fights harder to win her over, she eventually gives in, sexy times occur and all that good stuff.'

Huffing out a laugh, I finished putting on my sandals and straightened up. 'Left bedside table, bottom draw.'

'Oh, you're a doll.' Eyes lighting up like they had the one time she had won a card game against our friend, and fellow Sol member, Rynelle, Meredith raced over to the bedside table.

'And you're a deviant. You know the rules: bath water flowing so no one can hear that it's just you having a drunken erotic party for one; stay away from the balcony; and you're restricted to the daybed for your evening activities,' I stated absently as I gave myself a quick once over in the mirror. I have, in fact, gone through the rules routine too many times to count. We had established early on that the best way to ensure my visits home weren't discovered was to pretend that Mer and I were having a night in together. Sure it looked odd being she was meant to be my maid, but so far the Arlomans had chalked it up to being a weird Salistyan thing.

Meredith rolled her eyes. 'Yes, Mum. Gosh you used to be fun. This is how I know you need alone time with him. How long has it been anyway? Two months?'

'I stopped counting when it became depressing,' I muttered.

Lying back on the daybed with the fabulous book in hand, Meredith opened a champagne bottle. Deciding to completely forego the glass, she took a massive swig straight from the bottle. It reminded me of the fourteen-year-old girl I met all those years ago, a complete juxtaposition from the lethal assassin she had become.

After chugging what looked like a good quarter of the bottle, Meredith looked up. 'Alright, get your sexy ass out of here. Everything is under control, and I'm two seconds away from finding the best parts of this book and having a good old time. I know it hasn't been that long since we were in the barracks, but I'd like to think we've moved past sharing common spaces for moments such as these. But if you want to take a trip down memory lane, be my guest and take a seat.' With a wink, Meredith proceeded to open the book.

'Thanks, Mer, I'll see you in the morning just before the sun rises.'

Before turning to leave, I couldn't help but add some snide to my goodbye. 'Oh, and Mer?' I said innocently.

'Mmm?' She didn't even look up, too engrossed in finding all the good stuff.

'Remember; you're my maid and must clean all the sheets tomorrow. If there's shit out of place, you can count on all your gold that I will spontaneously decide all areas of my royal quarters need a deep clean.' I smirked.

Looking up with an expression on her face that promised revenge, Mer grabbed the champagne bottle and was about to throw it directly at me. 'You little …' but I was faster. Saying a quick, 'Love you,' I was still laughing as I swiftly teleported out of the room and straight to my real home.

CHAPTER 3

Muggy air enveloped me immediately and a relieved breath of air escaped from my body. I had landed at the same spot I always did when teleporting to the Isles, in the heart of the Temple of Wystia. While other mages teleporting from the mainland to the Isles had to arrive just outside the Temple, I had the luxury of skipping the ten-minute walk to reach this spot. Even after receiving their gifts, mages were unable to access them inside the Temple, meaning physical presences couldn't be detected and teleportation straight here wasn't possible. Inside the Temple. I was the only mage able to use my gifts, I suspected likely due to my strength. Not that there was a lot of action to be had here as it was a place for worship, not warfare.

Every morning, the Solistan's gathered here to pray, to acknowledge the Goddess Wystia and to give thanks for their gifts. As a trainee, I was forced to come here with everyone else and follow this ritual. Sure, I was thankful for my magic, but did I really need to worship the Goddess *every* day to show my gratitude? I wasn't sold on the notion then, and I still wasn't now.

The centre of the Temple hadn't changed at all since the first time I saw it. The large room looked like an amphitheatre, with a flat, central area enveloped within an ascending circular rock formation that acted as seats. They were able to hold up to three hundred people, which was a bit excessive, really, considering when I was gifted my magic there was a total of five people bearing witness to it, none of whom were trainees. It was the second new moon that month, a rare occurrence. The Solistans called it a black moon, and I was the only one who received gifts under that new moon, having been the only trainee to turn sixteen in time.

Raising my eyes, I took in the looming statue of Wystia in the centre of the large room. I might not buy into the frequency of worshipping, but there were Solistan customs that I did follow. I kneeled, kissed my three middle fingers and placed them on the foot of the statue. 'For the doers, the defenders, and the dreamers. To the devoted, the divisive, and the divine.' I stood, bowing my head and moved my fingers to my chest. 'For the Goddess Wystia, and the Queendom of Salistya.' Lifting my head, my eyes closed, I placed my middle fingers on my third eye. 'Protect our family.'

I felt a surge of power run through me from where my fingers were placed on my third eye. Time stopped, the power holding my body upright, while showing me a vision of bright, fuchsia eyes and the outline of a body that was undoubtedly male. The rest of the vision was dark and the man stood completely still, staring straight at me so it was impossible to distinguish any further, notable features.

When I was gifted my magic, I developed what I've named my 'knowing'. It told me when someone was lying, diverting my attention away from a particular course if it didn't serve me, or warned me against betrayal. It wasn't active at all times like my physical senses, which I learnt to shut on and off during training on the Isles. Instead, I could generally call upon it when required. But sometimes, like now when I felt a caress in my mind, as though someone was asking to come in, my knowing kicked in unexpectedly, letting down a mental guard I wasn't aware was up.

I saw another flash of the fuchsia eyes, this time with a gleam of satisfaction in them. Before I could speak, a force pushed my eyes open. I was still standing at the foot of the statue, fingers placed to my third eye. Removing them from my brow, the surge of power I felt seemed to move, rippling up and down my neck before settling on the triangular Royal Mark below my ear in a humming, soothingly warm pulse.

The Royal Marks, much like a tattoo, were present from birth on every person in a royal family. Where the Salistyan's was a triangular shape pointing to the back of the body, the Nyarellean royals bore the same pattern pointing to the front. The Arlom Kingdom's was a line curving up at the ends, while the Marlyst's mark was the opposite with the line curving down. I'd never understood the origin of these marks, or how they came to be. All I knew was that each Dom's was unique.

I took a step back from the statue, shook my arms and looked around. Nothing was out of place, no Mazyr or Rynelle around pulling a prank on me. But I didn't need that confirmation to know my mind wasn't playing tricks on me. I still felt the power humming below my ear, feeling like a gateway had been opened in my mind.

The question was, if a gateway had been opened, what was on the other side?

I teleported off the island as soon as I was outside the Temple and landed straight in the heart of Senora on the western-most Isle. Housing almost the entire Solistan population, Senora's location out west, far from the eyes of the rest of the continent, made it the perfect place to train and mould magic.

Looking around the town centre, which was marked by another statue of the Goddess, nothing had changed. There were five main cobblestoned streets that branched off the circular centre of the town. Several streets had a mixture of shops and residential houses spanning as far as the eye could see. Another street that led to the botanical gardens, which also held the Royal House used for royal visits, was on the other side of the town centre. Given that I had trained on the Isles and visited as often as possible, I had created a home for myself elsewhere so tended to stay away from the Royal House unless it benefited any secret meetings I may have had.

I walked up one of the streets that housed some shops, ignoring the awed stares of the crowds. I'd had nearly five years of becoming accustomed to people gawking at my lime green eyes. I had stopped being embarrassed by the way the Solistans spoke to me reverently, courteously stepping out of my way with a bow as I walked past. I figured they were free to believe the weird religious prophecy that prompted their stares. Just like I was free to never acknowledge it.

I grinned as I was engulfed by a dozen children yelling, 'Queen Valare, it's Queen Valare!' I smiled and played with the children, submitting to their demands to be thrown in the air – their parents looked on with a mix of terror and veneration at witnessing my unique magic. At one point, I had seven children up in the air spinning around in circles, while another five were hovering against the wall, air tickling their stomachs, eliciting cheerful giggles from them all.

These kids were around the age of ten, about the time where the call for magic would start to stir. It was at this stage that the children tended to act up and could be quite a handful for parents. For this reason, I started walking away, winking to the parents as the children began to cry that I was leaving them there forever. Pausing, I turned around to ask them, 'Will you promise to be well-behaved for your parents and try your hardest at school?' I chuckled when a resounding, 'Yes, Queen Valare!' came from all twelve children's mouths not a second later.

'Alright, if anyone breaks their promise to me, I will know about it.' I tried my hardest to adopt a menacing look as I brought the children back down to the ground, waiting for them to be steady on their feet before releasing my magic. And because I was a soft-hearted fool and felt bad for scaring them, I snapped my fingers, summoning sticks of fairy floss and used my magic to float the sticks, one at a time, towards the children. This should keep the kids satisfied for a while.

Squeals erupted as I made eye contact with the parents to check this was okay. I was met with their nods of appreciation. Nodding back in acknowledgement, I turned on my heel and continued up the road.

The familiar smell of my favourite bakery drew me closer. My stomach growled loudly at the thought of a freshly made scone or slice of bread with butter. As if he had heard my call, Iris popped his head out of the shop. Disappearing inside, he reappeared, quickly followed by his hand holding a paper box. Not being able to help myself, I teleported immediately to him, and snatched the box out of his hands with a grin.

'You're the best, Iris. One of these days I'm going to convince you to move to Amarald.' I sighed, taking a massive bite of the warm sourdough bread lathered with what could only be the freshest whipped butter. This was my definition of heaven.

Iris laughed at my impatient display. 'You know I won't ever leave here, little Val. You need a reason to come back and not forget about us.' He smiled ruefully, placing his hand on my head, ruffling my hair like I was still the fourteen-year-old girl who skipped class to eat his goods fresh out of the oven.

'It's been difficult to find time to return without raising suspicions of my whereabouts. You know I would never forget about you all. Plus, Arlom isn't all that bad. Better than the Salistyan Queendom if I'm being honest.' I spoke around mouthfuls of bread, not caring that, as a queen, I should probably conduct myself better in public. But I grew up with these people. They knew me as a trainee, basically just another civilian, despite the ones who believed whole-heartedly in the prophecy.

'Yes, but would they force us to call ourselves Arlomans? My ancestors went through one of the battles with Salistya. The stories were enough for me, and I don't intend to go through one in my lifetime. Sometimes it's better the devil you know, little Val,' he predictably responded, just as he always had.

Centuries ago, the Queendom of Salistya claimed they had a right to the Solista Isles. From all reports it was a bloody battle which ended with intense negotiations. One of the conditions was that the Solistans would train all Salistyan teens in combat and magic. In return, the people of Solista would not call themselves Salistyans or recognised the Salistyan royals as their own. However, they would treat them with respect, same as any other royal. Apparently, the lack of recognition had something to do with their religious belief in the Ophiscair Prophecy and the Goddess Wystia. They insisted on teaching all students their beliefs from the moment training began, but I didn't know the specifics of it, as me and religion had never mixed. Instead I skipped those classes and became a taste tester for Iris. A far more preferable alternative.

'I need to get going, sorry Iris. My time here is short tonight. Do you happen to have any other things you'd like me to taste?' I asked, giving him my best puppy dog eyes.

Iris pulled his other hand out from behind the door, grinning as he thrust a big bag into my hand. 'Of course, little Val, I can't have you going back to that kingdom empty handed.'

My eyes lit up like it was the Spring Solstice as I snatched the bag out of his hands. 'What's in there?' I asked, but before he could respond, I held up my hand. 'Wait! No. Don't tell me. It needs to be a surprise.'

True to character, Iris simply laughed as I teleported the bag far away before Mazyr or Rynelle could get their filthy paws on it and make me share.

With a hug and a promise to return soon, I hurried up the road, spending the next hour popping my head in to say hello to the local Solistans who had become my extended family over my teenage years. Once I had satisfied the social requirements that were often demanded of the Solistans, I cut through back streets and made my way to the last main street of Senora.

It was hard to misidentify this street, as it was the only one in Senora lined with the identical communal accommodations referred to as the barracks. Decorated in a deep, muted green that reflected the Salistyan colours, the barracks held all current trainees ranging from the ages of fourteen to nineteen. This was, for many years, the place I called home.

Not far along the street, I felt two of my Sol's presences land on either side of me. I didn't so much as flinch as I kept walking up the street towards the training arena. I knew the stocky build on the right was Mazyr, whilst his twin's lithe frame gave her away.

'Look who finally decided to show up. You know, ever since becoming a queen you've taken the fashionably late excuse to the next level,' drawled Mazyr.

'You know, ever since becoming a cook you've taken the let's-be-grumpy-for-no-goddamn-reason to the next level,' I threw back with a glance, taking note that he hadn't heeded my suggestions to cut his hair. Apparently the long brunette hair he always wore in a braid was all the rage. I thought it was a bit of a stretch considering I hadn't met any other person who rocked this ridiculous hairstyle. But Mazyr was going to do what he wanted to do. I kind of loved that about him, not that I'd ever admit it to him.

I swung my head around to my left after hearing a melodious chuckle. 'Hello, darling Amire, my favourite twin.' I smiled sweetly.

I heard a faint, 'Fucking suck up,' from my right, but chose to ignore it as Amire replied in her graceful tone. 'Hello, my favourite queen. I've missed you.'

'I've missed you too. I've been meaning to come by the Amarald Palace gardens during the daytime. Who would've thought you'd take to gardening so well?'

Amire nodded, fussing with her short bob and fringe that fell close to her eyes. 'I find myself quite enjoying the gardening, and I think it's a beautiful contrast to my training here. Where the former inspires caretaking, growth, nurturing, the latter is more destructive, violent, final. It's enjoyable to have that balance.'

Right. A contrast indeed.

Despite training alongside Amire for years, I still hadn't quite worked her out. She'd always had a gracefulness about her that

27

heavily juxtaposed the lethal assassin hiding in the shadows that is Mazyr. I had no idea how she was even related to Mazyr, let alone his twin. The two were chalk and cheese.

'Well, I'm glad everyone is having a great time with their roles at Amarald. I, for one, just absolutely adore making your beloved husband's scrambled eggs every morning. Not as much as Rynelle enjoys having to deliver it to the pompous ass, but it's a close second,' Mazyr drawled. 'When can I poison him, again?'

'No one is poisoning Eliasson, Mazyr. Not yet anyway,' I replied. 'I also think Meredith's role is worth a shout out. She does have to clean up after me, remember.' Mazyr laughed at the same time I did.

'True. But then again, is she cleaning up after you or herself?' Mazyr threw me a knowing look.

'Eh, minor details.' I waved my hands, dismissing his question. The five of us were a tight group, ride or die until the end, but Meredith was my best friend, my closest confidante. Always had been, always will be. It was a no-brainer positioning her as my maid and second-hand.

'Speaking of Rynelle, I assume he's getting in a training session at the arena?'

'Correct,' Mazyr nodded. 'And before you ask about Dwyla, we've checked in with her teachers. She's doing well, excelling in all classes, and has acquired strong magic. Not to the extent of yours, of course, but she can hold her own with water and air.'

I threw Mazyr a curt nod, the only sign I had heard his report as I came to a stop in front of the large black doors of the training arena. I technically wasn't supposed to be updated about her progress. Standard Solistan procedure was that the family of trainees were kept on a need-to-know basis.

'Are you ready, Your Highness?' Amire asked.

I pushed the doors open, figuring the action was response enough, and walked down the dark, narrow corridor. As we walked further into the building, sounds of shouting became increasingly louder. Coming to the end of the corridor, I stepped through the last door on the right. My eyes took a minute to adjust to the overwhelmingly bright light.

The room was a typical viewing space with a modestly sized lounge placed against one side of the wall and a table and chairs on the other. However, the large balcony that spanned the length of the entire space was the main feature. I stepped onto it, moving to the barriers. Looking out, I finally understood why these platforms were often used by the Solistan trainers to observe the best and brightest of the groups. You could see everything in the massive arena.

From this vantage point, I could see the enormous gym in the left-hand corner, with the archery area set up next to it. Close to me was a small area exclusively for magic training – only last years with stable control of their magic were able to practice in the arena. Newbies were prohibited from using their magic or training on this island. Instead the Solistans had a whole other island dedicated to that.

The last corner of the arena was where the trainees sparred. Luckily for us, this was where most of the action was tonight and, right in the centre of the sparring ring, where I spotted the girl Mazyr had given an update on earlier.

I watched enraptured as she fought her opponent. She was so graceful she made fighting look like a dance, her dark hair swirled around her with every movement of her body. Her opponent, an Arloman, danced with her, eyes fixed on every step she took. I noticed he never took an offensive move, only defending her attacks. Interesting. As if she knew this, the girl feigned a step to the left and darted to the right. Before he could defend himself, she teleported behind him and brought her sword to his throat. She whispered in his ear. An amused grin formed on the boy's face as he tilted his head to hit her forehead. Laughing, she released the boy before he connected, threw a teasing wink at him and sauntered off. His eyes never left hers.

What. The. Shit.

'Is anyone else seeing what I'm seeing?' I spat out through gritted teeth.

Dead silence. It was a rhetorical question, but they should know me well enough to know that I was always after some sort of acknowledgment.

I looked to my left and gauged Amire's response. As typical, neutral. Looking to my right, Mazyr's eyes looked like they were about to escape his head all together. Well, that was reassuring.

'Right. Thank you Mazyr for the confirmation. So, I did just see my innocent eighteen-year-old sister not only taunting an Arloman, but outright flirting with him.' My eyes stared accusingly at Mazyr. 'Where was that piece of information in your little update, Mazyr?'

Mazyr took an audible gulp. For all the banter we threw back at each other, he knew not to push me when it came to my over-protective nature. 'I don't know what to – '

'That, my dear Valare, you can blame on me,' came a drawl from behind me.

Shelving my annoyance for the time being, I swiftly turned into Varqel's arms, giving him a fierce hug. 'How long have you been in the room?' I asked. Damn Varqel, his magic was able to shield him from others knowing he was in the room. It was a rare gift that other magic wielders didn't have, not even me.

'Not too long. I was going to knock on the door but thought I'd see how much of your training has stuck. Clearly you need a refresher, dear. Those Arlomans are softening you,' Varqel taunted.

I let out a curse, annoyance re-emerging, pushing away from him, and resumed standing near the edge of the balcony. I turned, leaning against the barriers, and faced him once again.

'I'm softening, am I? Maybe this is more of a reflection on your training, V,' I threw back. 'Care to share why Dwyla is flirting with an Arloman?'

'I feel it may be remiss of me not to point out that it looked like more than flirting. I feel intimate familiarity are the correct words for it,' Amire interrupted, in her signature matter of fact way.

Closing my eyes momentarily, I took a few deep breaths, controlling my instinct to react to her bluntness.

'Yes, about that,' Varqel said, no trace of taunting or amusement left in his voice. 'I wanted to talk to you about this personally rather than through Fyriane whispers. No offense, Mazyr.'

'None taken, chief. Not upset at all that I didn't deliver this one,' he chuckled, scratching the back of his head with his hand, like he still couldn't believe what he just saw.

Before Mazyr realised what I was doing, I had stepped to the side and jabbed my elbow straight into his stomach.

He crumpled over with one hand on his stomach and the other on his knees. 'What the fuck, Valare. I thought we agreed no more cheap shots. Did you really have to throw extra magic into that one?' he wheezed out between deep breaths.

'We *had* an agreement, before you failed to report on Dwyla. That is for not keeping your spies in line, Maz. I shouldn't have to wait to hear from Varqel about my little sister publicly prancing around with a boy, and an Arloman no less. Maybe we should focus less on Meredith's late-night antics and more on the heir to the Salistyan throne,' I said, anger sharpening my tone.

He took a few deep breaths, before straightening up with a slight wince. 'In all fairness, Meredith is banging the right-hand man to your husband. That's kind of a big deal,' he muttered.

Before I could deliver an elbow to the other side of his stomach, my whole body, besides my head, stiffened. I stared furiously at Varqel, the source of the magic, who had paralysed my body.

'If I may, Little One?' He may be the army general and chief trainer of Solista, as well as my personal trainer as a teen, but Varqel knew as well as I did that his magic was no match for my own. His gaze never left mine, acknowledging the only reason I allowed myself to stay trapped was out of utter respect for him.

'Can you please release me before you start to tell me what I can imagine will be every reason as to why I am wrong, you are right, and that I shouldn't be angry with Mazyr?' I sighed.

Seeing him about to open his mouth to object, I hurriedly added, 'And no I will not go for another round at Mazyr as soon as you release me. I promise.'

Despite my promise, I shot Mazyr a glare. He sent me an amused grin in return, safe in the knowledge I wouldn't break a promise to Varqel. Mer was right. He was a little shit.

Varqel's magic withdrew, and I walked over to the other side of the room, unceremoniously slumping onto the lounge. Best to have a bit of distance between Maz and I.

I directed my eyes back to V, whose side-eyed glance told me this was a conversation best had between the two of us. With a subtle nod, I looked at Amire and Maz. 'You two can go. Make sure to be back in Amarald before the sun rises,' I ordered. 'Oh, and Maz, why don't you have a little chat to your spies. I suggest starting the conversation at the sparring ring to ensure there's a mutual understanding on what constitutes important information.'

A wolfish grin overtook Maz's mouth. He was a complete advocate for disciplinary training. 'As you wish, Queen.' Grabbing Amire's hand, the pair teleported out of the room.

Sighing, I brought my knees up to my chest, shifting towards Varqel as he sat down on the lounge next to me. I patiently waited as he crossed his left leg over the right, leaning back to brace his arms on the top of the couch.

'Where to begin?' He paused. 'As you saw, Dwyla is a natural with magic and her combat skills are second to none. For the first two years of her stay on the Isles she was surrounded by fellow Salistyan and Solistan teens, as you know, with the first crew of Arlomans coming on board just after she had been gifted her magic. Considering we had taken on fifteen-year-olds, some of them turned sixteen shortly after arriving. Because of this, they were behind on their combat training. We had to add on extra hours of training to get them up to speed. Not ideal, but it was a once-off.' He cleared his throat. 'Tarn was one of the Arlomans that received his magic the first new moon he was here, and therefore merged into the classes that Dwyla was taking.'

'Tarn? Tarn as in my husband's younger brother?' I sputtered. 'How the fuck did Maz miss that.'

'Yes, that would be the one,' he replied solemnly. 'There is no doubting his power or that the Goddess Wystia acknowledges his royal heritage. He is a force to be reckoned with and the only person on this island equal to your sister's power. Naturally, she would be drawn to him.'

I let out a string of curses.

Varqel continued, used to my colourful language. 'Now, I will admit this is not ideal considering the position you are currently in and the demands of your older sister …'

'But?' I guessed.

'But I remember a girl arriving on these very Isles with much power and potential, but who was a product of the oppressive nature of the Salistyan Queendom without realising it. A girl who, after six months, finally wore an outfit that wasn't the prescribed Salistyan clothing. A girl who, despite being warned against it, fell in love with a common Salistyan trainee. A girl who was, for a time, able to be free, to live a life as she wanted, without duty weighing her down.'

'V –' I breathed out, clasping my suddenly shaky hands.

'Maybe Valare, your sister is a little more like you than you realise. Tarn is the only person on this island that can understand the duties of a royal and the yearning to be free. Whether you like it or not, he makes her feel free. Are you going to take that away from her?' he said, a soft, understanding smile on his face.

'There's just so much going on here. Slaviya is the ruler of Salistya. The death of the Marlyst King is bringing in a new royal. There's the mission to make a sole ruler ... There is too much uncertainty and instability in Fyriane now, let alone what is likely to come. This could all end so very wrong. I don't want her heart caught in the crossfire,' I argued.

'Funny, I recall having a similar conversation with your older sister about your growing love interest when you were training here.' Amusement layered his voice.

Surprise gripped me. I had not been expecting that. 'What? How did she know about that?'

Waving his hand in dismissal, he said, 'It doesn't matter, it's done now. The point I'm making is that she chose duty over her sister's wishes. Will you do the same and take Tarn away from Dwyla the way your lover was taken away from you?' he questioned.

'They didn't take him away from me, V. We are still together,' I denied, shaking my head.

'You married a king, Valare. You may see him on nights like these, and be able to sneak away for a few hours of privacy, but don't fool yourself. You and I both know things have not and will not be the same between you two. She took him away from you to fulfil a plan she could have very well terminated the minute she took the royal throne. Are you going to do the same to Dwyla?'

'No,' I answered, immediately, seeing what he was pointing out. 'I will not let her go through what Slaviya has put me through. Absolutely not. But this must remain a secret.'

'Oh, my dear Valare, you underestimate your sister. If you had continued to watch the sparring, you would have seen that she plays the same game with all her opponents. Male or female,' he chuckled.

'What a little flirt,' I huffed in return.

'And that is why Mazyr's spies have not relayed this information, as they assume this is just a part of her personality and nothing more to look into.'

I probably should've felt bad that I just sent off Mazyr to put them through the ringer, but hey, their line of work meant being kept on their toes.

'So how do you know her relationship with Tarn is more than that?' I asked.

'Well, for one, she gets the same glazed look in her eye as you did with yours,' he winked. 'And two, about eight months ago the maids of the Royal House started reporting that they suddenly had to remake ruffled beds despite no one staying in the house. It sounded suspiciously like when you were living here, so I investigated. No one else knows. Not even Slaviya.'

I knew the royal maids swore to the Goddess Wystia to always uphold confidentiality, so I was confident no one else would find out.

'It seems we're definitely more alike than I initially thought,' I laughed. 'Has she not learnt how to use her magic to return things back to their former state yet?'

His lips twitched. 'You're forgetting that little trick is a Valare specialty. Your sister doesn't have that luxury.'

Oh, right. 'Sometimes I forget what's normal and what … isn't.' I lifted a shoulder with a sheepish look. 'Anyway, I trust you'll continue to keep an eye on this situation and update me. No one needs to know. Especially Slaviya. And please for the love of the Goddess, can Lyz ensure she's receiving her contraceptive remedy? My plate is already full right now, I don't need a royal baby conceived out of wedlock thrown into the mix.'

'Of course, Little One. Lyzia takes care of your sister's health personally, just as she did you. There will be no unexpected offspring.'

Releasing a big breath, I nodded, satisfied. 'Good. On that note, I best be off as time is getting away from me and I have a very important meeting.'

Varqel's eyes flashed with amusement. Standing up, he pulled me into a hug, murmuring in my ear, 'It was good to see you, my dear. I know it's difficult, but please don't be a stranger. I'll pass on your greetings to the others. I know they're wanting to see you. Remember if there's anything you need from me, you're always welcome in my home. Your room looks the same as when you last saw it.'

With a last squeeze, I pulled away to look into the eyes of the man who had become more of a father to me than my biological one. 'I promise I'll try to come back sooner. It hurts me just as much being away from you. Please take care of Dwyla and send correspondence if my other sister steps foot on the island. I want to be across what she's doing.'

'Of course, Valare. Now, go enjoy yourself. Be with your man.' He smiled at me fondly.

'Thanks, V. I'll see you soon.' Kissing my fingers, and placing them to my heart, I teleported straight to the one place and person I had been desperate to see.

CHAPTER 4

Walking into my favourite room in the household set aside for visiting Salistyan royalty, I could feel Sir's presence in the corner, hiding in the shadows. At the foot of the bed lay a blindfold and a rope. My excitement escalated as I stripped out of my clothes, placed the blindfold on, and kneeled on the floor facing the bed with my hands held behind my back. This wasn't my first time. Nor was it his.

Using his magic, he swept air down my chest, circling and teasing my nipples as he came over to fleetingly caress my hands. This was the only gentle gesture I was granted before he roughly tied them together with the rope. He was definitely angry.

'Stand,' he ordered.

Taking in a deep breath, I stopped a moan from leaving my lips, and obeyed. I could feel him walk around to my front. My magic sensed that he had sat on the foot of the bed where the blindfold was a moment ago.

His hand suddenly grabbed the back of my head, pulling me forward so that I was hinging at the hips, head down and breasts falling onto the top of his thighs. Groaning, he cupped both of my breasts, lightly teasing my nipples. I inhaled sharply.

'Two fucking months is too long, Valare,' he grumbled.

I opened my mouth to reply, before my head was shoved further down to take his cock in my mouth. I let out a moan.

'Too fucking long,' he groaned, as he started to lift my head up and down, fucking my face in a slow, torturous rhythm.

I was completely at his mercy as he took what he wanted, letting out his pent-up frustration. I tightened my mouth, creating a suction on his cock, my sole focus bent on making him feel good. Using my body to ask forgiveness, to apologise.

Before I could react to what was happening, he pulled me off him and threw me on the bed. My back hit the mattress while my legs splayed out to the sides. Without missing a beat, he moved to straddle my chest, cupped my chin and opened my mouth, forcing his way back inside of me.

His thrusts quickened, his breath sharpening as he continued to move. Evidently, he had no regard for my comfort which, at this point, was heading straight to the uncomfortable zone. Tears leaked out of my eyes, my jaw opened to its limit, my gag reflex well and truly engaged.

I guess this is what I deserved. For him to take his frustration out on me. It's my fault that I couldn't find a quiet moment in two months to spend time with him. It's my fault I'm a royal. It's my fault that we fell in love.

It's all your fault. His words from our last conversation played over and over in my mind.

Suddenly, he roughly withdrew himself and moved down the bed. He shoved two fingers in my mouth, collecting the juices his thrusts had created before plunging deep inside my core. After a couple of quick, rough thrusts, his fingers were gone, replaced with his cock. Slamming into me in one hard, heavy thrust, I couldn't suppress the slight wince and groan elicited by his brutality.

Noticing my discomfort, his deep, dominant voice rose between the sounds our bodies made. 'So, are you going to apologise for being a bad girl? For keeping what's mine away from me?'

I could only moan in response, overcome with the pool of pleasure spreading through my core. A sharp smack landed on my clit. I shrieked.

'Use your words, Valare. Are you going to apologise for not prioritising me and my needs? For letting that fucking Arloman scum put his cock in what is clearly mine?' he roared. His thrusts sped up, a giveaway that he was close to reaching the edge.

'I'm …' I was breathing hard by now, tears building in my eyes at the sensations.

'Speak up, sweetheart, otherwise I'll find other uses for that mouth of yours.'

'I'm sorry, Sir, it's my fault. It's all my fault,' I sobbed.

'Good girl. It is your fault, but I still love you anyway. Because that's what love is. Seeing all of you, punishing you when needed, and keeping you in check.'

Holding my ankles with both hands and spreading my feet further apart, his thrusts became erratic, uncontrolled, taking everything, showing no consideration for my needs. Not this time anyway. I didn't deserve it.

'Open that mouth wide and tongue out. You whore of Arlom, you don't deserve my seed in you tonight,' he ordered.

Not one to defy a direct order, I did as I was told. A second later, I felt him slip out of me and a string of wet stickiness hit my neck, before landing on my cheek, tongue, and forehead.

He moved up to slap his drained cock on my cheeks, smearing more across my face before roughly shoving his cock back into my mouth with an order to clean him.

Moaning, I sucked and licked off every last bit of him, humming my pleasure for his graciousness in allowing me to service him, despite being an Arlom whore.

He pulled my mouth further onto his rapidly hardening dick, holding it still while he pushed two of his fingers back inside me, working me closer and closer to climax. I moaned and thrashed around, wishing I had my hands untied to feel him. But as always, he was in control.

He released my head, allowing me to suck furiously on his cock, my climax seconds away. My legs started to still, my pelvis naturally shifting upwards. My moaning ceased as I felt the overwhelming sense of bliss taking over my whole body. And that's when he pulled his fingers out.

I whimpered in disappointment, so close to the finish line. He slapped my clit once more.

'Your satisfaction doesn't matter, Valare. You're here to service me. And if I don't want you to come? You won't. I'll take what is mine and you'll give it to me willingly like the little slut that you are. And when you take everything I graciously give you, never forget that you did this; you didn't prioritise me and my needs,' he said oh-so-quietly. 'Does your darling husband know this is how you spend your evenings away from him? With me? Putting this dripping wet pussy to good use like the other Salistyan girls just waiting to be bred? Tied up and left to the mercy of the one that truly owns her?'

With that, he kept fucking my face, lasting only seconds before exploding in my mouth. Forcing his cock all the way to the back of my throat, I had no option but to swallow everything he gave me.

Abruptly pulling away, I felt him withdrawing to the other side of the room, next to the door. I heard the shuffle of clothes being put back into their rightful place.

'Wait,' I said, before he could leave the room. 'Aren't we going to talk? Aren't you going to untie me?' I could untie myself, but it wasn't the point.

He sighed and untied me. 'There. But don't expect more from me tonight. I love you Valare, but a two month wait is not something I can forgive after a tumble in the hay. Work harder to prove yourself to me.' He left the room.

I scrambled to sit up and take the damn blindfold off. Immediately, I wish I hadn't. There was a mirror in front of me, and I could see I was a dismal sight. My bare breasts were on display, legs spread wide open, neck and face heavily covered in his marks.

Maybe he wasn't far off. I sure did look like an Arlom whore.

But that was a thought I needed to shut down immediately, because he didn't really think I was a whore. He only said that in the moment to heighten the roleplay. He wouldn't actually treat me like a whore.

He loved me. Sure, things had changed since I married Eliasson, but that's only natural, right? He said he'd always loved me and always will. He said that sometimes I bring these things upon myself, with my impulsiveness and lack of foresight. And he said if he doesn't punish me, how would I learn?

Wanting your partner to grow was love. And sometimes the methods involved his gratification and my punishment. That's how I showed my love and commitment to him, he said. That's what he needed from me. And he would always be there, through thick and thin. Because he loved me.

CHAPTER 5

B ack in Amarald a few mornings later, I strolled towards the Royal Dining Room where Eliasson and I religiously had breakfast together each day – the unfortunate result of my negotiating no night-time Dom engagements unless it's unavoidable.

It was necessary, Eliasson told me, for Arlom royalty to be seen as a united front to their people, hence breakfast in the official dining room rather than the private one in our apartments. Although this made perfect sense, it was a far cry from how my parents and the generations before them ruled. The king took care of affairs, and the queen was merely a figurehead, ready to serve at the king's beck and call. It was a transactional relationship to produce heirs. Nothing more, nothing less.

In contrast, Eliasson insisted on my presence at all meetings, often asking for my opinion while openly collaborating with his most trusted advisors. He encouraged me to take the contraceptive remedy, wanting to get to know me first and eventually mutually agree before commencing efforts to produce an heir. It had only been the last few months where my scepticism subsided and I finally accepted this was, indeed, Arloman culture. The men were firm but fair, the women respected and with an equal seat at the table. The similarities with the culture of the Solista Isles were unmistakeable. It's quite ironic, really, that the latter was ruled by Salistya, whose culture is basically the polar opposite.

I stepped into the obnoxiously-sized room, which never ceased to amaze me. The high ceiling was a single, big piece of glass that allowed natural sunlight to brighten the whole room. In the corner was a stage with a piano and a variety of string instruments, neatly placed alongside a dance floor, often used when noble guests visited the palace. In the middle of the room was a long, twenty-seater table, unsurprisingly fit for royalty.

Making my way towards the head of the table where Eliasson sat, I noted his eyes travelling up and down my body, taking in the plunging neckline of my silk slip dress. His eyes widened with desire as they zoned in on my left thigh peeking out of the high slit in the dress as I walked. His lips twitched in obvious approval.

The revealing Arlom dress code was yet another assimilatory hurdle I had overcome, albeit quickly due to the warm climate of the Kingdom – not to mention, the Isles had done a good job of stripping away my former prudish Salistyan ways. The looks of appreciation from Eliasson when I dressed like this were an additional motivator, working as another tool in my arsenal.

Stopping to his left, and purely to stoke the fires of his desire – not at all because I enjoyed toying with him, of course – I leant in to place a lingering kiss on his lips, one hand resting on his chest and the other cupping his jaw. Eliasson kissed me back and traced his hand up my thigh to toy with the slit of my dress, teasing my skin while his other hand came to squeeze my right butt cheek.

A throat clearing brought us back down to earth.

Pulling away, I mustered all my seductive prowess to purr, 'Good morning, husband,' as I blatantly ignored the other presence in the room. Eliasson's blue eyes darkened, and a firm squeeze of my butt cheek confirmed the effect I had on him.

'Good morning, wife,' he responded, his voice deep.

With a smug look, I stepped out of his reach and sat beside him. My eyes lit up at the cup of coffee ready for me. Bringing it to my mouth, my eyes closed, a satisfied moan escaped my lips at the glorious taste.

A familiar groan was released nearby. Fluttering my eyes open, I met heated eyes watching my every move, Eliasson's teeth biting into his lower lip in undisguised lust. The look made my insides stir. Okay, maybe I wasn't as unaffected by him as I thought I was. Let's blame that on the lack of climactic release a few nights ago.

Before I could tease any further, the person sitting next to Eliasson, who I had chosen to ignore until now, decided to ruin the fun.

'One would think you hadn't just spent the last twelve hours together,' Fyrel muttered, shaking his head in exasperation.

Interesting. He didn't know that Eliasson and I had separate quarters.

'One would think you wouldn't chase a Salistyan maid around like a smitten pubescent teen. But hey, different strokes for different folks, am I right?' I shot back sweetly, pleasantly smiling at Eliasson's Second and royal pain-in-my-ass best friend.

'How do you –'

'I know everything,' I cut him off. 'Although you have an incessant need to think otherwise, I'm not just a pretty face.' I levelled him with a stare that, had he or anyone else outside of Salistya and the Isles known about magic, let alone that I wielded it, would have him quaking in his boots.

Fyrel scoffed. 'Self-proclaimed pretty face, sweetheart.' His eyes lingered on mine, unsubtly gawping at their unique colouring.

'Fyrel,' Eliasson interrupted, a warning evident in his tone.

'Oh no, it's fine Eliasson.' I waved my hand, dismissing the interruption, turning my attention back to Fyrel. 'No offense taken. Besides, I'm aware of his type, very different to me. The type, might I caution, that if he were to ever hurt in any way, shape, or form, would result in him having a little taste of my Solistan training. Friendly tip: not recommended.' I pasted on an innocent smile.

Fyrel's blue eyes narrowed, seeing the less than subtle threat for what it was.

Taking his silence as acknowledgement, I clapped in mock celebration. 'Excellent!' False excitement was thick in my voice. 'I love how we understand each other, it really does warm the cockles of my heart.' I sighed wistfully, curling my finger around a lock of hair.

It's really no surprise Fyrel couldn't stand me. In all honesty, I stopped caring early on into my marriage when I realised his scepticism towards me would never waver. Which, considering my intentions to Eliasson were less than desirable, I couldn't really blame him. Mer claimed he wasn't that bad. I guess I would have to take her word for it, because winding up Fyrel was one of my favourite pastimes and the greatest source of entertainment I had in Amarald. I wouldn't be giving it up any time soon.

Eliasson's chuckle cut through the stare off between Fyrel and me. He was completely unfazed that his wife and best friend refused to be amicable. 'Never a dull moment with you two around.' He shook his head. 'However, Fyrel, I intend to spend the whole day with my lovely wife, so please, talk to us about the important information that couldn't wait.'

I couldn't help exploiting Fyrel's disdain for Eliasson and I spending extended amounts of time together. My impulsive need to rub salt into Fyrel's wounds took over. 'Yes, Fyrel,' I crooned, 'what exactly are you doing here?'

Fyrel went to respond but was cut off by three attendants placing a plate of food in front of each of us.

The smell of bacon and eggs attacked my senses, my eyes found Rynelle's as he leant over and placed the plate in front of me. Strategically blocking Eliasson and Fyrel's view to me, he dropped a slip of paper into my lap with a warning look. I subtly moved the paper under the table before visualising the drawer of erotic novels back in my quarters. Holding onto that vision, the paper left my hand, teleported to the desired location.

The attendants returned to the kitchens, leaving the three of us alone in the dining room once more. Momentarily forgetting there was a reason for company, a comfortable silence fell on the room, broken only by the clanging of cutlery as we enjoyed breakfast.

After a few minutes, Fyrel leaned back into his chair and placed his hands behind the back of his head, elbows wide. I supressed the urge to roll my eyes at his obnoxious stance.

'I received correspondence in the early hours of the morning from the Kingdom of Marlyst, confirming their attendance at the Royal Forum. We had already received confirmation from both Salistya and Nyarelle months ago, so this was the final piece,' Fyrel reported.

'That's interesting. I was convinced we would have to push this one back, given the untimely passing of the King,' Eliasson mused.

'You and me both.' Fyrel nodded. 'Having said that, the coronation was held a couple of weeks after his passing. Clearly, the new King doesn't like to waste any time. My sources confirmed this is a tendency of his. I'm intrigued to understand his motivations for this swiftness so the Forum will be rather telling.'

A coronation within a couple of weeks? That was even quicker than Slaviya's, and the speed of hers had been fuelled by her need for total control. She really was a carbon copy of Father. For the millionth time, a wave of relief washed over me knowing Dwyla was far away from the witch. For now, at least.

Fyrel was right, though. The King's motivations were intriguing. I made a mental note to partake in some old-school late-night spying when the Marlyst King was in Amarald.

'Rather telling, indeed,' Eliasson agreed, before moving his attention back to me. 'I want the Marlyst representatives' quarters next to ours. This way, it'll be easier to invite them to our quarters for informal meetings to gain a better understanding of their motivations. What do you think?'

Despite how often he considered and asked for my opinion, I was often still startled by it. I guess you could take the girl out of Salistya, but you couldn't always take the Salistya out of the girl.

Turning to him, I responded. 'I have no issues with that, however, I would like to politely remind you of our ongoing agreement in relation to night-time activities.'

Fyrel raised an eyebrow, clearly having not been briefed on our agreement and thinking the worst. 'Seriously, Valare? You can't keep it in your pants for a couple of weeks?'

An amused smile and blasé shrug of my shoulders was the only response I gave him. Eliasson meanwhile let out a growl. 'Fyrel, what Valare does and does not do with her pants is no one's concern but my own.'

Oh Goddess, why did the hint of possessiveness just do something to my insides, even coming from Eliasson?

This is all your fault. Sir's voice rang in my ears. I subtly shook my head, releasing those thoughts from my mind.

'Now that that's sorted,' Eliasson continued, 'Fyrel, since it's only two weeks away, I'll leave you to communicate to the wider Kingdom that the dates have been confirmed. My darling Valare, will I leave it to you to discuss arrangements with Meredith for the other royal quarters?' It wasn't missed by either Fyrel or I that his direction was an order and mine was a question.

I shot Fyrel a triumphant, taunting smile. 'Of course, darling, I can take care of that. Unless, of course, you'd like to Fyrel?' I replied innocently. 'I know how much you love being on top of all things Meredith.' My smile turned into a full, wicked grin.

'Valare,' Eliasson cautioned.

'Fuck you and your smart-ass mouth, Valare,' Fyrel raged, giving into his frustration and cutting off what was most definitely going to be Eliasson telling me off. But I didn't care. I had won this round.

'Sorry, Fyrel, but you're just not my type, sweetie. But then again, the feeling's mutual, isn't it?' I threw him a wink. Before he could respond, I continued. 'You seem so *touchy* about this subject, Fyrel, so don't worry your pretty little head. I'll have a chat to Meredith.' The emphasis on touchy did not go unnoticed.

He released a deep, frustrated breath. Rage shimmered in his eyes. Damn, classic Meredith. Always drawn to the high-strung ones I loved to poke at.

'I don't know how you put up with that little wench. Twenty minutes in her company is twenty minutes too long, as far as I'm concerned,' Fyrel said, deciding to ignore me and talking directly to Eliasson.

I cupped my hands around my mouth, amplifying my next words. 'For the record, you grumpy bastard, I can hear you.'

Eliasson simply laughed. 'If you two weren't so entertaining, I think twenty minutes watching this back and forth would be too long for me. Anything else to report?'

'No, that was all. Am I dismissed? It doesn't matter how good this breakfast is, it's not worth it to be in her company for a minute longer,' Fyrel complained.

I rolled my eyes. So damn dramatic.

'Yes, Fyrel, you're dismissed,' Eliasson conceded.

Without a second glance, Fyrel was up and out of the room before you could say small dick energy.

I released a snicker, unable to hold it back any longer. Honestly, if the guy hadn't been such an outright dick to me since I got here, I might have felt bad. Okay, let's be honest, probably not. But I did enjoy that he couldn't completely hate me because of both Eliasson and now Meredith. It felt good holding the trump card, and even better that he knows I did.

'Valare,' Eliasson started.

I cut him off. 'Eliasson, we have two options here. Now, I'm going to preface this by saying I much prefer the second option.'

He stared at me, waiting, amusement in his eyes and fighting off a smile.

'One, you tell me again why I should be nice to him and how the only way to rebuild a relationship – which would require a relationship in the first place – is to be the bigger person and show kindness, so that kindness would eventually be shown in return. Which, knowing both mine and Fyrel's personalities, we would both rather walk over hot coals between Amarald and the Solista Isles than do that.'

Eliasson opened his mouth to respond, but I raised a finger to silence him.

'Option two,' I continued, 'You remember the feelings I stirred in you when I walked through the door today, add a dash of your exasperation towards me for being the gorgeous, irritatingly witty specimen that I am, and take me back to our quarters before we carry on with our day.'

By the time I'd finished my proposition, Eliasson's eyes had zeroed in on my left thigh which I had subtly crossed over my right to reveal a healthy amount of skin.

With a rough clearing of his throat, Eliasson came over and scooped me up into his arms. I released a surprised shriek, throwing my arms around his neck before he dove in to place a scorching kiss on my lips.

'I think the second option will suffice for today,' he said, before heading out of the dining room towards our quarters.

My laugh followed us throughout the palace, the picture of Eliasson moving swiftly with me in his arms enough to stop workers from their tasks. My gaze collided with three familiar, mossy green sets of eyes as we passed. Two of them held a mix of wariness and understanding, but the last set of eyes ... My laugh stumbled for a split second before I forced myself to continue like nothing had happened. The sweep of his fringe partly covering those eyes didn't hide the defeated, possessive look or the more than a flicker of anger there.

Closing my eyes, I turned my head towards Eliasson, burrowing into his neck and pushed all other thoughts other than the feeling of him away. I had a role to play as the Queen of Arlom, and no one could argue I wasn't playing my part well.

After all, he was falling right into the trap.

CHAPTER 6

Heart racing, I swatted loose strands of hair away from my clammy face as I disentangled myself from Eliasson and made to move away.

'Where do you think you're going?' His hand clamped down on my hip, pulling my body back into his and holding me still. We were both sweaty and breathing heavily, our chests rubbing against one another.

Looking at Eliasson from below my eyelashes, I could see pure male satisfaction shining from his eyes, and my cheeks unexpectedly heated in response. Since when did I get shy about these things? I guess it's a good place to start when the guy you're supposed to kill had just given you three orgasms in one session, but still. The universe hated me.

As if reading my thoughts, Eliasson placed a finger under my chin and lifted my face. My eyes dipped to his mouth, satisfaction also reflected in the curve of his lips.

'I think I should annoy Fyrel more,' I mumbled, eyes darting up to his, my cheeks becoming impossibly hotter.

Predictably, Eliasson burst out laughing, while his fingers started to trace a pattern up and down my thigh. 'That's where you're going after what is, undoubtedly, the best sex we've ever had?'

'Seems fair, no?' I sheepishly shrugged, not denying that it was indeed the best sex we'd ever had. Honestly, it was the best I'd ever had. Wasn't that just a spanner being thrown into the works?

'Hmmm.' Eliasson's fingers moved up to my chest, circling a breast one after the other. 'I can think of a few factors.' He casually flicked his finger over my nipple, eliciting a small, sharp gasp from me, before pulling away and sitting up. I watched the sheets pool around his hips, his arm muscles contracting as he flicked his long blonde locks behind his shoulders. I had to stop myself from drooling. And from questioning why my attraction to him was suddenly intensifying.

Clearing my throat, I followed his movements and sat up, determined to move on from the topic of conversation. 'You mentioned earlier you were spending the day with me?'

'Yes, I thought we could go for a walk through Amarald, escape the palace for a while. From all reports, the harvesting season was fruitful with the first load of goods arriving the other day. Maybe we could pick up some plants for the garden?'

My eyes lit up in excitement and I nodded. A day of no guards following us because Eliasson was with me? I wasn't missing out on this. The safety of Arlom really was a boon at times.

I jumped out of bed, flinging my dress on as I rushed out the door to my quarters, yelling over my shoulder that I'd be ready in fifteen minutes.

Soaking up the beautiful mid-morning rays of sunshine, Eliasson insisted we walk hand in hand, opting to stroll down the road at the front of the palace to the Amarald markets instead of riding on horseback.

The city of Amarald was undeniably beautiful, with the soft white sand and deep blue of the ocean to the right of our path. Judging by the large number of civilians at the beach, there must have been a number of land-locked farmers taking advantage of the trip to Amarald to enjoy its natural landscape. It must have been a fruitful harvest indeed.

To the left of our path, luscious rolling green hills surrounded the heart of the city. Houses were scattered and built in what could only be described as a non-uniform layout. Roads wound around the building in a way that indicated housing had come first and the roads were an afterthought. All of the cottages were unique, ranging in colour from yellow to brown, and in material from bricks to straw. I couldn't help the smile that crept on my face at the civilians enjoying the beach, the farmers actually wanting to come to the city and the chaotic clash of colours scattered throughout the hills. It's so very different to Salistya.

After our wedding, Eliasson had taken me on a whirlwind tour of the whole kingdom, insisting on the importance of knowing the Dom I was to rule alongside him. I had known the Arlom Kingdom supplied the other Doms with agricultural products, but it was only when we explored the whole kingdom that I recognised the sheer magnitude of its operations. Hills and valleys were common, rising amongst flat plains of rich and fertile land. No matter which direction I had turned, my gaze was met with either rows of planted vegetables, fruits, or grazing livestock. Seeing it firsthand, I wondered how the Salistyan's could view the Arloman Kingdom as the weakest link. The Arloman farmers fed the entire continent.

A squeeze of my hand pulled my thoughts back to the present. Looking over at Eliasson, his questioning look told me I had missed something.

'Sorry, what was that?'

He smiled patiently. 'The ship is docked, ready for the Solista Isles. I believe they'll be leaving this afternoon. Is there anything you'd like to have sent over to your friends?'

'Why would I –' I started, confused, completely forgetting for a moment that he wasn't aware of teleporting.

I assumed a regretful look. 'That won't be necessary. Most of my friends have returned to Salistya,' I responded.

'Of course, not to mention that communication isn't allowed,' he nodded solemnly. 'I haven't spoken to Tarn since our wedding, and it's killing me. When I went through combat training in Arlom we were still allowed to go home over holiday breaks and receive messages. The Solistan way is hardcore, no?'

'Hardcore is one way to put it, but I guess you don't become a strong enough army to protect all of Fyriane by not being hardcore. They believe that cutting trainees off from the outside world is necessary to simulate the reality of war. Ultimately their end goal is to train everyone as a warrior, so they break us down piece by piece to recognise our true potential.' I shrugged. The concept was normal to me, but judging by the look of outrage on Eliasson's face, maybe it wasn't.

As we approached the port of Amarald, market stalls could be seen lined up on the ocean front walkway. Excitement buzzed inside me at the prospect of picking up a Nyarellean book or a new sword from the Marlyst Kingdom. I quickened my stride.

'How did you find not talking to your family? Did you struggle?' Eliasson asked.

What would he think if he knew not only was I able to talk to my family, but that in fact the only time they showed an ounce of interest in my life was when they had insisted on regular progression updates? And that Varqel took over the correspondence to give me a break from their suffocating demands? Every part of me wished there had been a hard and fast no communication rule for me like there was with everyone else.

I held his gaze, allowing the brutal honesty of my answer to show on my face. 'I didn't grow up in a family that openly displayed any type of emotion, let alone love or care. Salistyan's don't express themselves, nor do they place value on dwelling on matters of the heart. Everything is transactional, cool and calculated. The minimisation of familial contact was a blessing in disguise. Rest assured, Eliasson, my time on the Solista Isles were the best years of my life. If I had it my way, I would have never left.'

Eliasson opened his mouth to respond, but closed it quickly when a group of children ran towards us, having instantly recognised their king.

'Your Highness!' The children surrounded Eliasson with bright smiles. Giving me a nod to tell me he would catch up with me, Eliasson turned his attention to the children, forever the loving and involved king.

Growing up, I would have been lucky to have my parents give me attention, let alone see them walking the street interacting with civilians. It was so damn different.

Making my way through the crowd, I ignored the stares that often followed me wherever I went. I was used to receiving stares of bewilderment because of my eyes; being a Salistyan-born Queen in Arlom just amplified it.

I aimlessly drifted through the market, smiling and waving at passers-by who were brave enough to hold my gaze. Some of the stalls were as simple as a piece of fabric with advertised goods laying on the floor, while other merchants had large carts where buyers entered to view products – the latter were usually owned by Marlyst merchants.

When I spotted a modest stall with a handful of tables covered in books scattered around the tent, I made a beeline towards it. On the tables, the variety of books were no doubt from the Queendom of Nyarelle. My gaze landed on burnt orange eyes of the stall-holder staring back at me as I took in the space. The edges of her face revealed harsh, weathered lines, lines that could only be born from living so close to the Hudrielle Desert.

'Greetings.' I nodded politely before looking towards the books, keen to break contact with the all-knowing eyes.

The woman bowed her head, recognising another Dom's royalty. 'Was there anything in particular you were looking for?'

'Just browsing, thank you.' Smiling, I turned away and started sifting through the books.

The collections were quite impressive. The merchant had books on everything from agriculture to adventure to history. It wasn't a surprise considering the Queendom of Nyarelle's main purpose was to document the history of Fyriane. The Dom had an extensive library filled with archives and books, not to mention all of Fyriane's authors were from Nyarelle; no other Dom had the time or the means to sit down and write a book like the Nyarellean's.

Historically, the Doms worked in isolation, each contributing to the continent in their own, separate way. While Nyarelle recorded the history of the entire continent, the Marlyst Kingdom was responsible for providing weapons for Salistya's army and farming equipment for Arlom. In turn, Arlom fed the whole continent and Salistya fought the beasts in the Tidal Seas, preventing their entrance to the Pass.

Eventually, I settled on a new romance book, one that looked like it would be suitable for both mine and Meredith's tastes. How did she describe it? Guy chases girl, girl denies him, he fights harder to win her over, she eventually gives in. Yes, this ticked the boxes. It also sounded a lot like mine and Sir's story, but I always chose not to read into that.

Turning around, I headed towards the merchant, intending to buy the book and find Eliasson when I caught something from the corner of my eye.

The black book was quite plain-looking, aside from the vibrant lilac eye in the middle, which gripped my attention. It looked like it was glowing.

The World As It Was. No author. I was intrigued.

I handed the Nyarellean five gold for the two books, smiled and gave my thanks.

'Your Highness,' she spoke, just as I was turning away. I looked back expectantly.

'Knowledge finds those who are meant to see.'

'Excuse me?'

'I suggest you use that magic of yours to deposit that book somewhere safe. It chose you; it is for your eyes only. Make sure it doesn't fall into the wrong hands.'

I froze. How the hell did she know about my magic?

I looked at those damn all-knowing eyes, making a split second decision. 'I have no idea what you are talking about,' I lied.

She gave me a cunning look. 'We both know your husband is only a minute away. Hide the book, Valare, or I will have to take it off you.'

I sifted through my magic, gauging all presences around me and latched onto Eliasson's. Fuck, she wasn't wrong, he wasn't far off. But how did she know that? How did she know my name? More importantly, who was this woman?

'Valare,' she cautioned, using my first name again like we were the best of friends and hadn't just crossed paths with each other a whole five minutes ago.

Looking at my surroundings, there was no one close who would see it, but the risk was too great. I shoved both books in my bag, ignoring the part of me that screamed to listen to the Nyarellean.

'Who are you? What is your name?' I quietly demanded, not wanting to make a scene.

'I am a simple Nyarellean merchant,' she stated. Well, obviously. Her burnt orange eyes and darker skin were a dead giveaway that she hailed from the Queendom of Nyarelle.

'What is this you say about magic?' I pressed her, pretending I knew nothing.

'Knowledge finds those who are meant to see, Valare.' A highly ambiguous response. Perfect.

I could feel Eliasson coming around the corner. Time was up.

'You do not repeat this encounter to anyone. If you do, I will serve your head on a platter. Mark my words,' I threatened.

The woman smirked, a glint of approval in her eyes. 'Until we meet again, Queen.'

'There you are!' Eliasson put his arms around me and pulled my back into his chest. 'Sorry I took so long, time just got away. Do you want to go get some of those plants for the garden?' he asked, kissing my cheek.

I continued to stare at her, my threat in my eyes. Credit to her, though, she didn't break eye contact once.

Mentally shaking off the events of the last however many minutes, I smiled at Eliasson, kissing him while placing one of my hands on the black book in my bag. I envisioned the only place I knew the book would be safe. A second later, my hand felt empty air.

'Yes, let's go get some plants.'

I turned around and took his hand as we walked back to the main street to be instantly engulfed in the busy crowd, all while feeling the burning stare of those orange eyes in the back of my head.

After a few more hours at the markets, we trudged back to the palace, both of our hands filled with plants. I was excited to add to the collection in my quarters. We walked straight to the back, entering the royal gardens.

To the left, the kitchen door was strategically placed next to the large, sprawling vegetable gardens. We followed the path through the gardens, taking in the variety of produce ready for harvest just in time for the Royal Forum. I caught eyes with Mazyr in his chef's outfit, picking some vegetables in the garden. We childishly poked our tongues out at one another behind Eliasson's back.

In the middle of this part of the gardens, a path branched out from the left directing pedestrians through to its centre. Eliasson gave my arm a soft nudge and nodded in that direction. I obliged, taking the turn to walk deeper into the gardens, a comfortable silence falling around us.

We walked under a hedged archway that spanned out to create a huge circle shielding the centre of the garden. It was completely private, away from peering eyes, unless someone were to venture down one of the four archways leading off in different directions.

Eventually, we stepped out of the lengthy walkway to an area housing a pond. My eyes darted to the statue of the Goddess Wystia in the middle of the pond. Water was trickling out like a waterfall from the palms of her outstretched hands, and in front of the water feature was a blanket and a woven basket which could only be filled with food.

A smile spreading on my face, I zoned in on the bottle of wine and two glasses next to the basket. Excited, I hurried towards the blanket, gently placing the plants and bag down before taking a seat.

Eliasson released a soft chuckle. 'It doesn't take much to make you happy, does it?' Shaking his head with a smile on his face, he placed his lot of plants next to mine before sinking onto the blanket next to me.

'Can you blame me? They weren't jesting when they told me wine from Arlom is hands down the best in all the Doms.'

'I guess we have the Goddess to thank for our fertile lands and desirable climate. And also the fact that we are the only Dom that makes wine.'

Planting a quick kiss on my lips, Eliasson reached back to grab the bottle, pouring an equal amount in each glass, and passed me one.

'To the Goddess Wystia,' I said, lifting my glass.

'And the Kingdom of Arlom,' he added, clinking our glasses before taking a sizeable swig.

'So, what do I owe the pleasure of your company for a whole day, husband?' I asked, getting straight to the point.

Sighing, Eliasson looked around and noticed Amire appear inside one of the walkways, pruning away at the hedge. Apparently satisfied she was out of earshot, though I knew better, he turned his gaze back to me. 'Can it not simply be that I want to spend time with my beloved?'

My eyes narrowed. 'Although I believe that's true, I also know you well enough to hedge my bets against that being the sole reason for this.'

Eliasson opened his mouth to refute my statement, but I held my hand up before he could proceed.

'I tell you what. If I open this basket and there aren't warm scones with freshly whipped cream and my favourite raspberry jam, I'll apologise for thinking ill of your intentions.' He knew I loved baked goods, even more so when raspberries were involved. This would be obvious that he was trying to get me on side for something.

He looked guilty before I even moved towards the basket. 'Valare _'

'I don't even need to look, do I?' Of course, I still looked. I wouldn't be me if I didn't.

My eyes fluttered closed, the smell of freshly baked scones taking over my senses. 'You never play fucking fair,' I moaned. Diving into the basket, I lathered a scone with ample cream and jam and devoured it.

I reached into the basket for a second helping but Eliasson pushed my hands away. 'Allow me.'

Well, if he was going to ask me something I didn't like, he may as well earn it.

I leaned back on my hands, watching his meticulous application of the condiments. 'It needs more cream. What's a scone without an equal amount of cream?' I thought I had trained him better than this.

Eliasson didn't reply, merely rolling his eyes and placing more cream on the scone. He scooted closer, crossing his legs. He reached out, placed his hands on my outstretched legs and pulled me closer. My backside brushed his feet, legs wide and settled on the tops of his thighs.

'Open wide,' he commanded as he lifted the scone to my mouth, a shimmer of aroused anticipation in his eyes.

I held his gaze and obeyed his command, enjoying the burst of flavour in my mouth. He pulled back, lifting his free hand to my mouth, a finger scooping up residual cream lingering there. My tongue expertly licked his finger, taking what he offered. His eyes turned a darker shade, showing he was becoming increasingly aroused. I had him right where I wanted him.

'So, to what do I owe the pleasure of your company for a whole day, husband?' I repeated.

Eliasson shook his head and cleared his throat, gaining control of himself. He placed his hands on either side of my hips, fingers lightly stroking.

'I know the next two weeks will be very intense in the lead up to the Royal Forum. There is much to plan, living quarters to be arranged, menus to be decided, venues for conversations, the list goes on. I wanted us to have some time together, knowing we wouldn't have a proper opportunity for at least another month. I'm hoping this Royal Forum doesn't go over the two-week mark, like the last one did,' he said.

Ah, yes. The Royal Forum was planned over two weeks. But the last Forum in the Nyarelle Queendom was a lengthy one, spilling over to be almost a month. Trade agreements were negotiated for days on end as tensions grew between the rulers, mainly due to Salistya and Marlyst. Salistya had the army, but Marlyst created the weapons, so it was a tense relationship. Here's hoping there wasn't a repeat of that.

'Plus,' Eliasson cut off my thoughts, 'We also need to consider the new royal at the table. It would be inappropriate for us not to spend time showing him Amarald and providing an in-depth understanding of our Kingdom as a whole.'

With luck the new King of Marlyst would be less of a dick than his father. Then again if he was worse, perhaps I should consider giving him a medal as that would be a tough act to beat.

'What do we know of the new king?' I asked.

'His name.'

I paused. My eyes flicked over to connect with Amire's, confirming with her heighted sense of hearing she knew what was being discussed. 'Okay, you're on first name basis. That's always a good start, but what else?' I couldn't help the snarky tone that entered my voice.

'Well, I'm not on first name basis with him just yet. I found out through the messenger announcing that His Royal Highness Xylan Marlyst was crowned the new King of Marlyst. That's it, Valare, that is literally all I know,' Eliasson admitted sheepishly, running a hand through his hair.

Oh shit. 'Well, that is …' I stuttered, trying to find the right word.

'A problem?' He supplied.

'I was thinking more along the lines of undesirable. But yes, it's a problem. A big fucking problem. How do we, as royals, not know anything apart from the name of one of our counterparts?' I was completely baffled.

'The late Marlyst King, as you probably can recall from the last Forum, was a difficult character.'

'Understatement of the year,' I scoffed.

His lips twitched, his only sign of agreement. 'Xylan was never brought to any of the Royal Forums, which is unusual as it is quite normal for an heir to attend. It seemed his father didn't place any such importance on transferring his knowledge to his son so he would always attend the forums alone. His children and their mother were nowhere to be seen. It was like that for as long as I could recall, even when my father brought me to the forums as a child. No one dared to make any outright comment for fear of it significantly impacting their negotiations and ability to trade in the future.'

Well, that made sense. Who would want to be in the bad graces of the king who supplied the entire continent with weaponry and, in Arlom's case, the machinery and tools to farm and provide a living for their people?

'Of course, the Queen of Nyarelle was in favour with the late King and the only person he showed a fondness towards. I remember watching the queen making all sorts of teasing comments as to why her favourite heir wasn't at the table. Her jabs always came across as holding a double meaning no one else other than the Marlyst King seemed to understand. Again, your father and mine never dared to question anything, often pretending they never heard the comments in the first place.' He shrugged.

I remained quiet for a moment, taking in all the information. 'So, this Xylan … we need to build rapport with him, fast.'

Eliasson nodded. 'Yes, which is what I wanted to talk to you about.'

'Ah yes, the reason for the scones,' I muttered.

Eliasson let out a laugh before he could stop himself. 'Always so sceptical, Valare. Does it ever occur to you that I may just want to make you happy?'

'No.'

Rolling his eyes, he returned to the previous conversation. 'I need you to get close to Xylan and his people, find out what motivates them, what it is they want. His father was easy to read; he wanted money and a lot of it. Which was fine, I could work with that. But without knowing who this new king is, I don't know where to begin on playing the game with him. We know Nyarelle is still in his back pocket, and I am hoping, as you are a born Salistyan and married to an Arloman, that he may reveal more of his cards to you as you have sway over not one but two Doms.'

Having sway over Salistya was a bit of a stretch. No one had sway over Slaviya. But here we were again, me being just another political pawn in the game. I understood where he was coming from, and I would do it. But only because this helped my alliances once Eliasson was no longer in the game.

'How do you see me getting close to this Xylan?' I asked, intrigued to hear his response.

'In any way you see fit in order to get to the end result,' he replied instantaneously.

'In *any way*?' My jaw dropped in shock. I felt Amire's body stiffen at the insinuation, clearly still within hearing distance for a mage. Maybe I had read him wrong this whole time. Maybe he was like the men I grew up with in the Queendom, not seeing an issue with using a woman's body in whichever way it pleases them.

'What is that look for – oh! Not like that Valare, what do you take me for? A man who is comfortable with using his woman's body to further himself? Absolutely not. You are my wife. Goddess, that is despicable to even think that.'

I couldn't help but sigh out a breath of relief at his genuinely appalled reaction.

'It's not like I haven't seen it done before,' I muttered quietly, feeling defensive. Memories of my mother crying in her room, broken over my father's actions, flooded my mind. The sounds of fighting, her screams, his shouts, orders to do what he was telling her. I shuddered, staring pointedly at the arch behind Eliasson. I might put on a good front, but deep down I held an intense aversion to conflict that even my training hadn't been able to completely eradicate. It didn't take a genius to work out why, not with my horrid upbringing, which Eliasson proved even with his limited knowledge.

Fingers grabbed my chin, inching it up to hold his gaze. 'I am not Salistyan, nor am I anything like your father. Please remember that always, Valare.'

I refused to cry, trying to not let my mental armour crack. Not in front of him.

My responsive nod must have been deemed satisfactory as he moved his hand away to assemble another scone to my specifications. I took the momentary distraction to lock down the lingering thoughts of my mother.

He waited until I had taken a bite of the scone he held out. 'Now that's settled, moving on to the next topic of conversation. I would like to discuss you moving into my quarters permanently.'

Woah! Fucking asshole with his timing! Forcing me to chew and actually think about my response, or risk choking.

I swallowed the scone and the lump in my throat, calling upon all my restraint not to yell at him every reason under the sun why that wasn't a good idea, starting with the simple fact that I liked my own space and I hated sharing a bed. Oh, and I needed space to plan his demise, but probably best not to mention that.

With all the diplomacy I could muster, I kept my tone even as I enquired, 'And where has the need for this discussion arisen from?'

'Well, we've just celebrated our first anniversary. Some space was an understandable request to have as you became accustomed to your new home, the Arloman culture and way of living. I respected that when you first moved in. Now I feel we've got to know each other on many levels and aren't strangers as we once were. But I think we should re-look at our commitments and duties as the rulers of this Kingdom. I feel that, if we were to sleep in the same quarters, we'd have more opportunity to work towards fulfilling those duties.' His eyes took in my body, landing on my stomach.

Fuck. He wanted an heir. He wanted an heir, and he wanted it soon. In the foreseeable future. Not long-term anymore but short-term.

Fuck.

'And by duties, you mean …' I trailed off, wanting to hear him say what he was implying.

'We need to start trying for an heir.'

Alright, this was not ideal. I couldn't come off the contraceptive remedy, ever. I wasn't sure I wanted children, much less with the man who's supposed to be out of the picture soon.

'I understand we have commitments to uphold, one of those being an heir. But do you think this is really the right timing, considering we'll both be distracted with the Royal Forum? Also, is it really necessary for us to be in the same quarters? I don't think anyone could accuse us of not having ample practice in creating an heir.' I smirked seductively at my last comment, trailing my hand up his thigh in the hopes it would distract him.

He placed his hand on mine, intertwining our fingers, stopping my deliberate movements. 'I'm not saying we need to try tomorrow, Valare, only that we need to start planning. I think it's reasonable to start once the Royal Forum has concluded and the royals have left. As to our sleeping arrangements, I have been lenient enough.'

Right. Looks like no distractions were going to work, which left me with negotiation as my only option. But first, flattery.

'You're being very reasonable Eliasson, so I can agree to trying for an heir. As to our sleeping arrangements, you know I don't sleep well when I share a bed, and I think with everything at stake it wouldn't be a strategic move. I should be at my sharpest when conversing with Xylan and his entourage. Having said this, I'll agree to move into your quarters once the Royal Forum is over and life goes back to normal.'

I had to buy myself time. My Sol hadn't even discussed our strategy for move number one, having been focussed on assimilating to the Arloman culture and setting ourselves up here. I needed to be able to stay in my room for this to work.

'I'm not happy about the sleeping arrangements, Valare,' Eliasson warned. 'It's embarrassing to think my wife doesn't want to sleep next to me at night. What would others say if they knew?'

'Happy wife, happy life?' I jokingly replied.

Eliasson let out a frustrated breath. 'Your wit is one of the things I love and despise about you, Val.'

He was quiet for a while, mulling over what I said. 'Fine. I trust you'll do your part and advise the healer of the decision to stop your contraceptive within the next two weeks.'

Stop the contraceptive remedy within the next two weeks.

This is all your fault.

Bright fuchsia eyes.

Knowledge finds those who are meant to see, Valare.

Over and over these recent encounters repeated in my head, fuelling my growing anxiety and knowing that something was coming.

'Valare? Verbal confirmation would be the appropriate action right now.' He sounded pissed. How long had I been lost in my thoughts for?

'Yes,' I squeaked before clearing my throat. 'Yes, Eliasson, I'll do what needs to be done.'

With a satisfied smile, Eliasson pulled me towards him, pressing his lips firmly to mine. I melted into him, arms looping around his neck pulling him closer, trying to shut my mind out from everything that was catching up to me. Trying to play the diplomatic wife. Trying but, ultimately, feeling like I was failing.

Sometime later, we walked back to the palace. On my way, I passed Amire. The sympathetic look she gave me was confirmation enough.

Things were about to get messy.

CHAPTER 7

'Oh, here she is. Queen Valare Arlom has arrived. Everyone bow before Your Tardy Highness,' Mazyr taunted as I landed on the Isles' Training Island.

'You know, he was starting to question my ability to send a simple message, Valare. Not cool,' Rynelle teased as he sat on a massive boulder, quickly twisting a dagger around in his hand, the blade glinting in the light. He ran his other hand through the top of his hair, scratching the side that was buzzed almost to his scalp.

'How many times did I tell you to say 9pm on the note instead of 10pm. But no, no one listens to the best friend.' Meredith sighed, looking exasperated as she leant against a tall willow tree.

'My darling Amire, would you like to put your coppers worth in, while we're at it?' I walked towards Amire and took the seat next to her, completely undeterred by the jokes thrown my way from my tight-knit Sol family. These assholes weren't to know that I had honestly tried to get here on time. Turns out negotiating to stay in my quarters didn't sit as well with Eliasson as I had thought. He had all but demanded my presence in his bed immediately after dinner. Judging from his lengthy performance, I was guessing tiring me out to the point of sleep was his end game. I then had to wait for him to fall asleep before using my magic to ensure he remained in a deep slumber long enough for me to get back before he woke up. The wife life wasn't easy.

'I'm good. Considering the conversation I heard earlier today, I'm quite impressed you were even able to make it tonight,' Amire replied sympathetically, while also throwing me in the deep end.

'What conversation?' Mazyr asked, forever the busybody.

I groaned. 'It doesn't matter, it's not relevant to what we're discussing now.' Honestly, I just wanted a distraction from the events of today, not to rehash them.

'Amire don't make me –' Mazyr started.

'Enough! You're not pulling that twin magic shit,' I growled.

Four pairs of concerned eyes landed on me, followed by complete silence.

'We're here to discuss our plan for how we're going to kill Eliasson. Then I have somewhere else to be. So, let's focus on the task at hand.' All playfulness had left my voice. My directive was met with four stern nods.

I began to relay the information I'd received regarding the Royal Forum, the Marlyst King and Eliasson's expectations of me, minus the heir talk.

Rynelle nodded, oddly seeming pleased with that information. 'Mazyr, Amire and I managed to get away to Salistya yesterday. Queen's orders. She's getting toey, insisting the assassination takes place before the end of the Royal Forum. That way, all Dom representatives are in the same location and could be pinned as the suspect. So we will need to do it in a way that could be done by anyone.'

'Why didn't you tell me she ordered you to visit?' I asked, offended they didn't bother to tell me, but also felt a familiar tingle of unease grow. I had thought I was taking too many precautions, keeping my true plans just between Mer and I. But maybe my unshakeable sense knew there was more going on, some weight behind the unease. An unknown, shifting loyalty slithering into my subconscious.

As a group, we were in an odd situation regarding who it was we answered to overall. I was technically loyal to the Kingdom of Arlom, seeing as I was their Queen. But as Sol, we were all loyal to Solista above all else. As the Isles sat under the Queendom of Salistya, we were supposed to be loyal, and answer to, Salistya. But the Solistan people, including Mer, didn't recognise Slaviya as their ruler. Apparently, I was deserving of their allegiance, despite technically being an Arlom. Further complicating it was the fact that, as their leader, the four members of my Sol should've answered to me. For three of them to have been summoned without my knowledge, and without telling me, an unknown element had been added to an already complex web. And I didn't need to be questioning their loyalty while things were being set in motion.

'You've been busy, and I knew we'd see you tonight. Considering there was nothing of great importance, we didn't think it would be a big deal.' Rynelle shrugged, toying with his lip piercing. His lip caught on the spiked end of the metal, a lick of blood beading up.

His tongue swiped over the red trail, laving his cut lip and clearly revelling in the stinging sensation.

I didn't miss the wary glance Mer threw my way at his comment. Apparently, I wasn't the only one uneasy about this situation.

Deciding the last thing I needed was a blow up between my Sol, I let the issue slide, storing the information for later examination. 'Alright, in the future please let me know of any correspondence with Slaviya. I prefer, where possible, to not be on the back foot with her.'

I received a curt nod in response, which did nothing to settle my creeping anxiety. Why would Slaviya contact my Sol directly? As a courtesy as their leader, I should have been informed.

Never one to disappoint, and sensing the awkward silence, Mazyr simply said, 'Well, if we're throwing out killing ideas to get things moving, you all know I'm a big fan of poison and I'm in a great position to execute it. Pardon the pun.' He winked at me.

As expected, we burst into laughter, successfully breaking the tension.

'Let's start at the beginning with the methodology.' I cleared my throat, wanting to focus on the task at hand.

'Disguise. Deceive. Derail,' Amire stated.

Every trainee Sol had the Solistan Assassination Methodology drilled into them in the early years of training. The elite Sol prided themselves on the idea that this methodology, when utilised effectively, underpinned every successful assassination. In our case, the first two factors had been played earlier and solidified as time went on. Our disguise was each Sol member posing as palace staff, all placed in different areas for maximum coverage. The deception lay in the union between Eliasson and I, but the last section needed a bit of fine-tuning.

Mazyr wrapped his arm around my shoulder comfortingly, pulling me into his side.

Meredith nodded in defeat, my silence speaking volumes.

'I know I need to work on my controlling tendencies,' I blurted out, not being able to stand it. 'There's just so much on the line here. I wanted to minimise collateral on our end as much as possible.'

'We all understand that you're coming from a good place, Val,' Meredith relented. 'But you also need to see it from our side. Slaviya has been breathing down our necks wanting a plan and becoming increasingly more volatile. We could have been drip-feeding her information the last few months and saving our hides. You have a bit more leniency now you're technically an Arloman, but we don't have that luxury.'

The others nodded but remained silent.

'I'm sorry. I'll work on it,' I promised, mentally crossing my fingers.

Amire wrapped her arms around my waist, snuggling in beside me, creating a true twin sandwich. 'Don't apologise, Val, we just want to be more involved.' My eyes met Rynelle's. He stared back intently, almost as if he didn't quite know what to do with me.

I nodded, removing myself from the twins' embrace. 'Heart to heart aside, are we all in agreeance with the proposed assassination?' I asked.

I received a resounding, 'Yes!'

'Now, I have places to be. I'll see you all in Amarald at some stage or another. If there's anything pressing, send word and I'll try to make myself available. With the Royal Forum approaching it'll become increasingly difficult for me to get away, so make it worth my while.'

'Have you got another rendezvous planned?' Mer asked, curiosity filled her voice.

Strategically avoiding all eyes on me, I shook my head. 'No, I have more pressing matters to settle.' In truth, upon reflection, that night with Sir had rattled me. His treatment of me had opened up my eyes a little and made me question the authenticity of our relationship. It wasn't just him in the situation, and telling me it was all my fault was becoming hard to justify to myself. No, I didn't want to see him. Honestly, I wanted to avoid him at all costs.

Not waiting for a reply, I teleported out of there.

I landed on the other side of the island in a familiar front yard. It was a welcome sight as I hurried up the stairs to the porch, making my way inside without bothering to introduce my presence. They already knew I was here.

Through the narrow hallway, I entered the beautiful open plan kitchen and dining area. I ignored the expectant gazes of the couple sitting at the dining table and walked to the glass wall at the end of the room. From there I saw a stunning view of the cliffs which revealed the edge of the island. Dark blue ocean spanned from there to the horizon, Spreading as far as the eye could see in every direction.

I let the view calm my mind as I breathed deeply. Already despising what was to come, I braced against the hit my ego was about to take before I even said the words.

I turned to face the two people staring at me, no trace of surprise at my dramatic show. It wasn't the first time I'd stormed in like an unannounced wrecking ball.

'I need your help.'

CHAPTER 8

'So, he's finally pulled the royal duties card on you.' Amusement laced in Varqel's voice. 'Credit where credit is due, the man has more patience than I originally thought he had.'

I rolled my eyes, crossing my feet on the chair as I reached over the table to serve myself yet another round of fish soup. No one's soup beat Lyzia's. I shut my eyes as I took another ridiculously big spoonful, groaning in delight at the party in my mouth.

'I'm glad I listened to your suggestion to make a bigger serving, dear,' Lyzia laughed, her burnt orange eyes lighting up as she grinned at Varqel. Lyzia was the only Nyarellean that had been granted access to the Isles. Having studied healing her whole life in the Queendom, when she met Varqel and fell hopelessly in love with him, she moved to the Isles, and was welcomed thanks to being an exceptional healer. Around these places a healer was a hot commodity. Usually, Salistya had strict rules surrounding people from other Doms living in their jurisdiction.

'Well, she does have an uncanny ability to show up unannounced the nights that soup is on the table,' Varqel stated dryly.

'In my defence, I do have a one in seven chance of landing on soup night considering this is a staple on your weekly menu,' I said in between mouthfuls, no doubt looking very unattractive. Good thing V and Lyz were like parents to me.

'I see your table manners haven't got much better since you've become a queen,' he snickered.

'I blame my lack of table manners on the ridiculously good food. No time to think, all the time to enjoy.' I shrugged unapologetically.

'I'm flattered you enjoy my food so much, Little One.' Lyzia smiled fondly at me. 'But back to the matter at hand.'

I choked on my food, remembering my reason for being here. I had temporarily forgotten it in my enjoyment of the soup.

Varqel rolled his eyes before handing me a glass of water. 'Honestly Valare, you knew this was coming. It amazes me that you're surprised at this development.'

'I think it was more the demand that I stop the contraceptive remedy. The two-week time frame really hit home for me,' I huffed.

'In two weeks?' Lyzia exclaimed, roughly brushing her long copper curls off her face, eyes widening.

I nodded vigorously. Now she finally understood the urgency behind my request.

'And you said this conversation happened today?' Varqel queried, rubbing his hands soothingly down his wife's back.

'Yes, this afternoon. He then proceeded to not let me leave his sight until I eventually had to knock him out with my magic to be able to come here,' I explained, highly irritated that Eliasson had been this smart.

'He knows that, given space, you can be quite resourceful. Smart man,' Varqel laughed approvingly.

'Hey V, friendly reminder that you're supposed to be on my side,' I emphasised.

He simply smirked at me, his lips spreading wider when I childishly poked my tongue out at him.

'I need to get to work if I'm going to have the longer lasting contraceptive remedy potent enough for you to start taking in two weeks. How is your power feeling, Valare?' Lyzia questioned.

All remedies were stronger the longer they're brewed, which was important as, the more powerful a mage was, the stronger the remedy needed to be. For someone with my power, two weeks was the minimum brewing time. Although he didn't know why, Eliasson knew it took two weeks for my contraceptive remedy to be ready. Which was why he'd given me the two-week deadline today. The smart bastard.

'From a physical magic perspective, strong as usual. From a knowing perspective, it's getting stronger. More definitive when I use it.' Outside of Mer, these two were the only people I would divulge the extent of my knowing to.

Varqel nodded understandingly while Lyzia cursed quietly.

'Come see me in two weeks, Valare. I'll ensure it is ready. Always good to see you, dear,' she said before turning to her husband and giving him a kiss on the lips. 'Honey, I'll leave it for you to arrange the rest?' she asked, before walking out of the room without waiting for a reply, already knowing Varqel would handle things.

'What would you do without the head healer in the Solista Isles?' Varqel teased.

'Have an Arloman child?' I quipped, but my grimace gave me away. 'I almost want to see this come to fruition, purely to watch Slaviya have kittens,' he laughed, eyes twinkling with delight.

'Can you imagine. My life, quite literally, would not be worth living.' I couldn't help the twitch of my lips though. The visual was amusing and I did enjoy pissing off my sister, but not to the extent of having a baby. One had to draw the line somewhere, and I felt this was a pretty good point to do it.

'Ah well, merely a funny thought. Lyzia and I won't let that happen. Not unless you want it to,' he stated seriously. 'Speaking of what you want, have you worked out what you're going to do once you've fulfilled your sister's desires? You'll be flying solo, after all. What's your next step?'

'Well, it depends on how the assassination plays out.'

'You have a plan, do you not?'

'I do.'

'And have you communicated this plan to your fellow Sol?' He knew me too well.

'I just did, before I came here.'

He rolled his eyes, not surprised I left it to the last minute. 'And?'

'And they had no feedback apart from annoyance at the fact that I withheld this information from them without collaborating.'

'What was your reasoning for only telling them now?'

I loved that V knew me. He knew there was a reason behind my actions. 'The same reason Eliasson only gave me two weeks. I didn't want to give anyone time to be resourceful, not even my own Sol. I want to have full control over how this plays out.'

'You've had a premonition,' Varqel stated, realisation lighting up his face.

I pursed my lips. 'Not sure I would call it a premonition. More an extension of the knowing?'

Varqel waited patiently while I collected my thoughts.

'I can't shake the feeling that something bad is going to happen and I won't be able to stop it. Something feels wrong. It's driving me nuts that I can't put my finger on it,' I shook my head. 'Maybe I'm overthinking it. You know I tend to do that when I'm overwhelmed or stressed. I'm following my training, putting in place contingencies. I'm doing everything right. But I just can't help feeling I'm not doing enough or I have missed something. Does any of that make sense? Am I going crazy?'

'You're not going crazy, Little One. I understand what you're saying, more than you know.' Varqel smiled softly.

'You do?' I asked, hopeful.

'I do.'

'Well, at least that's something,' I let out on a breath.

He leant forward, elbows on the table and hands clasped in a fist under his chin. 'What's the plan?'

'Well, I refuse to accept the hand that has been dealt to me. I plan to beat Slaviya at her own game. If she is not going to divulge her intentions, why would I simply go along with her orders blindly? Ultimately, I want my choices to be my own.'

'Good.'

'Good?'

'Yes, I raised you better than to be someone else's pawn, Valare. I was simply waiting for you to decide you didn't want that, either.' Varqel's voice was filled with sincerity; his face radiated with fatherly pride.

I turned my head, distracting myself with the ocean view. I didn't want him to see the tears welling up in my eyes at his declaration. After a few minutes of quiet contemplation, Varqel's voice interrupted the silence. 'So,' he said conversationally.

I turned to face him with a questioning look.

'What do you need from me?'

I jumped at his invitation to divulge all my thoughts on the matter, going into far greater detail than I did with my Sol members. Varqel sat back and listened calmly. As head trainer and the Solista army's general, he took every piece of information I gave him with serious thought and consideration.

After I finished, he simply nodded, acknowledging my rationale.

'So, what do you think?' I gnawed at my lip, self-doubt kicking in.

'I think you're right.'

I felt the tension in my body leave immediately. I had not realised how much I needed his approval.

'I trust you're happy for me to discuss this with Lyzia?' Varqel asked.

'Of course,' I rushed out. 'I trust you two with my life.'

He reached his hand out to grab mine, giving it a squeeze. 'I'm so glad we can be that for you, Little One. Know that we also trust you with our lives. You are like the daughter we never had. Nothing will ever come between us, promise me.' Despite the comforting squeeze, his eyes looked troubled.

'I promise.' I didn't know how to ask what was wrong. V was always capable, always calm, so I let it go for the time being.

With one last squeeze and a smile, he pulled away, stood up and started to clear away dinner. I followed suit, taking the dirty dishes to the kitchen to wash up.

'You've had a big day, just leave it there Valare. I'll take care of it.'

'Are you sure? I don't mind.'

He simply nodded, nudging me towards the end of the counter before taking my position by the sink.

'In that case, do you mind if I stay for a bit longer? I wouldn't mind spending some time in my old room for a while. Being away from reality sounds like a great idea right now,' I said.

V chuckled, reading between the lines. He knew full well that I regularly needed my own space. 'Stay as long as you like, Little One. Your room is exactly how you left it last. If I don't see you before you go, stay safe, stay sharp, and remember what I taught you.'

'You're the best,' I grinned. I headed back down the narrow hallway, up the stairs to the right, and into the humble room I called my own.

When Varqel initially realised the potential of my power, he insisted on private training sessions with me at his estate. As time went on and we discovered more of my abilities – including being able to teleport much further than anyone else, levitate both myself and other objects, conjure items from thin air and send them off to a chosen location, move the contents in a room at will, and creating wards that shielded rooms– the more prone I was to being too fatigued to teleport back to the barracks. Despite Varqel's ability to teleport me back himself, Lyz and V gave me my own bedroom. From there, the fatigue-induced-sleepovers turned into dinner after training and breakfast the next morning. Before I knew it, they essentially became my adopted parents. Apart from Dwyla, they felt like the only true family I had. It hurt not to count my own biological mother in that, knowing full well that my father's control had significantly limited her abilities to be a good parent, but that didn't change her lack of involvement or care.

I hurried to the floorboards beside the modest single bed. Hovering my hand over the slightly discoloured floorboard, I reached my magic under the floor, searching for the lock that would only recognise me.

Click.

Got it.

Heaving the floorboard up and pushing it to the side, I looked at the black book laid on the top, the glowing eye blinking as brightly as it had earlier. I grabbed it before clambering onto the bed. Legs crossed under me, I found myself leaning towards the book, intently staring at it like I was waiting for something to happen, almost like I needed permission to open the book.

Knowledge finds those who are meant to see. The words the Nyarellean woman spoke earlier came back to me, but this time it was a male voice. At the same time, the mark below my ear flared up with the same humming pulse I had felt in the Temple. I guess this was as good a sign as any that I needed to read this book.

I opened the book, surprised to see a blank page with nothing but a title on it. Flipping through more pages, I found the same format throughout. Strange.

With a flick of my wrist, the pages turned until the book was back open to the first page, aptly named *The Beginning*. Training my fingers over the title, the further I went, the more I felt the pulse of my tattoo warm. Much like in the Temple, I felt a surge of power enter me. Eyes closing once my finger had finished caressing the last letter of the title before I could stop them, my mind was launched into a spiralling, black vortex. The sensation of my body fell away as my mind was sucked into a hazy scene.

CHAPTER 9

A shriek of giggles filled the air surrounding the daisy-filled meadows as a young blonde-haired woman, no more than eighteen years of age, burst out from behind the trees. She had her floor length dress pulled up so it fell around her knees. She glanced behind her frequently and ran at a pace that gave away her true intentions; she wanted to be caught.

The young woman ran further into the field of daisies, making it only a couple of steps before the man following her burst through the dense forest. He stopped at the entrance of the field. Bright fuchsia eyes glazed with desire, he focused solely on the woman who had turned to face him. She still held her dress as she braced to run at any moment. Her giggles slowly subsided.

'So, how are we going to play this, darling?' he crooned, taking a couple of purposeful steps towards her.

Her answer was to teleport a couple of steps back, smirking in response to the roll of his eyes.

'We've all got tricks up our sleeves, little Minx,' he reminded her, cocking his head to the side, watching as she inadvertently pulled the dress up to mid-thigh.

'You bastard,' she gasped, hands shaking in an evident attempt to stop them from moving upwards.

'Now, now, we both know you don't mean that, my love.' He wore a feline grin and moved towards her, his steps predatory. She released a deep moan.

Dropping her skirts, she flicked her wrist and the shirt he wore ripped straight down the middle, exposing sculpted abs and tight chest. Before he could react, his body was lifted up, levitating off the ground. The young woman teleported to stand in front of him and traced a single finger down the expanse of his torso, stopping an inch below his belly button.

'My future husband,' she whispered, biting her lip which elicited another deep, wanting groan, this time from him. The young woman giggled teasingly, levitating off the ground until they were eye to eye. 'I like the sound of that.' She reached forward, tucking a strand of his long, wavy, copper hair behind his ear.

'I'd be concerned if you didn't, considering the bureaucratic hurdles we had to clear to get the royals to give up their titles. But, it's finally over,' he sighed, eyes flickering closed in relief.

She took the opportunity to lean his body backwards, lowering him to the ground. She followed, straddling his hips, and placed her hands on his bare chest.

'I love you, too,' she said suddenly.

The smile he gifted her was one of complete adoration and love. It was the kind of smile that said he would run to the ends of the earth and beyond to protect her, to adore her, to love her. One of his hands cupped her cheek, the other wrapped around her waist. He brought her body towards his, crashing their mouths together. Their kiss was slow and passionate, conveying the deep love they shared.

They eventually pulled apart, his hand gently stroking her hair.

'Do you know what sounds better than betrothed?' he asked.

'The future rulers of Fyriane?' she teased.

He leant forward nipped her bottom lip in admonishment before resting back down on the ground. 'No, my beautiful tease. Our fated destiny. What we are and were always meant to be. That is what sounds better.'

She nodded knowingly and sighed in contentment as she settled on top of him, resting her cheek over his heart.

'True Infinite,' she whispered in quiet reverence, opening her eyes.

For the first time, her eyes were visible.

They were glowing. And lime green.

I woke with a start, eyes jolting open, rays of sunlight poured into the room. The room that was different to my one in Amarald. Which meant I was still at Varqel and Lyzia's.

'Shit! Eliasson will be awake now.' I scrambled out of the bed, straightening my clothes. My eyes searched for the book next to the imprint of my body on the mattress. Where did it go? Did I move it? It wouldn't be the first time my magic moved something in my sleep. Crazier things had happened. Like that dream.

I shook my head, as I raced to the floorboard to find it in its original place. I didn't have the luxury of entertaining what the dream was all about as I teleported back to Amarald and landed in my bathroom. The floating steam told me the bath had been drawn recently.

A second later, Meredith burst through the door from my bedroom, demanding to know where I had been.

'I fucked up. I fell asleep, I didn't mean to be gone past sunrise,' I interrupted her. 'Where's Eliasson? What's happened? How much damage control is there to do?'

Stance wide, Meredith had her hands on her hips, looking completely unimpressed. 'I came to check in on you about an hour ago to make sure you got back safe. Luckily I did because I sensed him wake up not long after. I started your bath before meeting him in the dining quarters, advising him that you'd woken up unwell and had summoned me. I bought you a bit of time, but it looked like he wanted to see you, Val. I insisted you were too self-conscious for him to see you in this state, which placated him a little, but I think he'll be coming around in the next half an hour if you don't show yourself before then.'

I cursed. An overbearing, worried Eliasson wasn't what I needed today. I hurriedly undressed, placing one foot into the bath, testing the water.

'I didn't know what other excuse to use, but I don't think he bought it. I didn't have much time and I had no idea when you'd be back,' Mer defended.

'No, you did great, Mer. Thank you. I'm sorry I put you in this position in the first place, it wasn't my intention. I planned to be back in his room before he woke up.' I put my other foot in, sinking into the luscious warmth, and let out a heavy sigh.

'It happens. That's what I'm here for,' she shrugged.

I cleared my throat. 'So, last night's meeting …'

Meredith started pacing, a sign she was unnerved.

'Interesting,' I finished.

She threw me a look. 'Interesting is one word. Unsettling, maybe. Downright sketchy are others. Slaviya's up to something. If she weren't, why wasn't I summoned with the others? She's not dense enough to think my loyalty to you would stray, but the rest of them? Does she see something we don't?' She shook her head.

'Who knows, but it's not as if we didn't expect this. We're still ahead of her, Mer. This could simply be her way of unsettling us. Or punishment for not having a plan yet. With Slaviya, there's always myriad possibilities, but the root cause is usually her shitting herself. So she makes a couple of petty moves to feel like she's in control again,' I shrugged. 'Standard behaviour. Nothing new.'

Meredith laughed in disbelief. 'How you can be so relaxed about this is beyond me.'

'Oh, I'm not relaxed at all. It's all a façade, darling. Call it the queen in me.' I winked, trying to ease the tension. 'Before I forget, excellent job last night. You played your part well.'

'Do you think they bought it?'

'You were essentially telling the truth, listing out all my flaws, so how could they not?' I joked, not mentioning the harsh truths had elicited real reactions in me, despite my prior knowledge of what would be said.

'Well, that's true,' Mer responded, calling my bluff.

'Ouch.' I placed a hand on my heart, feigning offense at her words and ignoring the lingering twinge in my centre.

'So, where were you last night if you weren't with lover boy?' she asked.

I spent the rest of my bath filling her in on the details I'd omitted last night: the contraceptive remedy, Eliasson wanting an heir, moving into his living quarters. By the time I'd finished she'd sunk down to the floor next to me. Her jaw had dropped open, and she gripped my hands tightly.

'You're reacting as if all of these expectations have been placed on you,' I commented, highly amused.

She stared into space for another minute or two, processing the information before shaking herself out of her stupor. 'So, you went to see Varqel.'

I nodded.

'Lyz has got you?'

Another nod.

'And you discussed things with him about –?'

'Yes.' I cut her off, wary about discussing details with Eliasson likely to appear at any moment.

'Good.' She released a relieved breath. 'That's good. Okay, we've had some wins, it's not all bleak.'

I laughed at her dramatic words, shaking my head as I stepped out of the bathtub, grabbing the nearest towel and drying myself. 'I can confirm it's not all bleak. Stressful and overwhelming, but not bleak.'

Before she could respond, a knock sounded through the room. 'Valare?'

Mer and I looked at each other. I'd hoped to have a little more time.

What do you want to do? She mouthed to me.

I raised two fingers, letting her know I needed a couple of minutes before I'd come out.

She nodded, heading into the bedroom. I heard the door open, and Mer tell Eliasson I'd be there soon.

I sighed, making my way to my wardrobe, and changed into the first dress I saw. As much as I would like to stay in my rooms for the rest of the day dissecting the events of the last twenty-four hours, I couldn't afford a day off. Not when the fun was just getting started.

I walked to the door joining my quarters to the dining area. Pulling my shoulders back, I took a big breath, pasted a smile on my face, and pushed open the door.

Just another damn day of playing the game.

CHAPTER 10

I couldn't help letting a groan out as I lay back on the shaded grass, hiding away in a secluded area of the palace gardens that no one, other than myself, visited. Goddess, I was tired.

The last ten days had been a blur; filled with Forum preparations, working with Mer to finalise the Royal Quarters, taste testing and approving menus. Meanwhile my nights were spent placating Eliasson, who'd become increasingly demanding of my time and affection, before I rushed to Varqel's until the early hours of the morning.

My time there was insightful as I worked my way through the book. The visions had shown me the lives of a young couple who wed and, soon after, became the leaders of Fyriane. I had learned that, apparently once upon a time our continent was united, the individual Doms seemingly non-existent. From what I had gathered, the King and the Queen were beloved by their people, almost as if they were a salvation their people were looking for. But, what did they need saving from?

The couple went on to have four children, two boys, Arlom and Marlyst, and, two girls, Nyarelle and Salistya – and I didn't think it was a coincidence they were the four names of the Doms today. No, I was beginning to think that the royals today were their descendants, ruling over the respective lands of their ancestors.

As the children grew older, it was clear they'd inherited the magic of their parents, who I'd figured out were the Goddess Wystia and the God Merlot. Merlot was the God revered in Marlyst and Nyarelle. I had never learnt why they had a different God, having merely been taught – or more to the point ordered – from a young age to never acknowledge this faux God. But I knew that just as Salistya and Arlom didn't recognise Merlot as a God, they wouldn't accept Wystia as a Goddess.

It was evident Wystia's magic was physical in nature, much like my own, and the eldest child, Salistya, and the youngest, Arlom, exhibited these gifts as well. However, Merlot's magic wasn't obvious in either him, or the remaining two children. Maybe he didn't have any? Or it hadn't been passed on? But even as I considered this, I knew in my bones that Merlot was a mage and Marlyst and Nyarelle had inherited it. I just didn't know what his affinities were or whether they appeared today like Wystia's did. I had never heard of any magic outside of the magic gifted on the Solista Isles. Whatever this magic was, could it still be alive in the Doms today? What would it look like?

Knowledge finds those who are meant to see. The Nyarellean woman certainly hinted at knowing more. How else did she know Eliasson was around the corner that day in the markets? I wondered what the Nyarellean Queendom was hiding, and what was I meant to see?

For the millionth time, I cursed Salistya and the lack of education regarding our continent's history. The Queendom simply didn't place value on teaching subjects that fell outside what was required to sculpt trainees into weapons; weapons that were utilised as the leaders saw fit. Such a damn waste.

I rubbed my eyes, my frustration grew as I wondered whether there was any point trying to understand what this all meant, or if it even was anything more than a potentially fabricated story and a market woman playing games.

But there was no doubt there was deep magic embedded in the book itself for it to provide those visions. My magic felt it. After all, like called to like. The question was, how was the magic stored in the book?

Having control over all four elements plus some additional magic, I was the strongest mage known on this continent, and even I didn't know how to store magic in objects. Maybe I needed to keep a close eye on the Nyarellean Queen at the Royal Forum, not just the Marlyst King. Maybe I could find out what they knew about Fyriane's history. Thank the Goddess for my ability to teleport frequently without needing to regenerate my power often – I didn't know how anyone could successfully spy without it. There were too many places to be, and not enough time.

On top of this, there were now the matters of my love life. Eliasson would be dealt with soon, so that was one down, but Sir? I had no clue what to do. Understandably, my marriage had changed everything. Our love story could be likened to the books Mer and I read. He'd chased me, and originally I was, quite frankly, not interested. Back then I was too busy enjoying my newfound freedom, and, having only been exposed to controlling and barbaric Salistyan men, my opinion of them, in general, was extremely low. Why would I tie myself to a relationship only to be treated as an object? A toy to be played with and controlled, never to be seen as an equal partner? No, thanks.

But he turned out to be different. His values and beliefs were in line with the liberal Solistans. He didn't show any Salistyan tendencies. Soon my walls had started dropping, and our love grew into one of adoration, respect, and, above all, equality. His touches were doting, his bedroom caresses sensual, always giving as much as he got.

Now our relationship had turned into something else. Something dark, accusatory, and resentful. It was a far cry from what it had been. Although I loved the rough, physical aspect to our relationship, I equally craved the soft touches we once shared, and the feeling of warmth, like being in perpetual sunshine, I would get when we made love. He was the only man I enjoyed making love to, the only one with whom it felt like it meant something. But we hadn't shared moments like those since my marriage.

That night on the Isles had left a bad taste in my mouth I hadn't been able to get rid of. The more I thought on his short rebuffs, his dismissal of my feelings, the increasing blame placed on me for anything and everything, the more I realised that in the last year he had never taken accountability for any of his less than desirable actions. And there were plenty of those to go around. Up until now, I had dismissed them, excused his actions for hurt; for losing me, in a sense, as I was unwilling to run away with him, to live a life in exile.

But that night? It awakened something. Forced me to look at things in a different light: instead of providing an excuse or an apology, he would place the onus of his behaviour on me and my actions. Whether I was not doing enough to earn his love, rubbing my relationship with Eliasson in his face, being too emotional to think logically, there was always something. And it would always result in a punishment.

The lines had become blurry. Sure, in the moment it was fun. But on reflection, the punishment didn't feel like a fun, sexual act fulfilling both our desires anymore. It didn't feel healthy between us now. He hadn't stayed. There was no after care, no talking it through, no checking on me. Nothing. And that was a problem. I was discarded how I always imagined the Salistyan women in the breeding villages were once the men had their way with them. It was awful, not something I ever wanted to experience again.

I needed to see him, though, to test the waters to see whether my realisations were correct. And if they were, well, I would need to have a serious think about how I would navigate us moving forward.

I clicked my fingers, summoning a piece of paper and pen before I could back away from the realisation that we needed to have a conversation. I wrote a note, scrunched it up, and felt it leave my hand, making its way to him. I couldn't let this linger anymore, not with the rulers of the other Doms days away from arriving. I needed all my focus there.

Sighing, I cast my magic wide, sifting through the nearby presences. Satisfied that the closest presence was far away enough to not see anything, I flicked my wrist around my head once in a circular motion. Earth magic sprang from my palm, manipulating the branches of the willow tree that I sat under, lengthening towards the ground. I'd need to undo it later or risk too many questions I didn't want to answer, but it effectively created a circular boundary around me, the branch walls unable to be penetrated from the outside. It also meant it was annoyingly dark. Maybe I did too good of a job calling on the branches.

I sat there for quite some time, waiting for him to appear. By the time he teleported, I was on edge, and had gotten up to pace back and forth.

'You called?'

I felt his hot breath on my neck and forced myself to physically hold in a shiver. I cleared my throat, taking a step away, and turned to face him. 'We need to talk.'

'About?'

'Us,' I exhaled, closing my eyes, running my hands down my face. Despite my hands covering my eyes, light began to infiltrate the cracks. Dropping my hands, I saw his two extended ones. A ball of fire in one was lighting up the space; the other held a bouquet of yellow roses.

'You forgot a light in your makeshift cave,' he smiled ruefully. It was a smile I hadn't seen on his face in such a long time that it made me melt into the sixteen-year-old girl who fell in love with him. Had I been overreacting about the other night?

'Show off.' I rolled my eyes, trying my best to not give him anything. Not until he apologised.

'And these are for you.' He stepped forward, forcing the yellow roses into my hand and not letting go.

I allowed the touch for a second before taking a smooth step away. 'Thank you. What drove you to buy me some flowers?' I asked cautiously, hoping it was his version of an apology.

'Well, I was hoping we would see each other today. I know you're going through a lot and roses are your favourite.'

The warmth I had felt curdled. Yes, roses were my favourite but not yellow roses. Red ones were, the roses of love. Yellow roses were the kind of flowers you gave to someone as a condolence for their grandma's death. Last I checked, my grandmother didn't die yesterday. She was long gone.

I took a good, hard look at the roses and noticed that out of the twelve, seven of them were already starting to wilt. I called my magic to the surface. Nostrils flaring, I zoned in on the wilted flowers. They lacked the sweet and spicy notes usually present in fresh flowers, So I knew they had to be cut around a week ago. Which meant they would have been on sale in the markets, about to be thrown out. Considering the time it took for him to receive my note and get here, I would put gold on him teleporting to some markets before coming, realising something was amiss. But he would have been disgusted at the steep price of red roses and settled for these dying yellow ones instead.

So in translation, it said, *I had no idea you would want to see me today. I know our relationship wasn't great right now, so I rushed around to grab you something. I didn't want to pay the full price for red roses though, despite having plenty of gold, but these yellow ones were on sale.*

The idiot shouldn't have bothered.

'Thanks.' That was the politest response I could give. And I must admit, I was proud of myself for not snapping.

'Honestly, Valare? I don't know why I bother,' he snapped, his emotions turning on a dime like they always did when I didn't react how he wanted me to.

Here we go. Well, at least he received one diplomatic response out of me before my temper snapped to the surface. 'You don't know why you bother? Are you hearing yourself right now?'

'I come as soon as I can, I give you flowers trying to be thoughtful, and the only response you have is thanks.'

'Well, you do come as soon as you can. Can't fucking argue with that part,' I muttered.

'Excuse me?'

'You heard me. You treated me like absolute shit the other night. Yes, I understand this has been hard for us both and we're limited in when we can see each other. But when we do? You call me a whore, deny me any real pleasure, and leave me high and dry without even talking. Not fucking cool, pal.'

His jaw clenched when I said 'pal'. It was a cheap shot, as I knew how much he hated it, but I didn't care. 'It was roleplay, Valare, and you loved it. You like being treated like a good little whore.'

'Yes, I used to. But now – '

'But now what?' he demanded. 'Your interests have changed now that you're with *him?*'

'No, not because I'm with him. This has got nothing to do with him. I don't like being called a whore or treated like one when it doesn't feel like roleplay. You left that night without discussing things. I know things haven't been the same over the last year. But not once have you ever walked away from me like that before.' I wrapped my arms around myself.

'And whose fault is it that we haven't been the same for the last year?' he accused, latching onto that part and dismissing the rest.

'It's neither of ours! This was out of both of our control and you know it! Why do you keep saying that this is my fault?' I cried, lips trembling.

Anger filled his eyes, his tone dropping. 'I'm not the royal here, Valare. Nor am I the one who decided to give us a shot. You could have refused me those years ago. You knew of the potential for your royal duties to separate us. Then you could have said no to your sister, provided another option. You could have ended us once the marriage was going ahead and saved us from all of this. But no. You're still so choked up on my dick that you couldn't do it, any of it. And I'm the idiot in love with you so I go along with it because I'd rather have something of you than nothing, regardless of everything else.'

True, he's not the royal. False, I did refuse his advances and he had continued to pursue me until I gave in. True, I could've said no to my sister, but the result would be living a life in exile, away from my Sol, V, Lyz, and Dwyla. False, I tried to end our relationship and he kept pulling me back in for more, holding our sexual attraction over me time and time again. True, he's in love with me. And knowing that part alone made my resolve waver. Every. Single. Time.

Fuck, I could feel the tears coming.

'Why are we putting ourselves through this then? There's no way out of this situation I'm in. When I'm not obligated to fulfil this mission, I'll be handling the fallout, figuring out what comes next. I don't know when we could properly be together. You and I both deserve more than this. We both deserve a chance to have a healthy relationship that isn't hidden in the shadows,' I whispered, wiping away a rogue tear.

He nudged my chin up with his fingers, forcing eye contact, his face softening in a way that didn't seem possible with his anger moments ago. 'When I ask myself why we bother, I remember how we created our own little tree house on the Training Island. The late nights lazing under the stars, wrapped around each other. I remember you handing me cards under the table, making sure I beat Mazyr and Meredith because you know I can't stand losing. I remember our first kiss. We were both excited and nervous, stumbling our way through it. Both pretending that it wasn't our first kiss, trying to impress the other,' he recalled.

I gave him a soft smile, my resolve wavering. 'That kiss was awful.'

'It was,' he laughed. 'But you know what?'

'What?'

'It was real. Our good times far outweigh the bad. Sometimes love isn't rainbows and butterflies. That is why I won't give up on us. I love you, Valare. I want us, no matter how long it takes. No matter how much I have to help you through your doubt.'

Memories of the good times rushed through my mind. We had grown up together, experienced so much over the years. I had missed it lately. Maybe once everything was over we could go back to that. 'I love you, too. I'm sorry. I'm trying to be good to you. I'm trying to make things better. I just don't know how.' I broke, tears running down my face. This was the best, most productive conversation we had had in a long time.

'Hey, hey, come here,' he hushed, pulling me into his arms and bringing us down onto the grass. 'It's okay, baby, I know you're trying. You're just dealing with a lot and it clouds your perception of things sometimes. But that's why I'm here, to balance you out. I wouldn't be good for you if I didn't call things out for what they are, would I, my sweet?'

'You're right. You do help balance things out. There's just so much and I don't know how to get out of it,' I whispered sadly, snuggling my face further into his chest, finding comfort in the man who had always been honest with me, always my equal.

He kissed my forehead as his hand brushed away loose strands of hair from my face. He pulled my face to his. Our lips came together in a sweet, patient kiss.

I knew it was risky to do this here, but I couldn't help myself, caught up in memories of our times together. It felt like old times as he laid me back on the blanket, hovering over me. Slowly, gently, he removed my clothes. We made love like it was our first time. Curious hands wandered over one another, quiet giggles and gentle caresses everywhere as we immersed ourselves in one another, the world around us forgotten. It was just him and me.

'I loved everything about that, but is it possible if you could, maybe, focus on my pleasure a little bit more?' I shyly asked afterwards, tracing my fingers over his stomach, enjoying the aftermath of our coupling and not wanting to ruin it, but needing to say it.

'I would if I could, Valare. We've discussed this though, you're so picky and hard to get off. I try. But how long do you honestly expect me to hold out for? It's pretty unfair of you to ask me this.'

Funny, Eliasson had no problem with it. I swallowed the lump in my throat, ignoring the unbidden thought, realising the confrontation it would bring would never change anything. Instead, I whispered a meek 'okay' in an attempt to keep the peace. It worked, but the moment was broken for me.

Eventually we separated. I remained on the blanket, a mixture of emotions swirling within. I watched as he quickly dressed, leaning down for a peck.

'I love you,' he said, running a firm hand through my hair. I didn't return the sentiment, nor did he wait for it. Instead, he straightened and teleported away.

I chose to stay amongst the branches, thoughts of our conversation playing on a continuous loop, the softness of our love rapidly leaving me. I was beyond frustrated that the conversation had gone exactly the way it always did. I went in knowing I had valid points, only to question myself and be roped back in with his memories of the good times we had shared. Like always, he left the conversation without apologising and I was left feeling like the worst person ever because I asked for what I wanted. Why couldn't I learn?

My head dropped between my knees, tears streaming down my face.

The verdict was in. The biggest loser award went to yours truly.

CHAPTER 11

I stumbled through the dining room in our Royal Quarters hours later only to be met by a dishevelled and alarmed Meredith.

'Thank Goddess you're here, I've been trying to find you to warn you that –' she whispered before being cut off.

'Well, hello sister.'

My body stiffened, a cold rigidity settling through my whole being at the sharp familiarity of the voice.

This was awful timing. Granted, there was never a right time to be in her presence. But especially not when Sir's scent was lingering on my body and my eyes were probably still swollen. Here's to hoping she didn't notice.

Pivoting, I faced the door to my bedroom where my older sister stood. My eyes trailed the length of her body. I took in the long-sleeved moss-green gown that covered her from head to toe, a look I only ever saw her wear during the Royal Forum. Ordinarily, she wore the mandatory hideous Salistyan-prescribed uniform, despite being the queen. Her sharp jawline and high cheek bones looked impossibly gaunt, much more so than the last time I saw her, and her brown hair was piled up into a tight bun on top of her head, not a strand out of place. Those wicked lips of hers were pursed in evident distaste, while her mossy green eyes shone with the unforgiving cruelty I knew she possessed. They were the eyes of our father.

'Slaviya.' My curt response was the only thing I could manage. I received an unimpressed eyebrow raise in response.

Forcing myself to expel the deep breath I was holding and loosen my shoulders, hoping she wouldn't notice the deliberate action, I sauntered across the dining table. I dropped onto one of the chairs and draped an arm over the back of another. 'To what do I owe the pleasure of your unannounced presence?'

'Is it unannounced or are your staff merely incapable of executing basic duties?' she countered.

It took all my willpower to not grit my teeth. I glanced towards Meredith, her tense body frozen in the same spot she was in when I had first arrived. 'You're dismissed, Meredith. Please ensure my sister and Bastra's quarters are ready for their stay.'

'Valare, I believe you need a reminder about who Meredith answers to.'

The damn controlling witch.

I mockingly placed a hand on my chest in false offense, sniffling, 'And here I thought you wanted to spend some quality one on one time with me, not train my already trained staff. You're breaking my heart, Slaviya.' Probably not a great move to goad her, but her controlling tendencies were already grating and I had been in her presence all of a minute.

Her eyes narrowed, yet she surprisingly conceded. 'I'm interested to see how the trained-assassin-turned-maid performs her duties. Make sure my quarters are to my standard and you need not bother with Bastra, I came by myself. You are dismissed.'

The condescending bitch didn't even look at Meredith, narrowed eyes never leaving my own.

I broke Slaviya's gaze to look at Meredith and she nodded, shooting me a look of thanks as she darted out of the room. At least one of us could be saved from this conversation.

I returned my gaze to Slaviya, waving my hand in invitation to the chair opposite. She proceeded to lean against the door frame and crossed her arms, maintaining her physical advantage, levelling me with a challenging stare.

I didn't supress the grit of my teeth this time. 'Come on Slaviya, are you really going to play it like this? Who are you trying to impress here? Look around, it's only us,' I said, gesturing to the empty room.

'What if I prefer standing?' she countered.

I shrugged, her stubbornness a familial trait. 'Suit yourself, but we both know your energy is drained after the teleport from Savast.'

My sister had trained as a Sol after her magic revealed she had strengths in both fire and earth. Despite her superior magic to the everyday mage, a teleport of great lengths was taxing on the body, unless you were travelling to the Isles, where the Temple of Wystia regenerated our energy immediately. I was fortunate that my abilities made teleporting great distances a breeze, so never missed an opportunity to prod Slaviya about that fact.

I waited to see if she would move to the chair. Her only response was to subtly sag further into the door frame.

'To what do I owe the pleasure of your unannounced presence?'
I repeated.

'I thought I would arrive a few days before the Forum commences
to see how things are tracking here.'

Translation, you better have an assassination plan for me.

'That's nice of you.' I smirked, deciding to make her work for the
information.

I caught a flicker of fire on the tips of her fingers, the only visible
sign that I was getting on her nerves, before she leant more heavily
against the doorframe.

I sighed, my magic latched onto her body, pulling her towards
the chair, not letting go until she was dropped onto the seat in front
of me.

'Valare,' she spat.

'Oh, save it Slaviya. This isn't a conversation to have when your
legs are failing you like a little baby lamb fresh out of the womb. At
least have the decency to sit down. Or in this case, to be physically
made to sit down. You're welcome.'

The bags under her eyes were more noticeable now that she was
closer. I didn't even know why I cared. I should've just let her fall,
a lesson for her stubbornness. But the softer side of me – which I
hated to admit existed even with Slaviya – didn't want her to hurt.
The rational part of my mind knew she wouldn't care if the shoe was
on the other foot. But I couldn't let it happen. It wasn't in my nature.

'You would have lasted one day as the Queen of Salistya before
someone came for your head. Vulnerability is weakness, Valare.
Did Father not teach you anything?' The ruthlessness of her words
paired with the sneer on her face caused an involuntary shiver to
roll down my spine.

'Oh, he taught me something, alright. Just not what you'd expect,'
I muttered. All of my father's advice, for lack of a better description,

was taken with a healthy pinch of salt. Whatever he suggested, I'd generally do the opposite. I refused to be like that bastard.

Her eyes wandered up my body, taking in the low-cut dress that showed off an ample amount of cleavage, my shoulders completely exposed. Her expression gave away her disgust, the provocative nature of the clothing a stark contrast to her modest Salistyan gown. She tutted in disapproval but had enough sense to not comment further. For now, at least.

'I trust you have an assassination plan in place?'

Finally, she cut to the chase. The real reason she came to Amarald early. The fact she chose to discuss this here, when Eliasson or another could walk in at any time, cemented her arrogance.

'Yes. It will be on the last night of the Forum when we have the closing ball. This will allow for negotiations to take place without distraction. When Eliasson heads to the bathroom, I will alert my fellow Sol, and follow him to execute the plan. I've set my alibi in place. It will go smoothly.'

She nodded her acceptance, clearly having zero regard for how it was executed as long as it was done. 'We need to discuss the next steps. I have soldiers stationed at the mouth of the Pass. They are awaiting my order to cross and enter Arloman territory.'

'What? You can't infiltrate Arlom the minute their king is found dead. Are you out of your mind?' I cried, forgetting myself as I digested this news.

'I can and I will.' She was completely unapologetic.

'You can't and you won't,' I countered firmly.

'Need I remind you, Sister, that the reason you are the queen of this Dom is because *I* put you there. There is a bigger game here, more things to keep away, and you would do well to remember what your part is in all of this.'

I watched her fingers clenched around the arms of the chair, as she attempted to restrain herself from lashing out. Knowing Slaviya, this kind of reaction would only arise if there were something out of her control, if she was relying on something or someone else. In this case, it looked like she was relying on me. Glee imbued my tone as I realised I may just have the upper hand. But my mind snagged on her comment about keeping things away. I took a stab in the dark. 'The beasts of the Tidal Seas getting a little bit out of control, are they?'

The tidal beasts. The bane of Salistya's existence and the reason for their army. I'd had many encounters with them when I lived on the Isles, often being interrupted during training sessions with Varqel to dispose of them. For some reason, they always showed up near his house.

They were awful creatures, ranging in size and shape, lurking in the depths of the Tidal Seas. They left destruction in their wake, easily able to take down unprepared or untrained mages whenever they appeared. They had always been an issue for Fyriane. However, in the last decades, the frequency of their visits to our continent's shores had increased significantly. I hadn't seen them as of late, given all my time was spent in Arlom. Usually, Slaviya was less than willing to share information; for her to be implying they had become more of an issue revealed the situation was dire.

'It's under control,' she replied coolly, but far too quickly to be believable.

'Your army is suffering,' I guessed again, my knowing was trying to tell me something.

'Suffering,' she remarked. 'No, Valare, we are not suffering. But the beasts are getting bigger and closer to our shores. They're making their way down the coast and heading towards Arlom.'

Well that wasn't good. Usually they stuck to the Solista Isles and Salistya.

'Let me guess, the Solistans refuse to help?' I asked, already knowing the answer.

She met my question with a cold glare and silence. So, this was why she needed me and the reason she had the army where it was.

The Salistyan Queendom's duty within Fyriane was to protect the land from the beasts and prevent them from entering the Pass between the Doms. It wouldn't be a good look for my sister if Salistya couldn't uphold its part of the agreement. If Salistya were to fail at this, it wouldn't simply mean the protection of Fyriane was compromised, but it would severely hinder Salistya's continued support from the other Doms. It would leave the Queendom vulnerable.

'I can have a chat to Varqel, see if they will provide assistance for a while until it's under control,' I offered, knowing that even if the request came from me, it was still likely to be refused. The Solistans were strict about upholding their part of the contract with Salistya, doing exactly nothing more and nothing less, including only dealing with the beasts when they came for the Isles themselves.

'That won't be necessary,' she replied stiffly. She always hated that I had a stronger relationship with the Solistans. Granted, it wasn't hard for me to to build a better relationship, considering she had refused to live at the barracks in her time on the Isles. Instead, she opted to stay away from everyone in her Royal House, pompous as ever. How she had thought it would make it easy for her as a ruler is beyond me.

'Between my Sol and I here, the beasts will be taken care of if you hold off the majority. I won't require aid on the Arloman side. Not to mention, I'm going to have a hard enough time as it is being accepted as the sole ruler of the Kingdom. Having Salistyans cross the border will only compromise my position further,' I pointed out.

'It's either that or the Arloman children on the Isles come home early to serve their Kingdom, Valare. I'm not willing for our plan to fall the minute the first move is complete. The army will ensure that doesn't happen.'

I knew what she was doing. Backing me into a corner, knowing full well I would not let children fight our battles.

'Absolutely not! They aren't even fully trained mages yet. I refuse to put innocent children out there to be slaughtered in the name of saving your hide,' I replied without thinking. 'And our plan? There is no our. You haven't even broached what this plan entails past my actions here. And you know what? I actually don't want to know. Don't include me in your warped schemes. You exercised your power as my former queen and put me in this position. I didn't ask to be here and I'm not a willing participant after the first move is complete. I won't risk Arlom when it'll already be destabilised, and that's what the army will do.' The more I spoke, the angrier I got.

'You really need to work on being less dramatic.' She rolled her eyes, dismissing my words entirely. Slaviya was so delusional she believed I would mindlessly go along with her plans and never question a thing.

'My powers alone are more than capable of keeping the beasts at bay here. If I require your help, I'll let you know. But for now, your aid is not required,' I said, finality evident in my voice.

'Valare –'

'They have always existed. The tidal beasts aren't news to anyone, Slaviya. If they are becoming more common and moving in new directions, maybe there's a reason behind this. You need to focus less on infiltrating Arlom and maybe place more emphasis on figuring out *why* they're moving further south,' I cut her off, diverting the conversation before we ended up arguing in circles. I may not be a born Arloman, but I would be damned if I saw untrained children sacrifice their lives, especially for something that was so unknown. I refused to rule like my father.

Slaviya was unable to conceal her worry at my question. She cleared her throat and shifted on the chair before stubbornly replying, 'No.'

I released a frustrated breath. 'You need to bring this up at the Royal Forum, Slaviya. Nyarelle can find more information in the archives. Where they come from, what they're capable of. We need to start talk about this if the beasts are becoming more of a question.'

'I can't. The Queendom must not look weak,' Slaviya refused, shaking her head.

'This is a Fyriane-wide issue, particularly if they are coming down more. It doesn't just affect Salistya or Arlom. Maybe this can form a stronger unity between the Doms, Slaviya,' I insisted.

'No, we keep this to ourselves. The only reason I've told you is for you to understand what we're facing.'

'If you don't bring it up, I will.'

Her face took on her usual scowl, any trace of worry was gone. 'Valare, don't use this information as an invitation to discuss confidential matters of my Queendom with the other –'

'Valare, are you here?' Eliasson shouted as he entered the room, suddenly interrupting us. I had been so involved in our conversation I hadn't felt him approaching.

His eyes landed on mine, before his body tensed up when he noticed Slaviya sitting across from me. 'Oh.'

I stood up and walked towards him, making every effort to ensure I came across as calm and collected.

'Darling, Slaviya decided to visit us a few days early, isn't that sweet? She must be getting soft in her old age. Apparently, she wanted to spend some quality family time before everything begins,' I smiled, placed a hand on his chest and gave him a swift kiss.

Eliasson stared at me, disbelief clouding his features. He knew this was unlikely to be the reason Slaviya had come, having known her for many years. But it turned out he was a much better actor than me as he slid his arm around my waist and faced Slaviya once again without flinching. 'That's so lovely, Slaviya. Thank you for coming early. It's a pleasure to have you here, as always.'

He was lying through his teeth – I didn't think there was anyone on the continent that disliked my sister more than him. Except Fyrel. Her stubborn refusal to learn the Arloman culture was a sore spot for someone as patriotic as Fyrel.

'Please, Eliasson, we're family now. No need for the formalities,' she said coldly.

Staring at the affectionate display with curiosity, she sniffed the air and zoned in on me, a cruel smile forming. 'The scent of Arlom sure has changed since I last came here,' she purred.

I stiffened at the way her eyes lit up with a knowing glint. It seemed, she too, had been distracted by our conversation, only just registering the scent of another man on me. I shot her a scathing look, warning her to keep her mouth shut. She responded with a predatory grin, knowing she had something over me. The bitch.

'Has it? How interesting...' Eliasson said innocently, probably thinking Slaviya was as strange as ever. I needed to get out of here.

'Slaviya, it was great talking to you. Perhaps you should retire to your room after your journey. I'm sure you're tired,' I stated, leaving no room for argument. She needed to leave before this turned into even more of a mess.

Slaviya sent me a withering look, aggravated by my dismissal but not pushing it further. 'I expect dinner will be at the usual time in the Royal Dining Room?' she said, as she stood and gracefully walked straight past us and out the door, not giving us a chance to respond.

The minute the door closed, I blew out a breath and walked away from Eliasson to slump back into the chair.

'What was that about?' Eliasson asked, concern in his voice.

'Oh, you know, just the big sister trying to control me. Same old, really,' I shrugged nonchalantly, deciding to keep the newfound information about the tidal beasts to myself for the moment. It was a problem that I intended to address when the time was right, and after the conversation with Slaviya, I didn't want that to be now.

Eliasson's eyes flashed in irritation as he growled, 'Your loyalty is not to her or Salistya anymore. You're the Queen of Arlom. If she has a problem with that, she can go through me.'

I felt my heart soften at his protectiveness. 'It's okay, Eliasson. She knows that. But she wouldn't be her if she didn't try.'

His shoulders visibly loosened with my reassurance, and I relaxed slightly too. It's always good to know I wasn't the only one on edge around Slaviya.

'Have I ever told you how thankful I am to be married to you?' he asked.

I couldn't help but burst out laughing. 'No, you haven't, but I'm trying not to take offense at the timing of it. If you mean to compare my sister and I, there really wasn't any competition to start with.'

'Alright, maybe that wasn't the best time to say that.' A cheeky grin lit up his face, mirth filling his eyes. 'But in all honesty, can you imagine Slaviya and I married?' He shuddered.

'That's a pretty comical image,' I admitted.

'Thank the Goddess it didn't come to fruition,' he replied.

Thank the Goddess, indeed. He would be dead by now otherwise. Unexpectedly, my heart sank at that thought.

Changing the subject, I asked, 'What did you come in here for, anyway?'

'Oh, I was warning you that your sister had arrived,' he answered sheepishly, scratching the back of his head.

I chuckled. 'Don't worry, you're not the only one who dropped the ball.' Sighing, I stood up and walked toward my bedroom. I needed space to process Slaviya's information.

'Where are you going?' he asked, a tone of concern in his voice.

'I'm going to lay down for a few hours to decompress and work myself up to sitting through dinner with you two.'

'Fair enough, I'll leave you be then. Would it make things better if I asked Fyrel to join?'

My eyes lit up at the prospect of Fyrel and Slaviya in the same room, knowing full well their history. I couldn't stop the mischievous grin that arose on my face. 'Please?'

He chuckled. 'Consider it done.'

CHAPTER 12

I'd been sitting on the ground, staring at the statue of the Goddess for what was probably a good hour, simply finding peace and calm in the solace of the Temple after our earlier dinner.

The dinner had gone as expected. Silence filled the room, the only sounds the clanging of cutlery on the plates as we ate. Slaviya, true to character, blatantly refused to talk to Fyrel, settling for shooting him hateful looks from time to time, which he returned fiercely.

Early on in our marriage, Eliasson divulged that Slaviya had made no effort getting to know him or Fyrel while they were betrothed. Fyrel, already wary of the union, did not appreciate her attitude. Apparently there were many heated arguments surrounding her blatant disregard and lack of respect for them and for the Arloman culture, which resulted in Fyrel ignoring Slaviya completely and vice versa. It seemed rather petty to me. I had always wondered whether there was something more that had happened behind the scenes to cement his contempt for her.

I hadn't thought it was possible for Fyrel to dislike someone more than me; alas, it seemed the damage had been done, and Slaviya solidified herself in the number one position. If I didn't know better, I'd say Fyrel was thankful I was the one to marry Eliasson in the end. Not that he would ever admit it, of course.

Eliasson and I, on the other hand, had shot amused glances at one another, silently bonding as we took in the tension of the room. Clearly, we were both a little unhinged, taking way too much sadistic enjoyment in this form of entertainment.

Not for the first time, I began to wonder what mine and Eliasson's life would have been like had the pieces not already been put in place. I felt a pang in my chest as I realised that we could have been happy together. Potentially a genuine love Could've blossomed between us, as we led the people of Arlom, a coven of blonde and brunette children running around at our feet. Would our children have inherited his eyes or mine? Would their magic have turned their eyes a different shade, like mine? How would he have taken that?

I shook my head, clearing the thoughts from my mind. There was no point in lingering on a future that simply would not, could not, come to fruition. It was times like these, I wished I could talk to Dwyla and tell her about the mission. Gain another perspective from someone who was not involved in it, and despite being the youngest, she had always been the stable one of the family. But I couldn't. Not with Tarn in the picture. Nor would I want to burden her with this secret. She was starting her final year in the Isles soon and had more than enough on her plate.

I rubbed my fingers over my forehead, smoothing out the worry lines. I was already exhausted, and the Forum hadn't even begun.

I had forced my focus back onto the statue in front of me when I felt a hum coming from the mark behind my ear. I felt the same knock on my mind's door as before, asking for entrance. The instinct to respond was as natural as breathing, similar to how I called upon my magic to enhance my senses. I released the barrier between my brain and the rest of my body, allowing this presence to step inside the room of my mind.

As soon as my barrier was down, my eyes shut and I was back in the darkness where the outline of the male body was present. Glowing fuchsia eyes stared at me again. An overwhelmingly powerful force surrounded me. This couldn't be ... no, it couldn't be Merlot, the same man from the book, could it? It was an outlandish thought, but, if not him, then who? Who could hold this much power?

At the same moment, I heard a chuckle in my mind. *Although I'm flattered, Green Eyes, I regret to inform that you're not talking to the God Merlot.* Delight shone in those fuchsia eyes.

I gasped. What was going on? Was this a figment of my imagination? But I found myself able to think, responding, *One, how are you in my head right now? Two, where am I? And three, who are you?*

We're in a place referred to as the Lull. It's a place that Queen Wystia and King Merlot created and sealed with their blood before their passing. It may only be accessed by the True Infinite. I take it you're at the Temple of Wystia? he replied, decidedly ignoring two out of my three questions.

The Lull, True Infinite, Queen Wystia and King Merlot – head officially scrambled. *How do you know where I am?*

Until we've physically met, for the Lull to be initiated, you need to be at the Temple of Wystia and I need to be at a certain location, too. Before I could interrupt, he continued. *To answer your other question, who I am isn't important now. What's important is that we're finally connecting. It will make things easier moving forward.* Desire filled those magnetic eyes.

Where are you? I asked, ignoring his sultry stare. The two men in my life already were proving to be too much.

That doesn't matter, he dismissed.

Alright, let's try a different avenue. *What do you mean by True Infinite? What is that?*

His whole body paused in bewilderment. *You don't know what the True Infinite is?*

Clearly, or I wouldn't have bothered to ask, I snapped back, giving into my irritation and confusion.

What are they teaching you over there, he muttered disapprovingly.

While he seemed preoccupied mulling over his thoughts, an idea sprang to my mind. Narrowing my eyes in concentration, I channelled my fire to create light within the space we were in. If he wasn't going to show me his appearance, I would force it.

But no light would come.

I wouldn't bother, he laughed. My ire rose as the sound of his laughter released a barrage of unwanted feelings within me. It was the most beautiful sound I'd ever heard.

What are you doing to me? I demanded.

I'm not doing anything, Green Eyes. You're in the Lull, a place fuelled by the mind, spirit and the stars. Your physical magic has no hold here.

Interesting. *Are you in my mind? And, if you are, does that mean I'm in yours?*

The outline of his face tilted to the side. *Not quite. I called you, invited you to this place.*

In that case, if I were to call you, I could invite you to this place?

It's a bit more complicated than that. But for all intents and purposes, simply put, you would be able to.

So, how do I –

He cut me off, pre-empting my question, *But you don't have the powers required for that yet. Unfortunately for you, you're stuck with me making the first move.*

I couldn't help the childish pout that formed on my face, which made him chuckle.

Patience, Green Eyes. You need to walk before you can run. Or, as was in your case, you needed to control your magic before you learnt to teleport.

How do you know so much about me? I decided there was no point in denying that he clearly knew more than I liked. Hell, I didn't like that the man had the power to pull me to this Lull. Whatever this Lull is. There was nowhere for me to hide.

Knowledge finds those who are meant to see, Valare. His tone mimicked that of the Nyarellean woman's.

My body stiffened. *That's not the first time I've heard someone say that*, I whispered.

And it won't be the last. Open your eyes, Valare. Seek the answers you require. They are closer to you than you realise. His body tensed as his eyes turned to his right, before settling back on mine. *I have to go.*

But –

His eyes somehow shone with disappointment, as though he wanted to stay as much as I wanted answers. *Until we meet again, Green Eyes.*

CHAPTER 13

We stood outside the Amarald Palace, waiting at the top of the stairs for the Queen of Nyarelle and the King of Marlyst to arrive. Their horses could be seen in the distance, making their way towards us.

I stood at Eliasson's side, his arm loosely around my waist, His fingers mindlessly drew soothing circles up and down my hip. Slaviya stood on his other side, keeping an appropriate space between us, her back rigid, signature scowl on her face. She wore a flattering moss green dress that circled her neck, bell sleeves flaring out to her forearms, the flowy material ending mid-way on her calf. Despite the requisite colour, her choice of attire surprised me, as the flash of skin was considered risqué for a Salistyan woman.

I moved from one foot to the other, gnawing on my lip, anxious. Eliasson squeezed my hip, drawing my attention to him. 'Stop it, you look stunning,' he muttered.

'What if teal wasn't the right choice? What if it sends the wrong message? Maybe I should've stuck to blue.' I groaned, nervously picking at the collar wrapped around my throat. The silky dress was held up by a simple tie at the nape of my neck. It fell to cover my body to mid-thigh.

'It's no secret you're a Salistyan-born Arloman Queen, Valare. Teal represents solidarity between the two Doms. It was a strategic decision and the right choice. Don't overthink it,' Eliasson soothed.

Don't overthink it? How could I not?

I took a few deep breaths, glancing at the people swiftly approaching us. From this distance, with my advanced sight, I could tell the horse on the left was ridden by a woman wearing a pink jumpsuit held together by ties around her bust. Her long, wild black hair trailed behind her, and would easily reach her backside. Her pale pink eyes stared directly at us in sharp concentration.

The dark-skinned man on the far right drew my attention next. His vibrant, burnt-orange eyes and neatly trimmed dark copper hair revealed his Nyarellean heritage. My mind actively searched for the name of the man, knowing I'd met him at last year's Forum.

'What's the Nyarellean man's name again?' I whispered to Eliasson.

'Ramone, Qynthia's Second.'

Ah, Ramone. That's right.

Meanwhile, Qynthia, the Queen of Nyarelle, sat on the middle horse in front of the new King of Marlyst. She wore an orange two-piece with pride, the colour beautifully complimented her dark complexion. Her curls were piled gracefully atop her head, loose tendrils framing her face, the copper tone glinting in the sun. Just how I remembered her. A picture of effortless beauty.

In the time it took for them to arrive at the Palace, I hadn't been able to get a glimpse of the new King apart from his arms, which were wrapped around Qynthia, holding onto the straps that guided the horse. Interesting statement on their part. A teal dress was clearly the least of my worries.

Ramone and the woman accompanying the King and Queen dismounted their horses, handing the reins over to our stable hands, before coming up either side of the remaining horse.

My breath hitched as the King gracefully dismounted and I got my first look at him. He was tall, rivalling the height of Eliasson who was a full head and shoulder taller than me. On the new King, I'd be surprised if my head even made it to the middle of his chest, a chest that I could see glimpses of through the thin linen shirt he was wearing. He was sculpted to perfection.

My eyes drank him up. His jawline was a gift from the Goddess herself, starkly prominent despite the five o'clock shadow peppered across it. His beautiful pale pink eyes were framed by thick black brows. What completely did me in, though, was the short buzz cut of his hair that accentuated his beautifully sculpted face, which lit up as he laughed at something Qynthia had said. He held out his hand in response, assisting her dismount. Holy hell he was stunning. And Eliasson wanted me to spend majority of my time with him? I could almost feel myself getting damper by the minute. Goddess, give me strength.

The entourage ascended the stairs, the King whispering something in Qynthia's ear, eliciting laughter and an intimate caress on his forearm. Very interesting.

Eliasson cleared his throat as the pair reached the top of the step, leaning in to chastely kiss the cheek of the Queen – 'Qynthia, a pleasure as always' – before raising his hand out to Xylan. 'King Xylan, it's a pleasure to finally meet you in person. Welcome to Arlom, I hope your travels were not too strenuous.'

Xylan's hand met Eliasson's. 'The pleasure is all mine, King Eliasson. Thank you for graciously welcoming us to your Kingdom. Your land is a delight to be seen. I have a newfound appreciation for the delightful food that I enjoy courtesy of your farmers,' he responded.

Oh, he's good, a true charmer.

'I'd like to introduce you to my –'

Slaviya interrupted Eliasson, holding out her hand in expectation to the Marlyst King. 'King Xylan, Queen Slaviya of Salistya. Pleasure to meet you.'

Xylan's unimpressed gaze landed on my sister, before moving down to her outstretched hand which he took and shook briefly. He stepped away as soon as was appropriate.

I felt the slight stiffening of Slaviya's shoulders at his response. She turned to Qynthia, placing a quick kiss on her cheek as the Queen responded in kind. 'Good to see you again, Qynthia.'

'A pleasure as always, Slaviya,' Qynthia replied, pulling my sister into a hug. Given Slaviya's dislike for physical affection, I was surprised she didn't rebuff the embrace, instead actually launching into a conversation with the Queen.

My eyes swung back around to King Xylan, only to see his were already on me.

'You must be Valare?' he purred, bringing an uncontrollable blush to my cheeks. Apparently, we were already on a first name basis.

'I am. It's very nice to meet you, King Xylan. Welcome to our home.' My voice came out a little breathier than I would have preferred.

His hand shot out to grab mine, lifting it up to his lips to kiss my knuckles. He lingered a tad longer than was probably appropriate.

'Please, call me Xylan,' he murmured against my hand.

I swallowed a gasp, pulling my hand away quickly. His reluctance to release me didn't go unnoticed. 'Alright, Xylan.'

His eyes lit up with an emotion I couldn't quite place. I felt the seconds go by, his stare refusing to leave mine, causing my cheeks to heat further. This was dangerous.

I cleared my throat trying to break the silence, glancing up quickly to see Eliasson taking in the exchange. His hand tightened on my hip slightly.

'Congratulations on, ah, the recent promotion. Sorry to hear about your father,' I blurted, immediately regretting it. Eliasson stiffened next to me. Shit, that clearly sounded as bad as I thought it did.

Xylan simply laughed, seemingly unfazed. 'Thank you, it's a pleasure to rule my Kingdom. And no need to be sorry, the God Merlot knows you're probably the only person in Fyriane to have thought his lack of presence a loss.' He waved his hand dismissively.

I couldn't stop the grin that rose on my face at his frankness. Well, at least we agreed that his father certainly wasn't going to be missed.

'Valare, lovely to see you again.'

I turned just in time as Qynthia came to embrace me with an affectionate squeeze. Eliasson quickly stepped away from us. Considering we had only met once, I didn't think the Queen and I were necessarily at this level of friendship, but who was I to deny her?

Pulling away, I looked at the remaining man.

'Oh! I'm so sorry, how rude of me. Valare, Eliasson, Slaviya, you remember Ramone?' Qynthia asked.

The man in question stepped forward to bow. 'Your Highnesses, a pleasure.'

Eliasson and Slaviya merely nodded.

'Good to see you again, Ramone.' I smiled at him, feeling that the others' lack of response to be a little cold and snobby.

'And this is my sister Orlandia. Orlandia, this is Queen Slaviya, King Eliasson and his wife Queen Valare,' said Xylan, gesturing towards us.

My gaze shot to Xylan's sister, eyebrows furrowing momentarily. Did I know her? I smoothed my features, smiling politely in acknowledgment.

Orlandia curtsied, copying Ramone's greeting before standing up and looking straight at me. My eyes narrowed slightly, then widened as I took in her features. There were uncanny similarities to someone I had briefly met before, apart from the pale pink eyes and lighter skin tone. I shook my head, dismissing the thought. There were plenty of people who looked similar. I was overthinking it.

Before I could probe further, Qynthia looped her arms through mine and Slaviya's, making her way into the palace. 'Ladies, please tell me dinner is ready. I'm positively starved. Not to mention I have been dying to drown myself in a healthy amount of that delicious Arloman wine. Gentleman, are you coming?' Qynthia called over her shoulder, not bothering to wait for them.

I swung my head around to watch the men follow, chatting casually. My eyes landed on those beautiful pink ones and found they were already starting at me, scanning the length of my exposed back, fixating on the scoop of material that rested daringly on the top of my behind. I forgot to breathe when his gaze made its way up to mine, unashamed that I caught him staring at me, and in front of my husband too, if the cheeky wink he threw at me was anything to go by.

'Valare?'

I swung my head back around to Qynthia, quickly realising she'd asked me for directions.

'The dining room? Straight through this first door and down the hall.'

My mind immediately jumped back to our interaction. What was this man playing at? He was staring at me like I was a prize to be won, and I most certainly wasn't a prize. I was off limits, not to mention married. If he continued with those smouldering looks, these next weeks may just turn out to be the longest of my life.

I needed a wine.

CHAPTER 14

'Another round!' Qynthia shouted for the tenth time tonight, raising her empty glass looking for the attendants. Rynelle stepped forward, halting his movements when Eliasson subtly shook his head. He stepped back, resuming his stance by the wall. His eyes briefly met mine, conveying his annoyance.

This was *not* how a Royal Forum generally went. I had envisioned it to be just like the last one – an awkward dinner filled with small talk as the royals attempted to pretend that their sole reason for being in the same room as one another wasn't to negotiate trade agreements like savages. It was amazing what a new, fresh-faced king, with a seemingly good sense of humour, and strong relationships with others, could do to the dynamics of a room. Despite seeing glimpses of her outgoing and affectionate nature at the last Forum, in the presence of Xylan's father, Qynthia would never have dared to turn the first night into a royal party – she had even convinced Slaviya to play a drinking game.

'Maybe that's enough, Qynth,' Xylan laughed while she leant towards him. Her eyes narrowed defiantly as she went, literally, head-to-head with him.

'Xylan, honey, remember the last time you tried to cut me off?' she threatened.

Xylan shot her a look of warning. I couldn't help the grin that rose to my lips. I sure as hell wanted to know all the juicy details of what happened last time.

'I'm going to bite. What happened?' I eagerly leant forward, unfazed by the frowns of disapproval from Eliasson and Slaviya. I was too many wines in at this point to care about what was or was not correct behaviour, and Xylan was clearly nothing like his father.

'It's not relevant –' Xylan started.

'I stole one of his favourite books!' Qynthia blurted.

Xylan groaned, running a frustrated hand down his face.

'Oh,' I replied, the answer wasn't what I was expecting. 'Is that all?'

'It's not so much that it was a book, darling Valare. More so, the book's *genre*,' Orlandia piped up, mischief written all over her face.

Xylan downed the rest of his drink, peering out the window. His tortured stare made the dining room's glass window seem like it could crack at any moment. 'To the God Merlot, why do you insist on surrounding me with insufferable women?'

'Based on the character in your book, we thought insufferable women were just your type,' Orlandia scoffed into her wine.

'What was the book?' I interrupted.

Before Xylan could shut the conversation down, Qynthia placed a placating hand on his chest and stared at me. 'I'll make a deal with you, Valare. I'll tell you the name of the book if – Nuh-uh-uh,' Qynthia placed her hand over Xylan's mouth as it opened, 'if you get us some more wine.'

'Done.'

'Valare,' Eliasson cautioned.

I turned to face him rubbing my hand up and down his thigh just the way he liked. I fluttered my eyelashes at him. 'Husband, would you really deny your wife a good time?' I crooned, seeing his eyes flare with desire as he noted the double meaning. I could sense another set of eyes boring into the side of my head.

'I'll get more wine.' His words came out rougher than usual as he tried his best to subtly rearrange his pants before heading towards the kitchens, Rynelle in tow.

I could feel the satisfaction settle on my face as I met Xylan's stare only to see what could only be described as jealousy. I furrowed my brow in question, noting Qynthia leisurely running her fingers up and down his forearm. Why that elicited jealousy was something I didn't want to dwell on. Catching my expression, the bastard threw me an inquisitive look in return, his jaw clenched. Well, we weren't starting off on the right foot.

'As promised, wine for the Queen,' Eliasson announced, strolling back into the room to pour Qynthia more wine. Mazyr, donning his chefs uniform, walked in with a plate of food. Why the hell was he here?

His eyes landed on Orlandia, curiosity piquing in those mossy green depths.

Noting his attentions, Orlandia pursed her lips and raised a challenging brow, earning a smirk from Mazyr in return. He placed the plate down right in front of her. Mazyr turned away, throwed me a playful wink, in response to my warning glare, and sauntered out of the room. I didn't miss Orlandia's eyes zoning in on his toned backside.

'Judging by your hesitance to talk about this alleged book stealing accident, I presume you are needing some of this?' Eliasson asked, not waiting for confirmation before filling up Xylan's empty glass. Moving around the room, Eliasson played host, filling up all the glasses, including his own, but left none for me.

'Hey –' I started. He pulled me from my own chair and straight onto his lap. His arm snaked around my waist, pulling me up against him while the other reached for his full glass.

'Drink, wife. I wouldn't want to deny you a good time,' he purred, bringing the glass to my lips and tipping the wine into my mouth. Chuckles littered the room, setting my cheeks on fire. Once he'd put the glass down, I slapped his hand in playful admonishment and cleared my throat. I focused on Qynthia and Orlandia, steadfastly refusing to meet Xylan's eyes.

'I've upheld my part. Your turn.'

Qynthia glanced at Xylan, seeking his approval before continuing. Xylan merely rolled his eyes and shrugged. 'Well, what are you going to do? Back out of your end of the deal?' The soft smile and her quick touch of his cheek had my eye twitching.

'The book I stole was *Once Upon a Woods*.'

My jaw dropped to the floor. His favourite book was a romantic-comedy, and not only was it a romantic-comedy, it was *the* romantic-comedy. The one Meredith and I were obsessed with and had constant debates over which character Louisah should be with. Hell, Mer and I stopped talking for a month when we couldn't see eye to eye on how it had ended. Of course, my guy was the one to end up with her, so I was right in the end.

I attempted to pick my jaw up off the floor to ask Xylan, 'Runaile or Nalu?'

His mouth curved upwards. It was the tiniest of movements, but it was there, nonetheless. 'Runaile, of course. Was there really any other option? Whoever is team Nalu needs to go re-read the scene in the woods and then look me in the eye and tell me he was really going to give her what she needed.'

'Right! And don't even get me started on that bedroom scene –'

'The absolute worst!' Xylan scoffed, shaking his head in disgust.

'Exactly! How anyone could have any sort of sympathy for Nalu after that is beyond me,' I said, exasperated.

'The ones that do need to reassess their life choices,' he agreed.

'Goddess, this is so refreshing. I need you to come and talk to Meredith with me. She's still team Nalu despite the debates we've had. Can you believe she just stopped talking about it all together after the end? Only a Nalu fan would do that. Team Runaile won't let it rest until every non-believer is converted.'

'Is your friend here in Amarald?' he queried.

'Yes, she's my maid.'

'Then we'll see her first thing tomorrow morning. This can't wait.'

I nodded in agreement, resolute.

Silence filled the room. In my excitement, I'd completely forgotten about the others. They were glancing between Xylan and I, clearly having no idea what we were talking about. I caught Orlandia and Qynthia's amused stares, which seemed to imply they were sharing an inside joke.

Eliasson cleared his throat. 'May I kindly remind you that we have the traditional Forum opening breakfast first thing tomorrow morning?'

'What time is it?' I asked.

'Eight in the morning,' Eliasson advised.

'Push it back an hour,' Xylan stated.

My hand flew to my mouth, smothering a giggle at Xylan's blatant order. He was definitely an upgrade from the previous King.

'We can't do that. It's always held at eight in the morning as per the tradition established by our ancestors,' Slaviya interjected. 'I think we ought to remember our responsibilities as royals and ensure that this is at the forefront of our decision making.'

As expected, Slaviya jumped in to be the typical party pooper. I rolled my eyes.

'Does six thirty work for you?' I directed my gaze at Xylan, and he nodded in return.

'Six thirty?' Eliasson scoffed in disbelief. 'You hate mornings. I was planning on bringing coffee and scones just to entice you out of bed in time for the damn breakfast.'

'Although I do appreciate the sweet gesture, I'll have you know that matters of the *Woodsverse* is no joke. As a ride or die Runaile fan I must do what needs to be done. Even if that does mean sacrificing my precious sleep.'

'You're not joking,' he sputtered.

'There's no joking when it comes to the great debate of Runaile vs. Nalu,' I said seriously. 'Am I right, Xylan?'

'It wouldn't be right to knowingly sleep under the same roof as a Nalu sympathiser,' he agreed. His voice held no room for argument as Orlandia snorted at our exchange.

Eliasson glanced between us as if we had lost our minds. 'You do realise you two may as well be speaking a completely different language. No one else here has any idea what you're talking about.'

We shrugged, before saying at the same time, 'If you know, then you know.'

CHAPTER 15

I pranced around my room, light as a feather and just a little bit smug from this morning's outcome. It had taken Xylan and I all of twenty minutes to convert Mer to the correct team in the *Woodsverse*. I had to give it to him, he could be very persuasive when he needed to be, and he unashamedly used every tool in his arsenal (including his devastatingly good looks) to achieve the desired result. Watching Mer crumble under his stare was brilliant, and it was very comforting to know I wasn't the only one who couldn't get a grip in his presence. Who knew a stunning man and a riveting debate would cure my hatred of mornings?

True to his word, Eliasson had had coffee and a ridiculous amount of scones delivered to my rooms while I was getting ready for breakfast. Could this day get any better?

'You don't play fair!' Mer whined as she fixed my hair into a ponytail, her grip a little tighter than usual. 'You brought a gorgeous king in front of my eyes – first thing in the morning while my defences were down, might I add – to do your dirty work? You just couldn't deal with the fact my stance on the matter wasn't wavering.' She shook her head with a mixture of disgust and awe, pulling my hair impossibly tight.

'Ow! Cheap shot, Mer!' I complained, whacking her hands away from me and threw a scone full of cream straight onto her face. Her stunned expression set off my laughter, tears streaming down my face. 'You should,' heavy breath, 'see you – your,' heavy breath, 'face,' I spluttered before succumbing to another round of hysterics.

'You're such a bitch.' She scooped the cream off her face, licking her fingers and laughing, finding the humour in the situation.

'And you're just jealous that when it comes to Runaile, you hadn't seen the light. It's okay. You can't always be right,' I smirked, shrugging condescendingly.

'I'm not going to entertain that with further comment. But what I do want to talk about is the babe that was with you this morning. Oof,' she said, fanning her face as if we were in the middle of the Hudrielle Desert at midday.

'Not too shabby, right?' I threw her a grin, turning back to the mirror so she could finish off my hair.

'Oh, my Goddess, not too shabby?' she sputtered. 'Did you *see* his jawline? His ass? His everything? I think he has the hots for you. How you're going to say no to that … all I can say is good luck to you, dear friend. It should be illegal to be that hot. I love Fyrel, but a girl would be hard pressed to turn down an offer of that calibre –'

'Wait. Back it up. You love Fyrel?' I said in disbelief.

'Oh. I – uh –' She scrambled for words as her cheeks flushed pink. Suddenly, all she could focus on were the walls around us, determinedly avoiding eye contact. I should've seen this coming. I'd lost count the number of times I had found them giggling in all sorts of compromising positions throughout the palace. Fyrel giggling was up there with the weirdest, most unnatural sounds I'd ever heard. As much as I enjoyed acquiring new ammunition against him, I decided I wouldn't use this one.

I waited for Mer to gather her thoughts, knowing from her past relationships – if we could even call them that – how big of a step this was for her.

'He confessed to me last night after a couple of drinks and I … I said it back without thinking. It felt natural. I know that it wasn't supposed to happen and believe me you don't have to reprimand me. I know how messy this is and I know it's not a good idea given everything that's happened already and … what is to come. Bu – But I can't help how I feel. Sometimes the heart wants what it wants. Surely you know this as well as anyone else –'

I lifted my hand to cut off her rambling and reached behind to place it over her hand that held my hair. She was spiralling, but I said, 'I'm happy for you, Mer.' And I was. She deserved this piece of happiness. Even if it was Fyrel.

'It's nice to know I'm capable of feeling this. Let's be honest, my track record isn't great. But with him … it just works.' She shrugged, perplexed as to how this had happened. 'For now, at least,' she added, soberly.

'We'll deal with that when the time comes. But for now? Enjoy it. Life is for making memories, pushing yourself out of your comfort zone so there's no space for 'what ifs'. We could all die tomorrow. It's important that we can look back on our life and know that we did the things that made our souls happy, that we truly lived. And spare me the lecture on how I should follow my own wise words. I'm working on it, okay?' I defensively added.

'I'll spare you just this once. Only because I love you, my favourite hypocrite,' she grinned. 'Speaking of 'what ifs', how's it going with your lover boy?'

I let out an annoyed groan. This was the last thing I wanted to talk about.

'That bad?'

'I much prefer talking about your thriving love life,' I replied, trying for a joke that Mer saw right through. She threw me a look that screamed 'start talking, or I'll pull your hair harder'.

I sighed, knowing there was no point trying to distract Meredith when she was hunting for information. She was like a dog with a bone when she wanted something.

'He brought me half-dead yellow flowers. And he hasn't made me come since I've been married. And Eliasson can. What does that say to you?' I shook my head, watching her mouth 'oh', understanding dawned on her features.

I continued without waiting for her reply. 'He keeps saying everything is my fault. That I've put us in this position. The further apart we drift, the more controlling he becomes. I don't know what's gotten into him, but he's not the man I fell in love with. I'm going to be a sole ruler soon and won't be able to just make us public knowledge. How's he going to take that? Am I going to be punished for the rest of my life for things that are out of my control? I'm trying to do my best, but he makes me feel like anything I do is never good enough. Nothing is ever his fault. Apparently, he's perfect. It's just me. I'm the problem.'

Now who was the one rambling?

A contemplative look fell across Meredith's face. She scratched her chin, a clear sign she was trying to work out how to deliver undesirable news diplomatically.

'What?' I asked, but she hesitated, clearly uncomfortable. 'I'm a big girl. Just say it.'

'I don't think he's good for you,' she forced out, taking a deep breath to steady herself. 'Once upon a time I thought he was perfect for you. He courted you, kept coming back despite your numerous rejections and worked on establishing a friendship with you before you … well, ended up where you've ended up. No doubt he's different now. For a while I thought maybe things had just changed because of our circumstances but looking back on it, Valare, I don't think he was ever a good guy.'

'Oh?' My gut churned with nausea.

'Think about it. How many times did you reject him? Ten, fifteen, *twenty* times? Shouldn't that have been a red flag, that he couldn't take no for an answer? And even more than that, every time you rejected him, his efforts became increasingly more calculated and forced. I know at the time we were teens reading romance novel after romance novel, thinking big macho males with domineering tendencies were hot. That it was someone we should look for in our lives, but are they really who we should be looking for? It's toxic when you think about it. And because of those novels, we swooned when he chased you. Revelled in it, even. We thought it was what true love looked like, when in actual fact we should've called Varqel to put him in his place.'

'Huh,' I mused, absentmindedly rubbing my Royal Mark. That was a lot to work through. I had been fixating on the changes in our relationship over the course of the last year, trying to work out when it had started to go downhill. But I hadn't stopped to think about what it was like prior. Were these patterns there before I married Eliasson? With my rose-coloured glasses, had I overlooked this? Mer's words caused so many things to take on a different meaning.

'Don't get me wrong, he puts on a good show laughing with us and being openly affectionate, all things we've come to appreciate about him. But there's something … off. I don't trust his intentions anymore. Not with you, not with us, not with what we're doing here. You need to keep your wits about you and play this strategically because my gut is screaming he's a ticking time bomb.'

The more I thought back on my encounters with him, the more I found myself agreeing with her. And that was scary. It meant I had to do something about it, and I simply didn't have the heart or the space to process the situation at this stage.

'I hear what you're saying,' I started. 'I think I've had these thoughts, more or less. But, let's just keep an eye on his movements. It's not at the top of my priority list to end things with him. Not now, at least. There's too much riding on the next two weeks to shake the boat more than necessary,' I explained, hoping I could work up the courage to confront him after the Forum was over.

'Oh good,' Mer breathed visibly relaxing. 'I'm glad you're seeing it for what it is, Val. And I'm sorry. It sucks and … I'm just sorry it's like this. But you deserve the type of love and loyalty you give to come back to you tenfold. And that guy? He's not what you need. If we're being honest – and I *loathe* admitting this – he's like Nalu. Nobody's got time for that bullshit.'

'No. Nobody has time for that,' I agreed.

I had no desire to linger on this topic of conversation longer than necessary, so I decided to circle back to Mer's previous comment in a not super subtle topic change. 'So, you think Xylan has the hots for me?'

'Oh, totally. He looks at you how I envision Runaile looks at Louisah. And those looks? Those are the ones to chase.' She sighed dreamily.

'Should we not be concerned he is openly ogling a woman married to another royal? I know my situation in all of this and what my relationship status will be. But he doesn't. It'd be damn bold of him if he were to make a play at me under Eliasson's nose.'

Mer remained silent, contemplating my words. 'Firstly, I can't blame the guy for being attracted to you, and he wouldn't be the first nor the last person I've seen sneak glances at you behind Eliasson's back. Secondly, he doesn't strike me as the person to care for what is and isn't appropriate. I think King Xylan takes what he wants. And you, dear Valare? He wants you *bad*.'

CHAPTER 16

I tried my best to hold it in, but when Qynthia groaned for the fifth time and placed her head on the table, an evil laugh slipped out before I could stop it.

'Why didn't you cut me off?' Qynthia groaned.

Who she was talking to, I had no idea. But Xylan apparently believed she was talking to him. He laughed softly, running his hands through her hair in comfort. 'We tried, Qynth. Multiple times. What were the words you used? Oh yes, "Xylan are you worried I'm going to drink you under the table? Is that what this is about? Your male pride can't handle being taken down a few notches?"' he recalled in a high pitch, trying and failing to impersonate Qynthia.

An amused snort left my mouth as Qynthia cringed in embarrassment. She slowly turned her head to look at me. 'You were keeping up with me. How the hell are you as sprightly as you are this morning?'

'I don't get hangovers,' I shrugged nonchalantly. One of the many perks of my unique magic. It had won me a lot of gold from disbelieving Solistans back in the day, much to Varqel's chagrin.

I changed the subject, unwilling to answer further questions on the matter. 'So, what's the plan for today?' I asked the table of royals and their Seconds. Glancing at the weary eyes of our hungover guests, I noticed Slaviya was the only one not feeling sorry for herself. Pretty standard really as she wasn't much of a drinker. Can't have that control slipping away.

'Matters of trade agreements and negotiations don't start until tomorrow,' Eliasson mused. 'Valare, since it's King Xylan's first time in Amarald, I thought you could show him around? The markets, perhaps? I would offer to tag along but I have palace matters I must attend to.'

'It's up to you, Xylan. I'd be happy to show you around. However, I understand –' I started but Xylan jumped in.

'That would be lovely. Orlandia, would you be interested in joining?' he asked his sister, before hastily adding, 'If that's okay with you, Valare?'

'Of course! The more the merrier.'

If I were being honest, spending on-on-one time with Xylan was dangerous. I found myself grateful that Orlandia would act as a buffer between us. Plus, I didn't want to turn down the opportunity to probe Orlandia a little more. I still couldn't shake the feeling that I had met her before. Her knowing gaze rattled me.

'That would be great. Qynthia, would you like to join us? Perhaps it would be good to walk out the hangover,' Orlandia teased.

The Queen rubbed her temples, wincing in pain. 'I think it's best for all of us if I spend the rest of the day in my quarters.'

Qynthia was a warm and vivacious character. She brought a spark of fun and joy to the Forum. However, I'd never seen or heard of her throwing caution to the wind like this. There was something about her relationship with Xylan that made her feel comfortable enough to do so. There had to be more to their relationship than meets the eye.

'Do you need anything before we leave?' Xylan asked her.

Not normally one to talk, I was surprised to hear her Second jump in. 'It's all taken care of, Xy. Go and enjoy yourself.' Ramone shot a reassuring nod to the King.

Xy. So that's what they called him. Good to know.

'In that case, meet you out the front of the palace in fifteen?' I directed my question to the Marlyst's.

'It's a date,' Xylan replied with a wolfish grin that absolutely did not make my heart flutter.

Denial was my new best friend.

I shrieked with laughter as Xylan sped past me on his horse. Hanging out with the royal siblings was a lot easier than I'd expected. They were easy-going and clearly up for an adventure. I felt like I'd known them forever, like we were old friends who had reunited after a long time apart from one another, instead of only meeting them yesterday.

Wanting to capitalise on a day without guards, we bypassed the markets completely and headed straight into the hills beyond the palace. We zipped in and out of the streets surrounding the civilians' houses. There were a mixture of startled glances and awe at the sight of me and royals from another Dom casually riding through the villagers' home. It wasn't long before we'd reached the edge of town, and could finally let the horses stretch their legs to sprint through the woods.

My hair blew in every direction, and I smiled, revelling in the wind wrapped around me. I could let my guard down, here in the woods, surrounded by nature. I took a moment to really acknowledge that this is what it felt like to be alive. To be free of reality that crushed and suffocated me. Out here I could breathe.

We reined our horses into a trot when we eventually cleared the forest, coming out on top of a hill. From this vantage point, we could see farmers working fields that spanned out into the distance. One poor farmer was having a hard time rounding up their cattle, a few strays deciding the grass wasn't greener on the other side of the field. What would it be like to lead such a life, away from the palace? No royal obligations or schemes to become an unwilling participant in? I imagined the hardest part of my day being a few stubborn cattle refusing to move. Honestly it sounded lovely.

'He's such a show off,' Orlandia muttered as her horse came up beside mine. She was wearing an all-black outfit which looked out of place in our current setting. Not to mention, she had to be sweltering under the Arloman sun.

'To be fair, if I'd taken the faster horse, I would've done the exact same thing,' I replied distractedly. My earth magic yearned to be let out. To create beautiful, coloured flowers in all different varieties to add to the browns and greens that surrounded us.

'Well, yeah, that too. But that's not what I was referring to.'

I had a feeling that if I were to look, I'd see a smirk on her face. 'Oh? What were you ref –'

My words stuck in my mouth, earth magic forgotten as I caught sight of Xylan and understood her comments. He had taken his shirt off and used it to wipe the sweat that had built up on his face and torso. He slung it over one shoulder, and my mouth watered. For all the built bodies I'd seen on the Isles, his put every one of them to shame.

Orlandia chuckled, no doubt reading me like an open book. 'The man can't help himself. He's just a big old flirt. Word of advice? Try not to play into it or it'll only get worse.'

'I'm a kept woman. It would be highly inappropriate for me to entertain anything of that nature,' I sniffed, willing myself to believe my words and stick by them.

'Good thing we aren't offended by inappropriate behaviour,' she called teasingly over her shoulder, making her way towards her brother. She was almost there before I could shake my stunned self into following her.

You are a married woman. You are still sleeping with your lover. You do not need a third man. I think this would be my mantra for the next fortnight.

'God it's hot out here. How are you wearing that outfit, Orla?' Xylan whined in discomfort as I met up with them.

'Because one of us doesn't feel the need to show off our figure every chance we get,' she said.

Well, she wasn't wrong.

'Hmm,' he tutted, 'Jealousy doesn't look good on you, sister.'

'What's there to be jealous of? That obnoxiously big head of yours? I think not, brother,' she retorted.

I watched on, amused, as the siblings continued their exchange, both unwilling to give in. If anyone were around to see this, they wouldn't believe they were royals. Their comments were that of any two siblings bickering and riling each other up. It was a little odd they were showing this part of their relationship in front of me, a person who was essentially a stranger. Maybe they felt comfortable around me as I did them?

In the meantime, I'd hopped down to place a picnic blanket on the ground and spread out the lunch we'd packed. Neither sibling had stood down from their argument and, from the look of their crossed arms, I had a feeling they adopted an agree-to-disagree mentality a lot.

'Lunch is ready!' I announced.

We ate our sandwiches in comfortable silence, but it took all my self-control to keep my eyes fixed on the landscape ahead rather than on Xylan's dripping body. Credit to myself, I was doing well until I reached for the raspberries sitting next to him. Xylan beat me to it, grabbing the punnet and holding it an arms distance away from me, which drew my eyes to his chest. A bead of sweat trickled down his abs. Orlandia was right. He was a flirt.

You are a married woman. You are still sleeping with your lover. You do not need a third man. I breathed deeply, leaned over to snatch the raspberries from him and scurried back to my side of the blanket, all without meeting his gaze, which was burning into me. I didn't want to see what was written on his face.

'You two aren't what I expected,' I said, determined to distract myself.

'What were you expecting, exactly?' Xylan asked.

'Well, for starters, I thought you'd come by yourself, Xylan. Secondly, you're both so … normal.'

'Normal,' Orlandia chortled. 'I think that's the first time we've been called that, Xy'.

'For the record, it was intended as a compliment,' I said, sheepishly.

Xylan's mouth twitched upwards. 'I think what she meant to say is that we're nothing like our father. And why wouldn't I bring my twin sister with me?'

Twin sister? That was news.

'Ah yes, Daddy Dearest,' Orlandia drawled. 'Well, I guess that's a compliment. Although it's not hard to think we're normal in comparison to him. He was an oddball.'

Oddball was an understatement. 'You're twins?' I asked.

'Don't get Xylan started,' Orlandia groaned. 'I've lived my whole life listening to him rub it in that I was one minute too slow to be crowned Queen. No matter how much I insist I don't want the job, big boss over here doesn't believe me. I think he's just in denial. He's the jealous type. Just an FYI.'

Xylan scoffed, dismissing most of her statement. 'What is there to be jealous over?'

'Well, for one, I don't have to worry about courtiers throwing themselves at me in the hopes they become royal,' Orlandia started, glancing my way. 'I guess I partly owe you thanks for my not being married. The King of Arlom was on my parent's radar for a while there, but you took the grenade for both of us. And now Xy is King, so I'm free to pick who I wish to wed.'

'You're welcome, I guess?' I mumbled, part of me wishing Orlandia and Eliasson's union had come to fruition. What a luxury it would be to choose who you marry. 'So, if you don't want anything to do with being a royal, why are you here?'

'Xy claims I need to be across everything in case something happens to him. You know, assassination attempts, angry ex-lovers, all that fun stuff.' She must have seen my mortified expression, as she added, 'It's completely dark and unlikely to happen. Well, maybe not the angry ex-lover thing. That Ophelie was a bit of a doozy.'

'Ah yes, good old Ophelie. Those were the days,' Xylan reminisced, his lips quirking in response to what was likely some nostalgic thoughts. Oddly enough, I felt like I'd been stabbed through the heart at that comment. Maybe his alleged jealous tendencies were rubbing off on me.

'Those were not the days, Xy. The girl was completely out of control.' Orlandia scowled in disgust.

'And who was the reason that I ended up in the situation, hmm? Don't fault me for being a good wingman and getting with the wild one to help your ass with the one you wanted,' he said.

Orlandia's cheeks turned bright red. Maybe the girl was spicier than I thought.

'Please tell me you at least got a little something-something out of it with the guy?' I grinned at her while Xylan burst into laughter.

'We don't need to continue this conversation. And for the record Ophelie had a twin sister, not a brother,' she said, looking away shyly.

'Oh,' I said. I didn't expect that. 'Sorry, I shouldn't presume.'

She waved off my apology. 'No need, I like men and women equally. I just happened to become overly … infatuated with this woman and Xylan decided to help, ah, speed it along.'

'Well, I'd say you've got a rather supportive brother then,' I smiled, going with the glass-half-full approach.

'Did you hear that, Orla? I'm a *supportive* brother,' he teased with glee.

'Please, you wanted to fuck the wildness out of that girl.'

Again, jealousy stirred, which was probably not healthy.

Xylan merely shrugged, not disagreeing with her. 'Every pubescent boy goes through it. I'm sure Valare knows all about that,' he threw me a wink.

I kept my face straight as possible, replying, 'I don't know what you're talking about.'

'Please, a woman with your looks? You were probably fending them off every day.'

He has the hots for you. Mer's voice rang in my head.

My face turned the same shade of red as Orlandia's had been. It was time to change the subject. I launched into the spiel about Arlom.

'So, this is the start of rural Arlom. As you know, it's about a day's ride north to the Pass. The surroundings throughout the rest of the Kingdom are as luscious as this. Bar the villages you stumble into along the way, our landscape remains much the same make up as this. Once you're within a kilometre or so of the coastline, there's naturally a lot more sand and less vegetation. My favourite time to be by the coast is when the humid winds blow in from the Isles.'

The change of subject wasn't my smoothest move, and when I shot a look at the twins, their lips quivered as they held back laughter. 'What?'

'You really don't know how to take a compliment, do you?' Orlandia commented.

'Well, I don't think there was a correct response to that. I'm a married woman. Letting him flirt like that is inappropriate. Plus, I was told to take you on a tour. Explaining the Kingdom's surroundings is a part of the tour,' I replied, flustered.

'I'd like to point out that I was merely stating a fact. If you took it as flirting, that's on you,' Xylan said. My cheeks flushed. Again.

Orlandia glared at Xylan. 'You don't have to pretend with us, Valare.' Her voice softened.

'Pretend what?' What are these two talking about?

'We know it wasn't your choice to marry Eliasson. Pretending to be loyal to him isn't necessary in our presence.'

Wow, that was a bold statement, even if it was true. I noticed Xylan had remained silent, intent on watching my every move.

'No, it wasn't my choice. However, he's a good man and an excellent ruler. He cares about his people and his people care about him.' Why did I feel like I was being overly defensive of myself? Of Eliasson?

'He's a good man, sure, but that doesn't mean you need to pretend that it's anything more than a good friendship,' she probed.

I wasn't sure what she was playing at, but I wasn't going to bite. Not when I'd known them for less than twenty-four hours. Maybe taking them on this tour was a bad idea.

'I tell you what. There's a waterfall with a swimming hole nearby that I can show you to cool off. If both of you can agree to drop this discussion, I'll lead you there. Deal?' I levelled them with a stare that told them to back off.

Xylan cocked his head to the side as he continued his intense assessment of me. He read my message loud and clear. 'Deal.'

With that, I hurriedly packed up the picnic blanket, thankful for the distraction.

When we arrived at the pool, Orlandia said – rather pointedly, I might add – that she wanted to explore the landscape, while Xylan stripped off. She hurried away before I could insist on her staying. As much as it was fantastic to see Xylan in only his briefs, I didn't trust myself without a third party nearby.

'What's taking you so long?' he shouted, having already submerged himself in the water.

I paused before I could start to strip. He picked up on my hesitation.

'Would you prefer I looked away?' he said. His tone may have been gentle, but his face told a different story. He was challenging me. And what was I going to do? Look weak in front of him? No way.

I held my head high as I took off my pants, folding them neatly on the ground next to his clothes, my top quickly joined the pile. I told myself that a bra and underwear was no different to wearing a bikini at the beach. Women wear nude-coloured bikinis to the beach all the time in front of guys they shouldn't find attractive and aren't their husband.

Welcoming the coolness on my skin, and avoided eye contact as I came up. I stood up, water trickled down my face and onto my chest. The water came up to my hip and I was very aware of my hardening nipples showing through my now translucent bra. I reached my hands behind my head, combing my fingers through my hair, allowing the strands to cascade down my back.

I smirked coyly as I met Xylan's desire-filled eyes, before diving into the water and swimming past him. By the time I surfaced, I was halfway between him and the waterfall. Looking back over my shoulder, I saw he was still staring at me.

'What's taking you so long?' I taunted him with his own words, swimming quickly towards the waterfall, intent on winning the race I just instigated.

I could hear the splash of water as he closed the gap between us. I pushed a bit harder, determined to win. With one last push, I dove under the waterfall, breaking the surface on the other side. There was a little cave under the waterfall with enough space for us to sit on rocks and catch our breath.

Pulling myself up, I hugged my knees to my chest.

'May I point out,' he huffed, pulling himself up out of the water, 'that you had a generous head start and I would've been the clear winner if we'd been on equal footing.' He slid onto the rock beside me, our legs touching in the confined space.

I had used a quarter of my strength, so as not to give away my powers, so there was no way he ever would've beaten me. 'Yeah, right. I went easy on you.'

He let out a disgruntled sigh. The man clearly was a sore loser.

We sat in silence, our breaths falling back into their normal rhythm. I was much too aware of our bare legs touching as the mark behind my ear began thrumming with heat. At the same time, from the corner of my eye, I saw him scratching the arc behind his ear.

'Do you manage to come here often?'

'Not as often as I'd like,' I admitted. 'Usually, I have a handful of guards nearby. I don't think Eliasson would be particularly happy with me flaunting my body in front of them.'

'Is that what you're doing?' he asked.

'What?'

'Flaunting your body?' he teased as his eyes took me in appreciatively.

In the safety of this cave, without any other eyes on me, I decided to give in to my desires. 'Well, you showed me yours. It was only right I showed you mine,' I threw back.

'How generous of you,' he said dryly.

'You'd prefer it if I didn't return the favour?'

'Never said that,' he chuckled, earning him a wry smile from me.

I twirled a stand of hair around my finger as I mused, 'Hmm, for a king you are awfully improper.'

'And you're not?'

I gave him a blank look, earning an amused smirk in return.

He seemed to mull over the rest of my words, debating his response. 'There's a time and a place to be King. And there's a time and a place to simply be a man enjoying a woman's company. The latter is relevant in this instance.'

'Will I have the pleasure of seeing you be King?'

He laughed darkly. 'You'll see plenty of that over the next few weeks, Valare. I don't hesitate to stand up and fight for my Kingdom when need be.'

Maybe the apple didn't fall too far from the tree after all. His father had always been ruthless in his dealings.

'I'll wait in anticipation then,' I said honestly.

'And you? Will you fight for your Dom when the time comes?' His tone grew serious, his eyes imploring.

'I'll do what is right to ensure my people are safe,' I replied, my tone matching his. I meant every word.

Xylan nodded in approval. 'Good. Fyriane needs that.'

'Fyriane?' I questioned.

'I mean –' He stopped, clearing his throat. 'The continent needs individual rulers who stand by their people. That's the only way as a whole we can run smoothly,' he said, scratching his head and looking away.

With his eyes focussed on the rock formation, I was able to study him a bit closer. I drank in his bared skin which had a natural tan. Every muscle in his body was lean, veins pulsing on his forearms, and he clearly worked out to maintain this kind of physique. I glanced down at the snail trail running between his belly button and down to the top of his briefs. At a leisurely pace, I took in his chest before slowly lifting my gaze to admire his face once more, only to find him staring back at me in open admiration.

'You can feel it. Can't you?' he whispered, as if afraid someone would hear him.

I swallowed deeply, licking my lips, drawing his attention before his eyes fluttered shut. Based on his reaction, I was happy I hadn't answered him. Everything becomes too real when you start acknowledging the attraction for what it is. And clearly he wasn't holding back.

'It?' Did that come out of me? I shouldn't be goading him. My body was not working in conjunction with my brain. The longer we were alone together, the more the palpable chemistry between us heightened.

Rolling his eyes, he said incredulously, 'You're going to make me say it? Fine. The attraction between us. The pull, the need to be close to each other, wanting to –'

Before I knew what I was doing, I closed the small distance between us, placing my lips on his. He responded immediately, his hand gently settled on the back of my head. The kiss was soft and sweet. He barely moved, perhaps afraid that if he took it further, I would pull away.

The warmth under my ear lobe grew increasingly hotter the longer we kissed, and I jolted away from him with a gasp. I couldn't look at him, knowing the desire he would be showing was a dangerous trap I wanted to fall into. Instead, we sat in silence for a minute or two, staring at the rocks. The crash of water from the falls broke the silence. It wasn't awkward. In fact it was far from it. It felt comfortable, too comfortable. And comfort was a deadly place to be.

After a while, he sighed. 'Should we go back?'

'Was that inappropriate?' I blurted, looking at him for the first time since the kiss.

'Inappropriate?'

The damn asshole was making me explain myself like I'd done with him before. 'The kiss,' I stated, in a deadpan voice.

He shrugged. The guy shrugged nonchalantly like it was nothing. What a way to knock a girl's ego down a few notches. 'It was barely a kiss.'

Barely a kiss? Was he challenging me? 'Should we do it again, then?' I countered, taking the bait.

'It would be rude not to,' he drawled, grabbing my head and bringing our mouths back together. He didn't hold back this time and took control of the kiss. His tongue swept over my lips, demanding an entrance that I willingly gave. Our tongues explored one another. My hands caressed the sides of his neck, paying extra attention to the area under his earlobe. Every time I ran my finger over his Royal Mark, his moans deepened, turned guttural.

I used this knowledge to my advantage, keeping my fingers there, to continuously eliciting noises from him, as I nibbled on his bottom lip, pulling it into my mouth. I pulled away from him to catch my breath before diving back in to claim his lips once more. I gasped when his hand ran over the warm spot under my own ear, a ricochet of desire spiralling down my body and straight to my core. My nails ran down his arms, the intensity of my grip increasing with his encouraging groans.

I panted as his lips left mine to travel down my neck, planting kisses along the way, causing shivers to run up and down my spine. Oh Goddess. I didn't know if I would ever get enough of him.

I grabbed his head to bring it back towards my mouth. Our lips had barely touched again before we heard, 'Where are you two? I didn't get the hide and seek memo or else I would've tried a bit harder.' Orlandia's teasing voice echoed around the cave as I pulled away from Xylan.

Our hands remained where they were, mine on his neck, his behind my head. We panted, trying to catch our breath, staring at each other in shocked wonder. This wasn't good. This shouldn't have happened.

'Fuck,' he muttered, taking his hands away from me to rearrange his hard bulge.

I giggled despite the situation, exceptionally satisfied that I had caused this reaction.

Deciding there was no point in giving him a lecture about the fact that no one could know about this, I slid off the rock slowly wading towards the entrance to the cave. As I was about to dive under it, I heard him mutter, 'Damn physical mages don't play fair.'

Physical mage?

My body went rigid. How did he know?

In a moment of impulsive stupidity, I threw caution to the wind and launched a torrent of water straight into his face, refusing to turn around despite the many curses leaving his mouth.

'That should help with the party in your pants,' I threw snidely over my shoulder, diving under the water and away from the temptation I left behind.

A temptation, I was quickly learning, that was proving impossible to resist.

CHAPTER 17

A sober mood surrounded our group as we made our way back to the palace. I was thankful for Orlandia, who had noticed the change in atmosphere and proceeded to ramble about the differences between the Arlom and Marlyst Kingdoms.

I knew I should have been listening. After all, gaining information on Marlyst was what Eliasson wanted. But I couldn't seem to pay attention to her. Not when it was solely focused on what happened in that cave.

That kiss.

I shuddered with desire as I recalled the feel of his lips on mine. His explorative touch. The burning sensation under my ear where my Royal Mark lay.

Eliasson and I had shared plenty of intimate moments. But I had never felt the burning hum of power I experienced when I merely touched Xylan. I thought back on these times, him kissing my hand, the high five we had exchanged when Mer conceded to being team Runaile, our thighs touching in the cave. Every time we touched, the feeling became stronger and stronger. It was an overwhelming pull to be near him. I'd never felt anything like it.

Maybe it was worth paying Qynthia a visit. Surely her scribes would have books on the Royal Marks and on connections like these. Maybe somewhere in that big old library there would be an answer to the strange sensations I was feeling. There had to be something, somewhere in Fyriane's history where this had occurred.

When we'd eventually arrived at the palace, I acted on instinct, passing the stable hand my horse. I threw out an, 'I'll see you at dinner,' to the twins before scurrying off. My focus was set on creating as much distance between myself and the Marlyst King as possible.

My daze lasted into the evening. I managed to put on a front during dinner with the royals, but I excused myself and returned to my quarters. When Eliasson gave me a weird look, I smiled and joked, 'Maybe I'm not immune to hangovers like I thought.' His face filled with compassion and he gently told me to get some rest. I didn't need any further prompting and made a beeline back to my quarters, squashing down the guilt of my infidelity. Once there, I sighed in relief at hanging up my Queenly duties for the night.

I may not have the means just yet to find out what my Royal Mark's reaction to Xylan was, or why it was occurring, but I did have the book with the story of Wystia and Merlot, and that was a tale I wanted to dive into right now.

Crossing my legs, I found a comfortable position on my, bed, calling the book to me. It instantly landed in my hand. Skimming through the titles of the pages, I tried to pinpoint where I'd left off. Finding it, I trailed my fingers across the title, *The Royal Forum*, and was welcomed by the book's familiar pull.

'A hundred years? Don't you think that's an unreasonable demand? There's only so many children a woman can bear in that timeframe,' Wystia exclaimed in disbelief, staring at the four figures sitting across the round table. Merlot sat to her side, running his hand up and down her thigh reassuringly.

'Wystia, you would do well to remember the reason you were brought into this world, and you will fulfil your duties,' the man straight across from her replied sternly, his tipped ears twitching in irritation. His emerald eyes would have been beautiful if not for their harsh depths. They were starkly contrasted with his flawlessly pale skin.

'But Dad –' Wystia started.

'It is Strahn to you,' he snapped. 'I am your sire and there is nothing more to it. You should be thankful that the Svaxlyn joined forces to even secure your position as the rulers of Fyriane. If I had it my way, I would have left you to your own devices to prove yourselves as fit for royalty.'

Wystia visibly flinched.

'Strahn, is that necessary? Show her a little kindness at least. Whether you like it or not, she is your daughter.' The woman to his left implored him with her midnight blue eyes, while her fingers curled around his in an attempt to pacify him.

Strahn pulled his hand away from hers, snapping, 'Areeya, I succumbed to your charms once. Don't expect it to happen again.' The man shook himself like he was trying to get a hold of his emotions. Despite his words, his actions revealed he wasn't as unaffected by Areeya as he claimed to be.

'And for once in your life you were a pleasure to be around,' Areeya murmured, her permanently pink cheeks turned a shade darker.

Wystia's nose scrunched up in disgust as she muttered a 'gross' that elicited chuckles from the other man and woman in the room.

The other woman's gaze turned to Wystia, her tangerine eyes filled with sympathy. 'I agree with Wystia. One hundred years is not a reasonable timeframe for us to start claiming our dues. We would be setting ourselves up for failure and find ourselves right back in the situation we are in now.'

'What is your alternative suggestion then?' Strahn spat condescendingly.

'The alternative Thais is suggesting, if I may?' The final man threw a questioning look at Thais, and received a nod to continue. 'An extended timeframe. Perhaps three hundred years? That would give the people of Fyriane an opportunity to procreate extensively. You need to remember that magic is new to the continent, Strahn. Wystia and Merlot need time to train and hone their people's abilities before we start demanding things. Honestly, this was an experiment for all of us. We don't even know the extent of the powers that will emerge. Only time will tell.'

Wystia and Merlot glanced at each other nervously and remained silent. Strahn quietly contemplated his words. Apparently, he only showed the courtesy of listening to men and not women.

'Two hundred years,' Strahn countered.

'Two hundred and fifty,' the man countered.

'Two hundred and twenty-five. And that is final, Kryol.' Strahn's voice dropped menacingly.

'Are you sure it's final?' Kryol flashed him a toothy grin, revealing extended canines. 'You know I could always make you.'

Small fire balls lit up Strahn's hands, his attention fixed on Kryol's. 'Let's see how far you get little blood sucker.'

'Alright, that's enough of that,' Areeya said, frustrated and ending their testosterone-fuelled battle by throwing water into both men's faces.

Strahn shook the water out of his hair, sending a scathing look towards Areeya that she met with an unapologetic stare.

'Damn nymphs,' he fumed.

'The same damn nymph that brought you to your knees,' Areeya crooned. 'You know where to find me when you decide to drop this domineering act you love playing so much.' The nymph smirked. Strahn's hands turned ghostly white as he clenched the table, causing it to splinter.

Releasing the table before he broke it, he returned his attention to Merlot and Wystia. 'Two hundred and twenty-five years. And you can count on me knocking on your door the minute this timeframe has lapsed. Don't let me down.' He turned away from them in dismissal.

Not wanting to stay a moment longer, Wystia leant over to kiss Areeya on the cheek while Merlot did the same with Thais, whispering, 'See you soon, Mum'. He turned towards Kryol who pulled him into a hug.

'Love you son. Don't be a stranger,' Kryol whispered, before pulling away.

Wystia grabbed Merlot's hand, teleporting them away from the room and back to a place that resembled a palace.

'That was a mess. Your parents are so much nicer than mine,' Wystia said, throwing fire balls into the garden, one after another, letting out her frustration and regenerating the flowers there as she hit them.

'In all fairness, it was better than I expected, Tia. You know how your father can be. And your mother tries her best given the circumstances. Although I'm not sure winding up Strahn was the best move.' Merlot circled his arms around her waist and pulled her tightly into his chest, producing an audible sigh from Wystia.

She snuggled further into his chest, releasing a content sigh. 'What are we going to do, Merlot? We can't let our children fall prey to their agenda. We just can't. It's not fair for them to suffer for it,' she whispered.

'We'll think of something,' he promised. 'But for now, I can hear our children wanting us. We've been gone longer than expected.'

She huffed out a laugh. 'Salistya has Arlom in a headlock again. I don't know what's gotten into her lately. I wish she could play nice like *the twins. And I wish Arlom would stand up to her a bit more.'*

'She'll learn. But you know what older siblings are like, they go through this stage. Arlom's the baby. He'll find his voice eventually.' He ran his nose up the side of her neck, nuzzling the mark underneath her ear.

Wystia hummed. 'I hope it's just a phase. If not, I fear for what his future may hold,' she whispered.

CHAPTER 18

I walked across the roof of the palace as stealthily as was possible while wearing a tight silk nightgown, trying to avoid the jagged edges of the tiles. I still managed to stub my toe though. I cursed quietly, wondering why anyone would think this shitty stone was suitable for a roof. It was probably to deter idiots like me sneaking around. And idiot I was – my damn toe was now bleeding all over the wretched tiles.

I had awoken from the vision in the early hours of the morning. I'd spent twenty minutes unsuccessfully willing myself back to sleep, already drained from the day, but then decided an old school spying trip was more productive than letting my thoughts run wild in the comfort of my own bed.

The new moon provided a small level of discretion, the lack of lighting allowed me to not-so-gracefully fumble across the roof to track Xylan's presence, avoiding the guards stationed below. I sent a blessing to the Goddess Wystia for the phase of the moon before I caught myself. Considering the new revelations from the book, I was unsure what I should call her. Goddess? Queen? Or maybe great-great-great grandmother? I had no idea how many 'greats' there should be as I didn't know how many years it'd been since that Royal Forum. I'd guess it had to be under the two hundred and twenty-five-year mark, as I had never heard of a sighting of the … Svaxlyn? Was that even the name?

But knowing the age of the training program in the Isles, the maths didn't add up to that. It had to be longer than that. I really needed to get closer to Qynthia and start getting answers from the Nyarelle archives. My mounting pile of questions was becoming overwhelming.

But that wasn't a problem for tonight. Tonight, I wanted to find out more about the king I had shared an unforgettable lip-locking session with.

I stopped directly above the window to Xylan's room. It had felt as easy as breathing to track him down, but the overwhelming pull to him was clouding my judgement. I battled the urge to enter the room and entwine myself with him again. That wasn't a good idea.

It took a minute to get myself under control, and once I had I recognised a second presence in his room, pacing up and down in agitation. I could sense Xylan was sprawled out on his bed, his body unmoving and relaxed. That other presence better not be a woman, or I swear to the Goddess –

I cut myself off. I didn't have a right to be jealous. I released a frustrated breath, closed my eyes in concentration and willed my mind into stillness, allowing my sharp hearing to take over.

'You did *what?*' A woman shrieked. Orlandia. Relief flooded me. The woman was his twin. Not a potential liaison.

'In my defence, I didn't do anything. She made the first move. I just … didn't stop her,' Xylan replied smugly.

'Seriously? Day one, Xy. Day one and you've already crumbled. I know we agreed we needed to build a strong relationship with her, but planting your lips on her at the first opportunity? Come on. She's a married woman. And now she's not talking to either of us,' she said. Oh. She was reprimanding him.

'Oh, and you think it was helpful when you questioned her loyalty to the man she's married to? Come on Orla, you know better than that,' he answered.

I sensed her body wince as she stopped pacing. 'In truth, it wasn't the best tactic.'

'*No shit*,' he retorted, sitting up straight. 'She's a physical mage. You know what they're like. They don't communicate like we do. Only with people they explicitly trust. And us? She doesn't trust us as far as she can throw us. We're royals from another Dom. She was raised as a Salistyan. You think a few years on the Isles and here in Arlom are going to override that appalling upbringing? You're a fool if you thought you would get the answers out of her by simply asking. But her body? A physical mages body doesn't lie. That's where you find the truth of her feelings. And I did.'

My breath hitched, overwhelming hurt flooded me. He knew I was a physical mage and he *manipulated* me with it? Lured me into that kiss to gain information on where my loyalties lie? To see if I would crumble into a heap at his feet?

No. I realised wasn't just hurt, I was furious. It took everything in me to hold my magic at bay. To stop the fire that desperately wanted to escape, the water that yearned to pour from the sky, the earthquake that hungered to emerge in a split second, the tornado that longed to rival any that had come before.

'What was that? Did you feel it?' Orlandia gasped.

I froze, my heart accelerated, awaiting his reply.

'It felt like her. But what would elicit anger like that? At this time of night? Unless …' His words died off as I sensed him jump to his feet. 'Please tell me you shielded this room before you came in?'

'Come on, Xy, it's not amateur hour here. It was shielded before I even stepped in the room,' she scoffed.

He released a sigh, sitting back onto the bed. 'Good. Maybe I'm freaking out over nothing. This connection is overwhelming my senses, more than I'd prepared for. I'm trying to fight the pull but … Merlot, give me strength. It's difficult. Give me a day of gruelling sessions in the ruins over this any day of the week.' I felt a caress on my mind as he talked, the same one I'd experienced at the Temple. I closed the barrier in my mind, blocking the entrance to stop the humming on my neck. Now was not the time or place for my mind to be taken over.

'You need to fight it. If you don't, there's no saying if we will get the result we want. You need to be honest as early as possible to gain her trust. You trained your whole life for this, Xy. This isn't just about Marlyst anymore, it's about Fyriane. We can't risk you royally fucking it up so early in the game,' Orlandia warned.

I don't know why I was so disappointed. I should've known. They may be fun to hang around with, but they were never going to be my friends. They were royals, after all. Every one of them had their own damn agenda.

'Easier said than done,' he muttered, so low I had to focus to hear it. 'I can't wait for the day you experience this. And on that day – mark my words – I'll be merciless when I remind you how you once told me to simply "fight it". No one can fight fate, Orla. Not even me.' His laugh sounded miserable.

'Not even for your Kingdom? For Fyriane?'

Xylan's body stilled. 'I would do anything for my people.'

'Then we need her on side. And then you can get what you want. Until then? Keep your hands to yourself. It's not just the husband you need to be worried about. I have my eye on the lover too.'

My face heated, furious. How *dare* they talk about me like this? As if I were a prize.

'That guy is a possessive piece of shit. I fucking hate the way he looks at her,' Xylan responded, revulsion thick in his voice.

'And he loathes the way you look at her. But she cares about him, so don't do anything rash. Pull yourself together. Don't turn into a jealous asshole like Father. You're better than that.'

With those parting words, I heard Orlandia leave the room.

I left too, teleporting to the Isles. Making it a step outside of the Temple, I unleashed a storm over the Isles that continued until dawn.

CHAPTER 19

The next morning, I ensured my expression was composed as I walked into the Royal Study, which was doubling as a meeting room. Eliasson's desk had been moved to the corner, creating space for the group to sit around the large square table in the centre of the room. A map of Fyriane hung on the wall above his desk, while the wall directly across from it held a detailed map of the Arloman kingdom. And, of course, the walls were painted blue.

It was a boring room with little character. I had had many arguments with Eliasson over the need to spruce it up a bit. I had even offered my assistance, littering the room with a few indoor plants. But I gave up pushing him when he insisted that his study had a purpose, and it wasn't to look pretty. He didn't want to give anyone

– including himself – reason to be distracted in the room, which was precisely why it had been chosen for the trade negotiations. I took my seat on Eliasson's right, courteously greeting everyone, meeting the eyes of Qynthia and her Second. Their playfulness had been replaced with a serious air – had they found out what transpired between Xylan and I? I shook my head. No. They wouldn't have. Not everything was about me. We were starting trade negotiations. It was always a serious time.

I nodded curtly at my sister, who sat directly across from me, and she returned it coldly. Her demeanour was nothing new. Ironically, with all the building uncertainties and questions, her consistent behaviour actually provided some comfort. I always knew what to expect when it came to her.

I wasn't the last one to show up. The Marlysts were nowhere to be seen, their assigned chairs empty. They probably slept in after spending half the night discussing how they were going to use me. Well, screw them.

I smiled gratefully at Eliasson as he passed me a cup of coffee, placing a kiss on my cheek. I may have only been to one Forum, but it took me ten minutes at the first one to surmise this was the boring part. Given a maximum of two representatives could be present for each Dom, I insisted Fyrel step in on my behalf. Naturally, Eliasson shot this suggestion down. *Apparently*, my absence wouldn't be a good look. I desperately wished it was a non-issue. Drinking until one in the morning? Absolutely, I was a sucker for a good time. Galloping around the countryside? Count me in. Talking politics and watching rulers fight over new deals? Drop me in the middle of the Tidal Seas and leave me to fight my way out.

The feeling of the twins presence interrupted my coffee. In five, four, three, two … one, the Marlysts entered the meeting room with a literal bang. Xylan shoved the door so hard it crashed into the wall. Both looked like they were about to murder someone as they rounded the table and sat in the last two empty spots. No good morning. No nods. Nothing. Just an assessing sweep of the room that weighed all the individuals. Well, it looked like the king was officially in the building.

I didn't miss that Xylan looked at everyone but me. Cool, cool, cool. Looks like we were going for full-blown avoidance. I should've followed his example and did the same. But I didn't. Nope, the stubborn ass I was decided to openly stare at him. Political schemes aside, if he was going to blatantly ignore me after what went down yesterday, I was going to make it difficult.

And I did. I kept my eyes on him throughout the whole introductory portion of the meeting. Eliasson, as the hosting royal, was obligated to chair the meetings. Per Forum customs, he went on and on through the introduction, listing today's agenda and housekeeping items. Funny, the housekeeping items were mainly around being professional – yes, he used the word professional – at all times. No screaming, no pointing fingers, no throwing things at one another; the list went on. I'd have loved to be present at the Forums that had caused the creation of these rules. It basically listed how to be a sensible person. We were royals, for Goddess' sake. We're responsible for the smooth operation of our Doms and Fyriane as a whole, including the livelihoods of our people. The blandness of the introductory items made the housekeeping list downright comical.

But the comedy of the list still wasn't as amusing as watching Xylan force himself not to look at me. He'd managed to maintain his stoic demeanour, apart from some tell-tale signs. He alternated between clenching his jaw so damn hard I thought he was going to break it, fisting his hands and biting his lip almost to the point of drawing blood. The others were in their own little world, zoning out during the boring part of the meeting, except Orlandia. She was well aware of what was going on between Xylan and I, shooting glares between us, watching the great standoff.

'And that concludes the introductions. Does anyone have any questions or concerns before we proceed?' Eliasson opened the floor and was met with complete, slightly uncomfortable silence.

I forgot how awkward these things could be. Everyone bit their tongue at the beginning, waiting for another royal to say something that would set them off. That's when it became fun. It was a shame we weren't allowed wine. I would love to sit back, sipping away, watching Xylan and Slaviya go head-to-head. It was bound to happen, considering previously tense exchanges between the Marlyst and Salistyan Doms. Xylan may be different from his father, but in this, I couldn't imagine either royals' stances changing.

'Alright,' Eliasson said, clearing his throat. 'Ramone, please begin the minute taking.'

As the Nyarellean Queendom's main role was to accurately record and preserve the history of Fyriane within the libraries' archives, Ramone's duty as Qynthia's Second was to ensure that the events of the Royal Forum were noted. In the future, the rulers of the Doms would be able to request information. Of course, the parts where we get a little drunk were often left out.

As soon as the Nyarellean had a pen in his hand, he nodded to Eliasson to proceed.

'Qynthia, would you like to begin by giving us an overview of the state of the Queendom of Nyarelle?' Eliasson asked.

'The Queendom's population is sitting just shy of fifteen thousand,' the Queen started, before giving the same information she always did. The Queendom was thriving, the history of the continent was being preserved, and children were being trained to carry on Nyarelle's legacy. Nothing changed in Nyarelle as it was the most stable Dom in Fyriane. Which made sense considering it wasn't directly involved in combat with the tidal beasts, risking lives every day. Nor were they finding new mining areas, or battling nature to harvest enough food to feed the continent. If I were to come back in another life, the life of a Nyarellean seems like a sweet deal.

But then I wouldn't have my magic. Would I really give that up for a safe, complacent life? I'd planned that kind of life on the Isles. But I would've still had my magic, still been called out on missions from time to time. The thought of not having it … No. I wouldn't give that up for a safe life. My magic was as part of me as were the limbs on my body.

'Any questions for Qynthia at this stage?' Eliasson asked, interrupting those thoughts. Silence.

'Slaviya. A report on the Salistya Queendom,' Eliasson said, hurrying to add a 'please' after she shot him daggers. Despite my husband's role as chairman, Slaviya could never shake her disdain for being commanded.

'Salistya's army is strong,' she started.

I held back my snort at the blatant lie.

'Our population is sitting at approximately thirty thousand, with roughly a thousand new trainees heading to the Solista Isles every year to commence their training. The average graduation rate of those trainees sits around the ninety percent mark, with seventy percent of that returning to Salistya to serve in the army.'

This meant a ten percent casualty rate, which sounded about right with the brutality of the training and the tasks involved. But twenty percent were choosing to stay on Solista? That was higher than I would've expected, and more than I thought Slaviya would allow.

Curiosity got the better of me as I interjected, 'Twenty percent retention rates on the Isles is higher than usual. Any reason for that?'

She stiffened slightly. Not enough for others to pick up on, but then again, we weren't surrounded by other mages. Her body's reaction couldn't escape my notice no matter how hard she tried.

'There's been a change to the requirements on the Isles,' she said. 'With the influx of Arlomans joining the Salistyan trainees, we require more cooks, cleaners and trainers to assist.'

I mulled over her words. It made sense, but not entirely. And my strengthening sense of knowing agreed with me on this. I continued to pry, guessing the problem was the tidal beasts, something the other royals needed to be made aware of.

'A plausible explanation,' I replied. 'But you don't require a hundred and eighty graduates for those roles when, over the last two years, Arlom have sent four hundred and twenty-seven trainees your way. And that's not to mention the plethora of experienced Solistans who would be an appropriate choice for trainers rather newly graduated mages.'

I felt Xylan's head whip towards mine, but my attention didn't budge from my sister's. I was determined to get to the bottom of this.

'Unless,' a wry smile formed on my face, 'the experienced Solistans are refusing to assist?'

'They're not.' Her answer was too quick for it to be believable. At least to me, anyway. Either she was lying, and they were refusing, or there's something else going on. Or it's both. The options weren't mutually exclusive.

'Alright, I'll believe that. For now,' I said, the last words a warning. 'The Solistans aren't refusing. So, I'll ask the question again; is there

any reason for the higher than usual retention rates on the Isles?'
My tone mirrored the uncompromising one our father used on us in
his many lessons. I knew Slaviya would recognise it. Her jaw ticked,
the message delivered. No doubt, I would pay for this later.

'Alongside the need for increased aid with the trainees in Senora,
there are more tidal beasts moving towards the Isles and further
down the coast heading towards Arlom. I allowed an increased
number of graduates to remain on the Isles to help if an attack
occurs,' she admitted.

There. That wasn't so hard.

'How far away from Arlom are we talking?' Eliasson's hand came
to grip my thigh, a little harder than usual.

'The last sighting was reported a few days ago. At that point,
they were about halfway between Savast and Amarald. The army
has provided decoys, which are proving effective. We have halted
their progress further south, and I have troops stationed across the
whole Salistyan coast right up to the mouth of the Pass on our side,'
she declared.

'And Varqel has Solista under control?' Between being the head
trainer and general of the small army based there, that was a lot
for even someone as capable as him. Why didn't V tell me this was
going on?

'He does now. I have permanently stationed Bastra as the Isles'
army general,' she replied.

The hairs on the back of my neck bristled. She put *Bastra* on the
Isles? The Salistyan's harshest and most ruthless killer? Well, that
explains why he wasn't at the Forum with Slaviya like usual, leaving
her as the sole representative of Salistya. Fuck, this wasn't good. I
needed to see Varqel. And kick Mazyr's head in for his spies' lack of
reporting. *Again.*

'Interesting move,' I commented. What the fuck else was I meant to say? Red flags were flying around in my head. I wanted to wipe that smug look off Slaviya's face.

'Who better than my trustworthy Second to assist Varqel in maintaining the integrity of the Isles?' she said, clearly goading me, enjoying the betrayal. She knew I hated Bastra. She knew I would protect the Solistans with my life. But how the fuck do I protect them from *him*? From his corrupting influence?

'Who better, indeed,' I replied, Refusing to display any type of reaction. But my mind was spinning. Something wasn't right. I was missing something. Story of my bloody life right now.

'The Queendom's breeding programs are strong. We are averaging three thousand births a year, which is a dramatic increase since I've taken over as Queen,' Slaviya continued, her voice smug. The pride she had while proclaiming that more people were procreating, majority against their will, under her reign, was disgusting. Clearly, she wasn't lingering on our previous conversation. It was almost as if she hadn't just shoved a sword into my back by placing Bastra on the Isles.

I took in the room, noting everyone else was equally disgusted by Slaviya's comments. The breeding programs were always a hard one to listen to. None of the Doms, bar Salistya, agreed with forcing women and men to have sex with others outside of a consenting relationship. But the Salistyan's knew better than attempting to leave. Not that some of them didn't try, and frequently. It was one of the reasons Salistya had the Sol. We exterminated the runaways.

Fyriane's population had always been low, no one knew why. Our shores required protection; for that to happen, we needed numbers. Salistya, until recently, hadn't allowed any other Dom access to the Isles to gain magic. And the other Doms refused to subject their people to breeding programs, having given it up long ago. From the tidbits Eliasson had told me, the debates to stop the breeding programs were always heated. And every time it left the Doms right where they started: at an impasse.

'Surely there's a better way, moving forward, for your people than subjecting them to these *programs*,' Xylan bit out with disgust. Here we go. The new royal was entering the age-old debate.

'I'll give you some grace by prefacing that this isn't the first time the topic has been discussed. And you will do well to remember that it is *my* Dom you are talking about. It is only *I* that chooses how it is run, Marlyst,' Slaviya sneered.

I sat up straighter, curious to see how Xylan navigated this.

'Slaviya, the purpose of this Forum is to relay information on the current standing of our respective Doms and negotiate trade agreements. I'm not telling you how to run your Dom, but I would be remiss as a fellow ruler not to lay out the facts,' Xylan replied with an equally icy tone.

I hope to the Goddess I was never on the receiving end of that tone. My sister's I could manage. Hell, I've dealt with it my whole life. But from him? I'd be shaking in my boots as much as Qynthia, who was fiddling with her hands, seemed to be. Eliasson, meanwhile, looked like he was about to grin in delight.

I snuck a look at Orlandia. Her lips quirked briefly, the only sign that, she too, was enjoying this.

Slaviya leant back in her chair, cradled her head in the palm of her hand, placing her elbow on the arm rest. She wore a mask of boredom, feigning a yawn, and motioned for him to continue.

To Xylan's credit, he maintained his composure. 'You've stated that the tidal beasts are moving further south and pose a threat to not only Arlom but the Solista Isles. It's been highlighted that more of your graduates, as you call them, are staying back to aid the army on these Isles. Which means you're down on your forces on the mainland. Which also means that if they do move further south into Arlom, you don't have the numbers to protect the coastal border, or the Pass.'

It was one thing for our coastline to be inundated with attacks. But the Pass? We could not allow the tidal beasts to infiltrate it. It was a key mode of transport between the Doms. Not to mention, the Palace of Fyriane sat in the middle between the Marlyst and Arlom Kingdoms. Despite being in ruins, the Nyarelle and Marlyst Doms insisted on preserving the site.

'Claiming I don't have enough numbers to protect the coastal border is merely speculation, not facts,' Slaviya pointed out.

'So, you're denying it?' Xylan countered.

His question was met with pause. I grinned. Oh, I so wish we could drink in this meeting.

'I am not denying that it would stretch the army. But we can hold our own.'

Silence followed as it sank in that the Salistyan army wasn't as strong as Slaviya first portrayed. I could see where Xylan was going, and based on the scathing look on Slaviya's face, I'd bet a healthy amount of gold that she could see it too.

'In that case, it's a fact that if the tidal beasts move further south into Arlom, your army will be stretched. Which will leave the Fyriane continent compromised,' he stated.

The way he was standing up to Slaviya made him that much more attractive, which was a problem. He wasn't joking when he said he showed up for his people. The man in front of me had done a complete turnaround from the tease I kissed less than twenty-four hours ago. And it only made me want him more.

'The continent will not be compromised,' Slaviya insisted firmly, impatiently drumming her fingers on the chairs' arm. She was wound up, despite her cool demeanour.

'How many shipments of weapons do you require for the next quarter?' Xylan pressed.

Slaviya stiffened. 'Three will suffice. We have left over equipment from the last delivery.'

Xylan hummed. 'That's a lot less than it was a few years ago. What did we get up to, Orla? Six? Seven?'

'Seven,' Orlandia confirmed.

'I'm no expert when it comes to running an army, but I'd guess that you don't require as many weapons because you don't have enough soldiers on the ground to wield them.' His words came out like a purr. It was predatory sound, like he was a cat that had a mouse exactly where he wanted it. He was ready to pounce.

'That's usually how things work,' Slaviya fumed.

'It'd be a shame if the Queendom couldn't uphold their part of the deal with the other Doms,' he mused.

'Unless you do have enough soldiers,' I blurted. I didn't realise I'd spoken out loud until all eyes had fallen on me. Well, it looked like I'd officially reinvolved myself in the discussion. 'The trained Arlomans will be back home in a few years. They'll be able to assist,' I supplied.

'Sounds like we don't have a few years,' Xylan quipped.

'I understand your concerns. That wasn't the extent of my thoughts,' I replied sharply.

'Arlom also need our youth back in the field. We can't have them all moved to the frontline, or we will have no way to maintain farming production,' Eliasson advised.

I turned my attention to Qynthia, my mind ticking over. 'The south-western lands of Nyarelle are a similar climate and terrain to Arlom, yes?'

Qynthia nodded. 'Yes, the land in the south-west and all along the Pass are very similar. Even into the south of Marlyst, but there are a handful of blacksmith villages there.'

'Which means, in theory, that the Arlomans could teach and assist the Nyarelleans to start their own farms,' I began. 'If Nyarelle was self-sufficient and provided food to their own Dom, there wouldn't be as much pressure on Arlom. It could free up some of the graduates to help on the frontline.' I was speaking out loud as I thought through how this would work. For some – mainly Salistya – this wouldn't be a popular option. But we only needed majority rules to make it happen.

'Salistya does not require extra aid,' Slaviya insisted.

'Is that your ego talking? Or the Queen whose duty and focus should be to protect her Dom, and have what is best for the Fyriane continent at the forefront of her decision making?' Xylan challenged, sending a disapproving look towards Slaviya.

'It is my Queendom's duty to ensure the tidal beasts are kept at bay. And we can fulfill this.'

'And it's our duty as your fellow rulers to remind you that at times we need to pivot,' Xylan replied. His attention broadened to land on the rest of us royals in the room. 'Having separate duties throughout the Doms has, debatably, worked for a long time. I often question the logic of this structure, an answer that evidently has been lost to time. Nonetheless, the way we operate as a continent could be better, and clearly times are changing and have been changing. We need to evolve. We need to learn from each other, use our strengths to assist and, above all, protect the lives of our people. If this means we need to break down the barriers separating what the Doms do, then we do it,' he paused. 'Honestly, if you don't agree with me, I suggest you take a good hard look at how you're ruling. Are you ruling for your people? Or for your own personal gain?' The last comment was very clearly aimed at my sister. Judging from her reddened face, she knew it too.

With that, Xylan stood up and left the room before Eliasson could stop him. Guess that meant it was break time.

The others got up to leave the room, drawing the same conclusion as me. I stood up to follow, but Slaviya said, 'Valare. A word.' This wasn't a request.

Eliasson looked back with worry, leaving the room when I mouthed, *I'll be okay.*

CHAPTER 20

As soon as the door closed, she pounced. 'What the fuck was that?'

'There is a lot to unpack from that discussion, Sister. You're going to have to be more specific.'

She was livid. 'I explicitly told you not to talk about the tidal beasts.'

I blinked. Didn't she realise that she brought it up? 'That was all you, Slaviya.'

'You forced my hand,' she seethed.

'I asked questions about graduate numbers. Because, quite frankly, you're acting fucking shady, and I don't trust your intentions. I didn't talk about the tidal beasts, you did. That's a fact.' I threw Xylan's rationale back in her face.

She gritted her teeth, nostrils flared. 'You made the Queendom look weak.'

'No, Slaviya. I didn't make the Queendom look weak. Nor did you. But do you know what does look weak?' I asked, meeting her glare. Oh, if looks could kill. If silence could kill.

'No? Not going to bite?' I taunted. 'Alright, Sister, I'll play. *You* exposed yourself with *your* ego and *your* need for control. You exposed that you would rather feed your own pride than ensure your people see another day by accepting help and considering a new approach to things. And by doing that, Slaviya? You made yourself look weak.'

I made my way to exit when a vine from the plant by the door slithered up my leg, holding me in place. A quick flick of my wrist snapped it in half, and it fell to the floor. I spun around, blasting a wave of air that forced Slaviya back into her seat. I called thicker branches from other plants to wrap around her arms, tying her to the chair.

A cruel smirk formed as I sauntered back towards her. 'I thought you would know better than to threaten a mage more powerful than you. I'll attribute it to a lack of control, and lapse in judgement.'

'But make no mistake, Sister,' I sneered, leaning down, our noses almost touching. 'If you ever come at me with magic again outside of a training room, you will feel the full wrath of my power. And it won't end well for you. I make every effort to be the opposite of our father, but rest assured there is a little piece of Dominiq running through me as well. I am just more selective on when I let that show.'

I stepped away and walked to the door, leaving her to figure out how to remove the bindings before the others rejoined.

'You need to help me get out of this fucking mess you've created. Starting with untying me,' Slaviya demanded with uncontrolled rage.

I snorted and opened the door as I said over my shoulder, 'That sounds like a *you* issue, Sister.'

I stepped out of the room to see Xylan and Ramone sitting nearby. The former had a mug in his hand, sipping on coffee, while the latter looked sympathetic. I caught Xylan's look of approval as I strode past.

They had heard it all.

And for once, I didn't fucking care.

'Are you okay?' Ramone's voice interrupted my thoughts as he took a seat on the bench next to me.

In my haste to gain some distance from Slaviya, I'd headed into the gardens. The smells and sounds helped to calm my racing heart.

I cursed quietly, gripping my shaking hands, willing them to still. Despite engaging in it frequently, I hated conflict. In the moment, impulse took over, adrenaline fuelled my words. But after? When I no longer needed to maintain the façade? I turned into a quivering mess.

'Not really,' I responded. There was no point in lying. My tear-streaked face gave me away. I hated the relationship I had with Slaviya. It was frustrating, how easily she crawled under my skin. How everything turned into a fight. Ramone hummed in acknowledgement, not probing further. Instead, he simply sat next to me, staring at the horizon. He wasn't much of a talker, and his calm, quiet nature soothed me.

The silence was comfortable. The chirping of birds, and the whispering of leaves swaying in the light breeze, provided an air of serenity. It was a welcome change from the busyness of the past few weeks.

'Do you have siblings?' I asked.

He smiled fondly. 'One. She passed away when we were younger. I didn't have the opportunity to learn the trials and tribulations of sibling fights.' His sly, knowing eyes briefly met mine.

'I'm sorry. That must have been hard,' I said. 'The fights aren't anything to be jealous over.' I laughed darkly.

'I'll have to take your word for it.' He paused, considering his next words. 'Would you like to know a secret? It might improve your mood.'

My eyes widened. I loved secrets, and I would love to shake the mood I was in. 'Absolutely.'

His returning smile was radiant. His darker complexion contrasted beautifully with the incredible whiteness of his teeth. 'That book you and Xy were talking about?'

Oh. Not where I thought this was going. However, I wasn't mad about it. I leant towards him.

Moving towards me, his lips were next to my ear when he whispered, 'I wrote it.'

I jumped off the bench, squealing in excitement. Maybe a bit too loud, judging by the way he cupped his hands over his ears.

'*No way,*' I rushed out. 'Wait a second. How? The name on the book is clearly female.'

Ramone blushed. 'I'm quite partial to romantic-comedies. One day I decided to write my own. However, being Qynthia's second, I wanted to keep my anonymity. Hence, I chose a pen name,' he explained. As an afterthought, he added, 'The initials of the pen name are my sister's.'

Damn. Ramone wrote *that*? And all those scenes? Whoever frequented his bed was a lucky person. The quiet ones were often dismissed yet were commonly the ones who knew how to throw it down. This placed my opinion of him in a whole different light.

'Okay, I must ask. There's so many whispers out there saying there is going to be a novella, an update on Louisah's and Runaile's lives. Can you confirm this?' I asked excitedly, bouncing on my feet in anticipation for his answer, wanting him to say yes.

A sombre expression clouded his face. Maybe I pushed the friendship with my question. 'No. I don't think there will be,' he answered quietly.

My heart dropped in disappointment and I sunk down on the bench. 'Oh, that's a shame,' I said. There was so much more that he could do with the story.

He cleared his throat and answered, 'With these things, we're always hungry for more information, more context of another's perspective, to see more of the story. But there's an art to accepting we may not always be gifted that. Instead, we need to find our own closure so we can move on for our own sake.'

Why did I get the impression he wasn't just talking about the book? I gave him a side-eyed look. He'd successfully distracted me up until now. 'Let me guess, Slaviya?'

He lifted one shoulder. 'You can make of my words what you will. I've been in this world for many years, young Queen,' he said warmly. 'You can't always control other people's thoughts and actions, but you can always control your response to it.'

He patted my shoulder and stood up. 'Do me a favour and keep what I've told you to yourself. Few people know how I spend my time outside of being Qynthia's Second. I'd much prefer to keep it that way,' he said softly.

I was shocked when he leant down to press a kiss to my forehead, much like I imagined a father would.

'It can be our little secret.' He winked at me before strolling through the gardens, back towards the palace.

CHAPTER 21

Breathing hard, I stumbled to my feet and resumed my fighting stance. Wiping away the trail of sweat running down my forehead, I stared down my opponents. In a two-on-one situation, it was best to observe first, defend second, and attack last. A plus of this situation? I'd trained with these two for years. The downside? They had pinned me to the floor more times than they should have been able to. I was out of shape. Served me right for bailing on my training session with Mer in the lead up to the Royal Forum.

'Didn't we say best of five? I think we've well and truly won, no?' Rynelle taunted, launching towards me, his fist aimed straight at my head. I ducked, swinging my leg under his knees. He fell to the floor. Mazyr was immediately behind me, arms coming around my neck. I lifted my foot and shoved it into his groin. He staggered back, surprisingly staying on his feet, but only for a second as I hooked my fist into his jaw, sending him sprawling into the walls of the training arena.

'We did. But I like the feeling of kicking your asses so much I decided to stop counting,' I threw back as they got to their feet and resumed circling.

My statement wasn't entirely true. They'd handed me my ass significantly more times than I had them in this session. But hey, I had managed to get a few knocks in there, and considering it was two-on-one with no magic allowed, it was fairly even. I had had to take magic off the table to even entice them into the ring with me. The Goddess knows I needed to let off some steam tonight.

Mazyr scoffed. 'I think you've been hanging out with your sister a little too long, Val. You're starting to sound as delusional as her.'

When he found me outside the palace after Ramone left, Mazyr stayed with me before I had to put my Queen hat back on and head to the meeting room. He used his knowledge of the fight to lash out at me now, intending to spark my rage. And it did.

I launched towards him. He raised his hands to defend himself before returning to engage in some old school hand to hand with me. At that moment, I felt Rynelle come up behind me so I stepped to the side and watched in amusement as he fought to stop himself from barrelling Mazyr over.

Capitalising on the distraction, I landed a punch under Mazyr's jaw, splitting the skin, and sent him to the floor right as Rynelle approached me. I noticed he was stumbling. Maybe I'd hit his legs a little hard. Oh well. I executed the same move as before, honing in on his weakness, knocking him down.

When it seemed they both wanted to stay on the floor, I allowed my bruised body to sink down too. I lay on my back trying to catch my breath, grinning as the two men groaned. I had missed this.

'They may have won the best of five, but I think overall performance has to be handed to you, Valare,' Amire called from the stands, casually filing her nails, not even bothering to look up at the spectacle. She'd been here the whole time, politely declining to make the match three versus one. She claimed tonight was her night for self-care, not self-destruction.

'Please, you just want to say you won the bet. Hand your coppers over, Amire,' Rynelle spat out.

'I specifically said that she'd have you on your asses crying like little schoolboys while she walked away relatively unscathed. Now, correct me if I'm wrong, but from my vantage point, you're lying on your asses moaning in pain and she's rather casually trying to level out her breaths. Plus she's got that sadistic smile on her face,' Amire stated, moving on to painting her nails.

Mazyr managed to roll onto his side to face me. The blood running down his chin didn't stop the tired, sloppy grin on his face. 'Do you feel a little better?'

A sound of contentment left my mouth. 'I feel amazing,' I replied.

His eyes crinkled at the sides, warm adoration shining in those mossy green depths. 'Good,' he whispered, resting his head to the floor.

'Another round?' Rynelle joked, tucking his anger away, receiving a round of laughs.

'With all due respect Valare, you're out of shape,' Amire commented when the laughter had died. I could always trust her to say what I didn't want to hear. And it was always the truth.

'Yeah, yeah. I'm getting weak in my old, queenly ways. Still managed to take these two losers down though.' Brushing off her comments was usually the best way to end the conversation. But not tonight apparently.

'How are you planning on defending yourself against your enemies if you're not training? Yes, you have your magic, but eventually you will need to rest and regenerate. Maybe not as quickly as us, but you don't have infinite power. You need to keep up your hand-to-hand combat as well,' she finished.

She was starting to sound like Varqel with how she was lecturing me.

'Says the assassin who chose 'self-care' over training,' countered Mazyr.

True to form, Mazyr had my back in these situations. With words, at least. With action? He was a bit useless on the best of days.

'It's a very important part of maintaining one's body. Which, if you'd attended the classes instead of hooking up with anything that had a pulse, you would know.'

Well damn, Amire. She wasn't playing.

'Alright, well, it's been a pleasure,' I interjected loudly, cutting off any further conversation. I'd reached my quota of sibling spats for the day. 'But I have places to be, people to see. You know how it is.' I brushed off my pants as I stood up.

'Why don't you ever stay around to hang out with us like the old times?' Rynelle whined.

'I promise once this is all said and done with Eliasson, I'll make time for us to hang out. I miss you guys, I really do. I know we see each other fleetingly but –' I cut myself off before I became emotional. 'It's not the same. And I acknowledge that. But I appreciate all your hard work. And there's only just over a week to go with the Forum, so we're almost there.'

It was true. I wanted nothing more than to find a rowdy Solistan bar and forget about all of this, even if it were just for a night. Just me and my Sol kicking it like the good old days.

'I'm sure you could make a bit more time for us,' Rynelle scowled.

Amire frowned, unimpressed with his comment. 'No need to explain yourself, Queen. Go do what you need to do. We'll be here when you need to let off more steam.' She shooed me away.

I looked at the boys, ignoring Rynelle's comment. 'Same time, two nights from now?'

'Can't wait,' Mazyr winced, clutching his rib where I had landed a nasty punch earlier. I might have broken it. Ah well, he'd been through worse.

'Your bacon and eggs were bang on today. Keep up the good work, chef,' I quipped.

The last thing I saw was a raised middle finger aimed straight at me.

I didn't bother changing out of my clothes, instead opting to land straight on the palace roof above Qynthia's room. After last night's successful (or not so successful depending on how you want to look at it) snooping, I decided it wasn't ideal to test my patience with another round of the Marlyst twins.

Varqel had told me off earlier in the evening for the storm I'd created throughout the Isles. Afterwards, the ground was so muddy the trainees weren't able to get outside for their usual classes, despite having multiple Earth and Water Mages working on the mess. I didn't bother pretending that it wasn't me. Sometimes a girl's got to let off some steam, and I sure as hell couldn't bring myself to use Eliasson as the usual outlet. Not after everything that went down with Xylan. The guilt was still gnawing at me.

'Well, this is definitely a look I haven't seen. Not going to lie, I'm surprisingly into it.'

Xylan's voice broke through my thoughts.

Where the hell had he come from? I hadn't sensed him at all.

'Just kicking back,' I quipped, sitting down, refusing to look at him and be distracted by his beauty.

'On top of the palace? In fighting leathers? Interesting place for that. Interesting time of hour, too,' said Xylan. He sat down next to me but kept an appropriate distance, so we weren't touching.

I didn't answer. I did not owe this guy any explanation.

'You have blood running down your neck.' I sensed his hand reach towards me, only for him to retract it quickly.

'I do?' I ran a finger down my neck, wincing at the bruise that must be forming, and pulled away 'Huh,' I said, noticing the blood.

'Shall I get you a healer?'

I swung my head, assessing him, accusation in my voice. 'Why do you care?'

'Probably not a good look strolling into the meeting room tomorrow all banged up,' he teased. I wanted to wipe that smirk off his face. Maybe I should've stayed longer at the arena.

'Well, I can always add a couple of battle scars to your face and we can stand in solidarity with one another, hmm?' I replied.

Somehow the snort he let out was attractive. 'You wouldn't be able to go through with it.'

Clearly he didn't know me very well. I could still use a punching bag to let out my frustrations, the sparring with my Sol had barely satisfied it. 'You want to test that theory? Because I easily have another ten rounds in me.'

I moved my neck from side to side, cracking it as I went, preparing for him to call my bluff.

'You're a bit wilder than I was expecting,' he mused. His appraising glances gave nothing away as to whether my being wild was a good or bad thing. I wasn't offended. It wasn't the first time I'd been called that, nor did I expect it would be the last.

'Is that meant to be a compliment?' I asked, my words spilling out a little too quickly.

I waited for the blow to come, the one where he admonished me like most other men I'd known. Aside from a select few, a lot of the men I knew felt it was their right to put a woman in her place. They were too scared we would be uncontrollable, wild, emotionally erratic.

I was surprised when my question was instead met with a feral grin.

'Absolutely,' he responded.

His primitive look made me pause. Xylan portrayed himself as jovial and carefree, flinging jokes around, giving as good as he got. But beneath the mask, I could now sense a thrumming, tightly restrained power. There was a ruthless, unforgiving edge to Xylan I was beginning to notice. It screamed 'fuck with me or mine and I will obliterate you'. Of course, he wouldn't be deterred by my 'wildness'. His look showed me all I needed to know. He wouldn't control me or my power. He'd match it. I longed to experience the beauty of that. To have an equal.

The noise of a door opening, followed by two presences, in Qynthia's room ripped my attention away from his captivating gaze.

I could tell clothes were being taken off at a rapid pace, lips mashed together in a heated embrace. I sensed a person on their knees, while another was lying down in front of them on the bed, legs wide open. Heavy moans soon sounded. A lot of 'Oh yes, right there. Oh, God right there. Oh, that's good. That's very good darling,' followed.

I felt my face heating. Looked like Qynthia had found herself a buddy in Arlom. And it wasn't Xylan. Not tonight, anyway.

'Well,' I quipped, breaking the awkward silence forming as we listened in on the fun. 'At least someone's getting a happy ending.'

His deep chuckle stirred desire in me.

No, it wasn't him. It was Qynthia and her friend stirring it.

'What's your favourite food?' Random question from him, but okay.

'Any baked goods. And raspberries. Oh, and chocolate,' I answered. My mouth started watering.

'That's more than one,' he noted.

'Well, you have a lot to learn about me. That question is like asking a mother who her favourite child is. Impossible.' I shook my head at him.

Surprise and a hint of jealousy lit up his face before he carefully masked his expression. 'You have children?'

'Well, no, but –'

'So how do you know?' he countered.

I rolled my eyes. 'This game's getting off to a good start.'

'If simply getting to know you is a game then I hate to say it, but you've got some trust issues.'

I scoffed, irritation spiking. This man was talking to his sister last night about getting me on side. And he was going to pretend being up here with me wasn't a game? And comment on me having trust issues? Un-fucking-believable. Of course, him not knowing that I knew, was irrelevant.

'Look, in case you aren't aware, I didn't come up here to be psychoanalysed. So, spare me,' I shot back. 'Which reminds me, what are you doing up here?'

He feigned innocence, 'Just taking in the serenity. What are *you* doing up here?'

'Oh, you know, leaning into my voyeuristic side. Strolling the roof hoping to listen in on someone getting lucky,' I said, biting my lip, dramatically moaning at the same time one sounded from the Queen. Qynthia followed it by releasing a scream, whimpering as she came down from her climax.

'*Fuck*,' Xylan groaned as he watched my every move, clearly reacting to the sounds and restraining himself.

I threw him a wink. 'See? It's a lot of fun.'

'Apparently,' he said, gritting his teeth.

I eyed him as he shifted his pants to make way for what looked like his hardening dick. Damn. I was joking but it seemed like he was right into the listening thing. I was into that. But I resisted the urge to store that information for a later date. 'It looks like you may have a problem there.'

'Are you offering? After the show you put on today, I'd say you're quite adept at resolving problems,' he purred, leaning into me.

I simultaneously hated and loved the challenging glint in his eye. 'I think I've had enough for one day. But I'll take the compliment, thanks.'

He huffed out a laugh before creating more space between us. 'Blue or Green.'

'Oh? We're going back to this, are we? Shall we place bets on us lasting more than one round of questions?' I really tried not to taunt him, but I couldn't help it. It was too fun. Plus, I was pretty sure he secretly loved it.

'Blue or Green, Minx.'

I guess that was a no. And I guess I had a new nickname. 'Blue.'

'Interesting.'

"Was it really?"

'Not for any political reason,' I rushed out. 'I just … I love the crystal clear ocean blue of the shallow waters of the Isles, right where the water meets the sand. The push and pull so great between the two that they are tied to one another, always coming back for more.

The sand is stable, unmoving, while the water is erratic, at times calm, gentle, lapping at the sand. And other times? It's fierce and untamed in its relentlessness to never stop moving. For the world to see it for the powerful force that it is. But the sand never cowers, nor ever tames it. It welcomes the water with an open embrace for everything it is. It's beautiful.'

My heart ached as I thought of the symbolism of waves crashing on the shore. It's how I envisioned my true love. Someone who would accept me in all my wildness, never diminishing my power, but rather holding steady and staying by my side through it all. Always having my back, never afraid or thinking I was too much. I had known deep in my heart for a while that person was neither Eliasson nor Sir. Definitely not the latter. That had become increasingly apparent over the last few weeks. And Eliasson? He didn't know the full extent of who I was. And if he did, I knew he wouldn't be able to handle it. He would constantly be on edge, bracing for a wave to hit, wiping him out along with everything else. It would never work.

Xylan watched me in quiet contemplation.

I broke the silence, not wanting to linger on the analogy of love. 'Pink or Orange.'

My question snapped him out of his thoughts. 'It wasn't a political question, for the record,' he clarified. 'But if I had to choose, pink, of course.'

'Wow. Someone's comfortable in his sexuality,' I joked, not pushing the political part any further. We'd made it all of two questions, I wouldn't want to ruin it when we're on a roll.

'Well yes, I am. Very comfortable, that is. But that whole pink is a girl's colour thing is bullshit. You get over it pretty fast and stop subscribing to that ridiculous notion when you have pink eyes.'

Those pink eyes were staring into my soul.

'Fair enough.' I winced at my less than great response.

'Pink reminds me of the sunrise over the Hudrielle Desert. As kids, Orlandia and I would often wake up early to catch the splashes of light pink. It complements the blue sky as the sun rises over the sand. The sight is … it's hard to explain how beautiful it is. It's one of those things you need to see to appreciate its beauty. My words will never do it justice.'

He'd relaxed as he started opening up to me, allowing me to see another side to him. It was … nice.

'Are you able to see the sunrise from your palace? Or do you have to venture into the desert to see it?' I hoped he didn't feel I was probing. After all, I'd never been to the Kingdom. I had heard the Marlyst Royal Forums were held in the blacksmith villages, rather than their palace. It was strange, but no one knew where the palace was located. I should've been gathering information, but I found myself simply wanting to know. I wanted to understand where he came from. And maybe … maybe it would help me better understand him.

'We see glimpses of the sunrise depending on where we are in the palace. The dunes on the outskirts of the city are quite tall though, so it cuts off the view a fair bit. It's best to be in the desert itself to see the full effect.'

'I imagine you'd have outposts in the desert then? If you have to get up so early to be able to see it. Or do you go camping?' I couldn't think of anything worse than camping, surrounded by sand, in that kind of heat. At least in the Isles there was plenty of cool water to dive into, helping to cut through the humidity.

'I've done my fair share of camping, yes. But these days I tend to stay in one of the … outposts when I can get away from royal duties.

I've spent too many hours in the cool climate of the Kingdom to favour the heat of the desert anymore.'

Interesting. I'd taken a guess mentioning outposts, as in truth, I had no idea if there was any infrastructure out there. I wondered why they would need buildings in the desert. There was nothing there.

'So, what I'm hearing is that you've become soft,' I teased. He raised an offended eyebrow at me. I held up my hands in an innocent gesture, 'Just reading between the lines.'

He chuckled. 'I suppose that's how your kind would view it. I tend to see it as favouring comfort over hardship.' He flashed a rueful smile. 'Sand in your clothes? Sticking to you as you sweat from the blistering heat? At least in the Isles you're surrounded by water to wash off. But in the desert? Waterholes are few and far between. It leaves us craving water, driven by this insatiable need to quench our thirst,' he said, voice dropping low, sensually. He leaned towards me.

Warmth spread through me, heating up my body despite the cool nip of the night air. My eyes lowered to his lips, remembering the feel of them on mine. The flick of his tongue, the bite of his teeth, his groans as he'd tilted my head, pulling me deeper into him.

I cleared my throat, mentally shaking myself. 'I guess you make a valid point. Water is important,' I responded lamely. Here I was worrying that my analogy had taken it too far. But Xylan? Give the man a little and he would run with it.

'It's as vital as our next breath,' he breathed into my ear, sending a warm buzz through my body. If I moved my head a fraction, I knew his lips would brush my cheek. I craved the contact like my body craved its next breath.

What I needed, though, was to get out of here before a repeat of our kiss happened. 'Well, sleep is also vital. So, on that note, I best be off,' I said, not particularly smoothly.

I felt Xylan cock his head to the side, gifting me a sliver more space as he listened to the activities in Qynthia's room. 'Are you sure? You're about to miss orgasm number four.'

'Consider my thirst quenched,' I paused, lingering on his perfect form. 'For now.' I shouldn't have said that last bit. I knew he would hold onto that.

'Suit yourself,' he grinned. 'Until the next rooftop hangout, my Minx.'

I didn't give him the satisfaction of a reply. I was too busy reeling over his last words. Oddly, the possessive 'my' didn't feel suffocating when it came from his mouth.

CHAPTER 22

O ur legs were tangled, our breathing working to fall back into its natural rhythm as we lay together in post-coital bliss. Curiosity sparked and my hand inched towards the mark below his ear that looked like an upturned mouth. He sighed as I caressed it. I waited for the warm, throbbing feeling to work through my body. But there was nothing. I may as well have touched his arm for the lack of reaction I felt.

'Does that feel nice?' I questioned. He responded with 'mmm', his head leaning into my touch.

'Can you describe it for me?' I probed. Maybe there was something wrong with me.

'It feels like … home? You know that tingle of anticipation you have when you've been away from home for so long and the knowledge *that you're close. So close. But the more it lingers, the more it's– there's something not quite right about it. It has a coldness to it. Almost like I want to go home, to taste the warmth of the sun, but the coldness is leading me away from it. But I don't want to be away from it. I want to go home –'*

He gasped suddenly, pulling away from my hand and looked at me with confusion. Like I was the one keeping him away, and he wanted to get as far away from me as possible.

'Eliasson? Are you okay?' I asked, shocked. He'd never looked at me like that before. Like I was an imposter. Like I was anything other than his wife. But if the markings were what I was beginning to think they were, his reaction would make sense. Because what he was describing wasn't the hum or warmth I'd become accustomed to. And if I wasn't his true home, it would explain his reaction.

His mark was rejecting me.

'Valare?' Qynthia's voice shook me from my thoughts of this morning with Eliasson.

I swept my eyes around the markets, taking in the carts and pop-up shops strewn along the side of the path I was mindlessly walking down. There were significantly less people in the markets than last time, with many of the farming community vacating Amarald to head back to their homes and ready themselves for the planting season.

After a week of negotiations where, not surprisingly, Slaviya and Xylan had continued to butt heads at every turn, Eliasson had called a hold on meetings.

Despite my discussion with Slaviya, she had completely ignored my words – and me, personally – and continued refusing to accept assistance from the Arlomans despite everyone now realising the threat of the tidal beasts. And she had been very vocal about her disagreeing with the Doms working cohesively, which had, naturally, set off Xylan and instigated a majority vote.

As per Fyriane customs, when there was a need for a vote of this magnitude, the royals were excused from meetings for two days to contemplate their decision. I had taken the opportunity to invite Qynthia for a stroll down to the markets. I needed her alone to get information. As expected, she was delighted to accept my invitation. Apparently, though, Orlandia also thought we were close enough to tag along. Not ideal. But I couldn't refuse her company without stirring up suspicions.

'Sorry, ladies, I got lost in my thoughts,' I sheepishly responded.

'Hmm, that's the fourth time you've done that in the space of an hour,' Orlandia commented with a sideways glance. 'Is there something on your mind?'

Yes and no. Everything and nothing. Where do I start?

I sighed. 'Just tired. This hosting thing is more demanding than I expected.'

I tried to shake it off like it was nothing, but the knowing look I received in return was evidence enough that it wasn't working.

Qynthia steered me towards a back alley, away from the crowds and merchant carts, Orlandia trailing behind. When we were alone, they turned to face me, standing side-by-side. For a split second, I thought I saw a shimmering glow encompass us before the feeling passed as quickly as it came.

'What do you need?' Qynthia demanded. The carefree expression of the affectionate woman I'd come to know was replaced with a solemn, firm look. 'Don't bother lying to me. I have an uncanny ability to see through fibs.'

And for some reason, I believed her. She might be the Queen of another Dom, and potentially someone to watch out for, but, deep down, I knew she had our best interests at heart. Through the course of the meetings, she hadn't spoken up much. But when she did, it was in solidarity of Fyriane as a whole. She wasn't self-serving –

I doubted she even had a selfish bone in her body. She led with empathy and demanded respect in return. I could only give her that respect if I was honest and trusted her.

But trust wasn't an easy thing for me. Without it, though, I wouldn't receive the answers I needed, which was a bigger risk than I was willing to take. It could be the difference between surviving as a sole ruler or crumbling.

Swallowing the nausea rising in my body, I threw caution to the wind and divulged, 'I need access to information that will help me understand the tidal beasts. If they're coming for Arlom, I need to be prepared.' I omitted asking for information on Wystia and Merlot, choosing to keep my cards close to my chest on that subject. For now, at least. Starting with the tidal beasts was a safe option. It was a well-known, more pressing issue.

Orlandia tilted her head in quiet assessment, while Qynthia nodded understandingly, eyebrows furrowed in concentration. 'From my time in the archives, I know we have some books on them,' she began. 'Whether they have what you require, though, I can't promise anything. If memory serves, these books are old. Like, *old* old Valare. I'm not even sure if they're in the language we speak.'

Well, that may be a problem. But something was better than nothing. I would work on the translator later. 'How fast could you get them to me?' I resisted the urge to ask exactly where they were and just teleport there.

She reached her hand out to clasp my wrist, squeezing it reassuringly, her eyes telling me she knew what I wanted to do. 'It depends on how much you're willing to trust me.'

My self-control kicked in to stop me from moving away from her touch at the insinuation in her eyes. It was as if she knew my first impulse. Which meant she knew about my magic. But how?

My body stilled. 'What are you insinuating?' I asked. The only thing moving was my rapidly beating heart.

'If I may?' Orlandia interjected.

Qynthia's eyebrows creased while the two looked at each other. It seemed there was a silent conversation passing between them. Then Qynthia reluctantly nodded.

What the hell was going on?

'Promise not to freak out?' Orlandia directed the question at me, and I responded with a confused frown. I couldn't really promise not to react to something I had no idea about, and I wasn't going to stand here and pretend I did.

Orlandia straightened her shoulders, looking me dead in the eye as her body shimmered with gold for a moment. I watched as her body transformed into the Nyarellean woman from the markets.

Holy shit. So, I haven't been imagining things.

'I knew I knew you from somewhere.' My words came out as an accusation.

Her smug grin told me she found this whole situation hilarious. 'I'd be lying if I said I didn't enjoy the baffled look you gave me when we first met,' she admitted.

Bloody asshole. Just like her brother. 'How did you do that and why did you do it?'

Orlandia hummed, working out an appropriate response. 'Have you heard of the Ophiscair Prophecy?' she asked.

My head reared back in familiarity. The Ophiscair Prophecy was what framed the Solistans religion. The prophecy, they claimed, was the reason I was the one they recognised as their leader. It was the reason for their loyalty. But what did it have to do with the tidal beasts?

For the first time, I wished I'd gone to those religion classes instead of stuffing my face with Iris' sourdough. Maybe then Orlandia's question would make a bit more sense.

'I've heard of it, yes,' I replied stiffly.

'Do you know what the actual prophecy is?' she asked, staring at me. She leant towards me so intently that our bodies were a breath away from touching, but it was the intensity of her voice that startled me more.

'No. I never subscribed to the religion of the Solista Isles. Quite frankly, I think it's all a crock of shit,' I sniffed, feeling oddly defensive – not to mention embarrassed – over my lack of knowledge.

Her melodious laugh startled and scared me. 'You didn't think it was important to at least understand a prophecy that's centred around your entire existence?' She shook her head in disapproval.

Back when my eyes had changed, I hadn't wanted to further exaggerate how different I was to everyone around me, so I avoided anything that could emphasise it. But maybe that had been a mistake.

'I just wanted to blend in. Be normal,' I muttered as it dawned on me that some of the answers I'd been searching for would've been found years ago if I had only been willing to listen and stand out.

Orlandia shot Qynthia a knowing look as the Queen closed the distance between us.

'Do you trust me?' Qynthia asked, her hands moving to clasp the sides of my face, energy emanating from her.

'I'm guessing I don't have a choice if I want the answers I'm looking for.'

Orlandia snickered and Qynthia's mouth twitched, fighting the smile that wanted to escape. Her fingers pressed to my temples, and I felt a caress in my mind. This didn't feel like Fuchsia Eyes; this caress had a feminine energy surrounding it. Qynthia's energy, I realised. Probing but soothing, it searched, requesting entry into my mind.

'Let me in, Valare,' Qynthia murmured.

Sighing in resignation, I allowed her to enter, and was pulled into a familiar setting.

Wystia and Merlot were standing in the heart of the Temple, in front of the statue of the Goddess. They were surrounded by people, undoubtedly Solistans.

'There will be many that will come and many that will go. You must do everything in your power to leave them better than they arrived. Fyriane requires your allegiance in paving the way for what is to come. We need magic wielders across the continent, strong and ready to defend.

'Teach your young the prophecy no matter what happens in the future. They will arrive when the time is right to lead and unite Fyriane once again. You must do everything in your power to ensure the path is lit for them. To show them the way. Do we have your pledges to carry out what has been asked of you?' Wystia asked,

A resounding, 'Yes, Your Highness,' swept through the room. The Solistans bent down on one knee before reciting the Ophiscair Prophecy.

'Opposing stages of the moon brings extraordinary gifts.

One for her, another for him.

On these nights, Fyriane will awake, a new destiny starts to shape.

Within the union lies myriad answers, a True Infinite bond to rule the masses.

Unlock this bond and there it shall be; knowledge finds those who are meant to see.

True Infinites, hand in hand, will rise above to take a stand.

Lime green and fuchsia meet, ready to take their seat.'

Wystia grabbed Merlot's hand, immediately teleporting them to a different place.

Here the layout was like the Temple, however, the walls were carved from rock and the floor was covered in orange sand. A statue of Merlot was now behind the couple, and they were surrounded by people with burnt orange and pale pink eyes.

Wystia and Merlot repeated the prophecy, asking for allegiance to carry out the duties. When they received confirmation from the others present, the couple looked at one another, tears welling in their eyes.

'I love you,' Wystia said in an anguished whisper.

'I love you, my darling. In this life and the next. Don't cry for us, for we will always be. My True Infinite. This is our path, our journey. It is our children's and their children's path now. Rest easy knowing we've done everything in our power to save them. And when they come, they, too, will save Fyriane.' Merlot combed his hands through Wystia's hair, comforting her as tears streamed down his own face.

Wystia nodded, leaning into him to press her lips to his for what was clearly the last time. 'For our family.'

'Until we meet again, my love. For this, I am sure.'

Suddenly, I was watching two scenes happening. Wystia returned to the Temple, placing her hands on the statue, and Merlot did the same on the other statue. As if they both knew when to start, they opened their eyes and spoke in unison.

'For the doers, the defenders, and the dreamers. To the devoted, the divisive, and the divine. For the True Infinite, and the continent of Fyriane. Protect our family.'

They kissed the middle fingers of one hand and pressed them to their third eye, their other hand remaining on the statues. A green light surrounded Wystia, while a pink light surrounded Merlot, and their powers drained into the respective statues. As the flow started to dwindle, their bodies were pulled into their statues. A glowing, lilac shield was propelled out of the statues with so much power it rippled further and further away, out of eyeshot.

My eyes flew open. I stumbled away from Qynthia in shock and braced my hands on my thighs. I took in short, sharp breaths. What in the hell did I just witness?

Is *this* the reason the Solistan's saw me as their rightful heir? There's one sentence mentioning lime green. One. And their conclusion is that it *has* to be about me, simply because of my eye colour? They're living on a different planet. Hell, a different universe. This isn't about me. They've lost their damn minds.

I looked up to see both Qynthia and Orlandia with one leg bent, hands over their hearts, heads bowed in reverence. This wasn't happening. This was a bad dream. A bad dream where people had lost their fucking minds. Wait until I wake up and tell Mer about this.

'My Queen, I pledge you my loyalty. I am at your disposal,' they said in unison. My eyes bulged at the sight of them. Seeing them kneel for me was too much. Not to mention it was completely misplaced.

I rushed forward, pulling them up to stand in front of me. 'That isn't necessary. Truly. I'm just Valare. No need for formalities. We are all equals here,' I spluttered.

Qynthia gave me a pitiful smile. 'This may take some time for you to get used to. Take all the time you need, the Dom of Nyarelle will be taken care of for you, until you're ready.'

Until I'm ready? What was there to be ready for? The prophecy said a True Infinite must unite to rule Fyriane. Hell, I didn't even know what a True Infinite was, let alone have one.

'I think this is all being blown out of proportion. That thing you just showed me,' I exclaimed, waving my hands around like a lunatic. 'Completely open to interpretation. Couldn't be any more ambiguous if you tried.'

'But –' Qynthia started.

'And my interpretation?' I cut in, 'Absolutely nothing to do with me.'

Orlandia shook her head in disbelief, arms crossed. She sighed, side-eyeing Qynthia.

I huffed. 'I just wanted to know about the tidal beasts,' I muttered. 'How did you do that, though? I mean, get into my head like that?' I asked, curiosity getting the better of me.

'We are psychic mages,' Qynthia stated simply, like it was common knowledge.

'Right, of course you are,' I muttered. 'And I suspect Mr Fuchsia Eyes is a psychic mage as well?' I asked.

They probably thought I was ridiculous. So I was surprised when they burst into hysterics. It took a while for them to recover from their laughter, shock and understanding slowly dawning on their faces.

'Mr Fuchsia Eyes?' Orlandia blurted out between cackles.

'Yeah, the man that does what you just did. Activating a Lull like that.' I waved my hands in between us in a dismal attempt to demonstrate a Lull. How they understood what I said was beyond me. But apparently, they were picking up what I was trying to put down.

Qynthia's mouth dropped open. 'Yes. He is a psychic mage. And that wasn't the Lull, Valare. I can't access that. Only the most powerful True Infinite mages can meet in a Lull. I was just pushing a memory onto you. But maybe you should ask him these questions …'

She looked away, suddenly finding the ground very interesting.

'Ask him? I don't even know him. So far he has just shown up randomly and walked into my mind whenever the hell he wants!' Exasperation filled my voice at that suggestion.

'Right. Yes, you're right. Hard to ask someone you haven't met.' Qynthia scratched her head nervously, still staring at the ground. Orlandia also avoided my eyes.

Judging by their reactions, I'd hazard a guess to say there was a good chance they knew who this man was. And suddenly it clicked.

'Unless I have met him,' I probed.

I was sure I knew who Mr Fuchsia Eyes was.

My eyes landed on Orlandia, waiting for her to speak on the matter, confirm my suspicions. She met my eyes and merely raised her hands as if to say, 'I'm not getting involved'.

'Well technically you have. In the Lull. Maybe you should activate it again and talk to him,' suggested Qynthia. Her answer was too quick for her ignorance to be believable, and her suggestion was most definitely trying to deter me from probing any further.

My head had started to ache, and I decided to leave aside my suspicion on Fuchsia Eyes as it was clear I wouldn't get anywhere with them.

'So, the tidal beasts. I can have the books deposited to you within a couple of weeks. Unless you would prefer to teleport to the Queendom with me. In that case, we can have them within the hour.' Qynthia ruthlessly pulled our conversation back to the earlier topic before I could ask more of them.

Yes. Right. The tidal beasts. 'A couple of weeks will suffice. Please throw in some books about the damn Royal Marks as well. I've got some questions about those, too.'

Qynthia threw me a knowing look but didn't push the subject.

'Does my sister believe in this madness?' I had to ask even though I knew it likely wouldn't get me where I needed. It had become clear the two of them seemed closer than I originally realised.

Qynthia raised her eyebrow, waiting for me to expand.

'Does my sister believe in this prophecy?' I explained.

'Your sister is concerned with the direction that best fits her purpose,' Qynthia replied. Cryptic. But also, not wrong. She was protecting her, Goddess knew why.

'You said I could trust you. You also pledged your loyalty to me, and now you're being cryptic,' I challenged. I might not believe in this prophecy, but it didn't mean I wouldn't shamelessly exploit it when it suited my needs.

'Being a psychic mage gives one access to … intimate thoughts and feelings of others. We live by a code of ethics to ensure we practice our magic with integrity. Your sister has her own agenda. I'm not telling you anything you don't already know. If her plans were detrimental to what needs to happen, I would speak up. But the one thing you should know, Valare, is that there is an art to what is told and what is seen. Your sister has her own path and her own lessons to learn. And for you? Knowledge finds those who are meant to see. Keep pushing to see, and you will find the way.'

I let out a frustrated breath, 'You're not going to give me any more information, are you?'

She pressed her lips into a thin line. 'I'm sorry, my Queen. We already pushed the boundaries showing you the memory. We need you to make sure this wasn't for nothing.'

I flinched, uncomfortable with another Dom's ruler calling *me* her Queen.

I could sense that she was conflicted and held a flicker of unease, so she wasn't lying. She may have crossed a line to provide me with insight, but I still had questions I wanted answers to. It wasn't fair.

I assessed the two women, taking in their uncompromising stances. This wasn't a conversation I was going to win today.

I plastered on a smile, showing I was letting things go. 'Well, it's a lovely day in Amarald. I wouldn't want to miss the last few hours of sunshine hanging out in a dingy alley. Shall we?'

I may have been smiling on the outside. But inside? A mixture of anxiety and rage was building as I began to suspect what I would need to do next.

I'd tried to live my life like an ostrich. Putting my head in the sand. Ignoring the unsubtle gazes of people staring at my lime green eyes. The whispers of awe as I passed by. Ignorance is bliss, the saying goes. And I believed it. Revelled in the thought that, if I didn't give energy to the whispers, the stares, the expectations of a sham prophecy, it would cease to exist.

But I never stopped to wonder, what happened when ignorance didn't equal bliss? When it turned around and bit you in the ass?

The answer to that question was now jarringly apparent. Ignoring things left you exposed. Floundering. Vulnerable. And had left me with the expectations of not only the Solistans, but also people from Marlyst and Nyarelle.

It was clear I now faced the formidable task of confronting the direction of my life. A life that, I had refused to admit, was a mask of delusions and denial.

The catch? I had only myself to blame. I put myself in this position.

And only I had the power to change it.

CHAPTER 23

'Another one over here! I need back up!' Shouts rang out as pure chaos unfolded before my eyes.

From my vantage point on the cliffs, I could see it all. Figures hurriedly moved along the shore to fight the two tidal beasts. Three of the fighters were strong with the earth element and were attempting to use trees from a nearby clifftop to ensnare the beasts without luck. I wondered who was heading up this fight and why they bothered bringing earth mages into it. The mages had poor form and the lack of strategy was making the fight harder than it needed to be. They were burning themselves out for no good reason.

At least the fire mages in the group were getting some hits in. But it wasn't enough to deter or stop the beasts. The orange creatures were on the bigger side, and each had two fins that had razor sharp ends sticking out of their backs. Their jaws only opened a fraction and lacked teeth. But their long tails, silver blades adorning both sides, could slice a person in half. That was without mentioning their highly venomous skin.

I'd seen beasts like these before. They were a frequent sight in the Tidal Seas. Varqel and I had taken down five of them by ourselves once after a particularly gruelling training session. I was seventeen at the time and still learning the ropes when we heard the commotion near the cliffs of his house. So given that, I was surprised at how the mages here were struggling. Granted, V and I were a lot stronger than these warriors. But there were ten mages and two beasts in front of me – well, seven mages because I'm ruling out the earth wielders as liabilities and not worth counting. Even then, they all looked like graduates, so it shouldn't have been difficult.

It was a serious concern if this was the calibre of graduates staying behind to protect the Isles. I couldn't help but wonder what Varqel thought of all this. More importantly, where was Bastra? As the general, he should have been on the front line of the attack.

The beasts were only a few metres from the shores now, close enough that if they were to flick their tail and hit one of the graduates it wouldn't end well. That thought concerned me, especially paired with the fact I was watching these amateurs colossally mess up a fight that should have been over within a couple of minutes.

I decided it was time to assist. I sent a gust of wind towards the beasts, putting a decent amount of strength behind it to ensure they were pushed away from the shore. Once I was satisfied they were far enough away that a tail couldn't deal a fatal blow, I envisioned a circle surrounding the creatures. I directed my energy into pulling the water away from the beasts in the space while simultaneously summoning and throwing green fire balls towards the middle of their bodies. The shots landed, and wails resounded throughout the cove.

Green fire balls could only be created by a Sol specializing in fire and air, as regular ones would simply land and burn a few seconds. But the green ones? The air in them made sure that, once they landed, the fire sunk into their bodies. This meant the creatures had about thirty seconds before their whole body would be burned from the inside out.

I watched the light of the beasts' eyes die as they crumbled to ash then relinquished my hold on the water. The beach returned to normal, calm waves lapping on the shore giving no indication of the fight that had just unfolded.

I stepped behind a tree as the graduates' heads flicked around to try and discern the mage who'd finished their job in mere minutes. Before they could sense me, I teleported out. Even if they'd worked out it was me that was there, none of them would be game to say it. Not if it showed they'd failed at their task. No, they'll take the credit for the kills, and that was fine by me. Hell, if I was in their positions, reporting the mission back to Bastra I don't think I'd be game enough to tell him there was outside help.

I landed in the middle of Varqel's kitchen, not bothering with using the front door. I wasn't in the mood for pleasantries. Not after the bombs Qynthia and Orlandia had dropped.

'Where's Lyz?' I asked Varqel, surprised to see him eating by himself.

He shrugged, picking at the chicken meat left on the bone in his hand. 'She mentioned something about staying late for a new potion she was tampering with. You know how she can be. When she feels she's onto something there's no pulling her away from it.'

I nodded in understanding. It didn't surprise me at all. Once while she was obsessing over a new way to heal poison bites, I hadn't seen Lyzia for a whole month. I may not understand the pull or her interest, but her devotion to the craft was admirable. Considering she gives me my contraceptives, and has healed me countless time from training with my Sol, I couldn't complain.

'So,' I started conversationally, taking the seat across from him. 'How long's Bastra been stationed here?'

He dropped the chicken bone, using his nails to scrape out the meat stuck between his teeth. 'Let me guess, Slaviya?'

'The one and only.'

He rolled his eyes. There was no explanation required, and no point bitching about it. Our thoughts of Slaviya were aligned. 'About two months or so.'

'And you didn't tell me, because …' I trailed off.

'Because there's nothing you can do about it. Plus, you've got enough going on. I can handle an inadequate man who thinks he's all that.'

I laughed at his condescending tone, but we both knew Bastra could be lethal when he wanted to be. And volatile.

'Well, you're not wrong. I just saw ten graduates try to take down two tidal beasts. Remember the orange ones with spiked tails we took down after training that time?' He nodded in confirmation. 'I watched the show for about half an hour before I handled it myself. The creatures were a few metres off the shore. Rookie error. What are you teaching the kids these days?' I raised a palm to my forehead in mock disbelief.

'Where was it? Who was leading the attack?' he demanded.

'A couple of kilometres out from the Temple. I felt bodies scrambling around like headless chooks, so I went to check it out. From what I could see, there was no leader. Just ten graduates trying to figure it out.' I tutted.

V shook his head. 'That's not good,' he said sharply. 'You're not the first person to tell me of an instance like this. I don't know what Bastra is playing at. There's no excuse for him to not be there. Especially with those juniors. Makes me wonder ...' he started, before stopping mid-thought.

We tended to think on the same lines, which gave me confidence to finish his sentence. 'Whether Bastra's presence on the Isles is not to only take care of the army? Because if it is, he's doing an awful job. He must be occupied with something else.'

We sat in quiet contemplation for a moment, both of us theorising the possibilities for his presence. Slaviya was up to something.

'The Solistans can take care of the Isles themselves. We have been for the last however many years. We have the experience to dispose of the tidal beasts efficiently with minimal to no casualties. Yes, there's been an influx of graduates staying back on the island, but I can still handle the army and the training. I haven't seen Bastra much since he's been here.' V was leaning the side of his head on his hand, tapping his middle finger on his forehead, deep in thought. 'I'll keep an eye on the situation and let you know of any findings.'

'Please do. Feel free to pull a couple of Maz's spies, if need be,' I offered.

He shot me a thankful look. 'I think at this stage it's best to keep it to myself. If I need to, I'll reach out.'

Staring at him, I suddenly noticed the bags under his eyes. And were those wrinkles I could see? V never had wrinkles. He must be tired. I refused to acknowledge they could be due to age. In my stubborn mind, Varqel was immortal. He would never leave me. I would not entertain the thought.

He caught my appraisal and pasted on a fake smile that I saw right through. 'Was the Bastra discussion all you came for? Not that I'm upset with your company, of course. You know I love seeing you.'

Also, classic V with the redirecting of conversation. In truth, I couldn't be annoyed. I'd learnt it from him and utilized it often.

'Partly,' I shifted apprehensively, nerves coming back in a heavy wave.

'You're giving me "I want to know this information, but I'm scared to say it or ask for help" energy. You know I'll always help where I can. What is it, Little One?' His gentle voice soothed me like I was a baby bear who'd been reunited with their mother after being separated for too long.

'Do you know what a True Infinite is?'

Varqel dropped the cutlery he was holding loudly on the ground. I didn't miss the scared shock on his face but he quickly covered it up, pasting on an expression of indifference. 'Where are you going with this?'

I wasn't about to reveal that a psychic mage, let alone a Queen, had projected a seemingly pivotal moment in our continent's history into my mind. I was keeping that information to myself.

'The prophecy?' I made sure my voice held a dash of naivety in there.

Based on the doubt written across his face, I didn't think he was buying it, but he bit. 'I was under the impression you skipped your religion classes for bakery taste-testing.'

I dismissed him with a wave of my hand.

He sighed in resignation. 'A True Infinite is a very rare and special bond between two people. They are life partners whose strengths and weaknesses complement each other. It's believed that True Infinites are the most sacred of fated pairings. Think of it like a soulmate, your one true love, but rarer. Extremely hard to find, those who find theirs are lucky.'

Damn. He explained it with such reverence. Like it was something to spend your life seeking. 'Are they always a love connection? Can it be a friendship?'

'Any good relationship starts with a friendship, Little One. And in a long-lasting relationship, such as a True Infinite one, naturally they become your best friend. I guess it could just be that, but the pull of a True Infinite relationship is hard to resist. Almost impossible. The bond is created in such a way that, even if the intention isn't romantic, it tends to fall into that.'

I couldn't say I was enjoying how this was turning into a cautionary lecture. But it was information, and I wasn't having to chase down answers, so I was keeping my mouth shut.

'You mentioned it was a rare bond? Is this bond only for mages? I don't think I've heard of any True Infinite bonds …' I trailed off, racking my brain and coming up with nothing.

A contemplative air settled in the room as he considered how to answer. 'It is, though many people have no idea about it. The True Infinite bond was supressed when Wystia and Merlot sacrificed themselves for the greater good of the continent. I don't think they realised at the time the ramifications it would have on the True Infinite bonds. It's believed that once the prophecy comes to fruition, the fated rulers of Fyriane will unite the Doms and unlock whatever spell was placed on the continent. Only then will couples know whether they are with their True Infinite.'

Fated rulers? I knew V believed in the prophecy, but he had never pushed it on me, so I didn't like the expectant look he was pinning me with, like he was trying to work out whether I was going to continue to skirt around the elephant in the room. I pinched my nose, gearing up to admit that maybe I shouldn't have disregarded the Solistan religion all these years, as well as the news I still hadn't quite wrapped my head around.

'Well, it is looking like I have a True Infinite. Which is kind of not great for me right now, considering the tidal beasts are becoming more of a problem, I'm supposed to kill my husband to become sole ruler, and I have a lover who isn't treating me well. Oh, and I'm pretty sure I've just met my True Infinite in real life, and I'm beyond furious with him because he knows all this information and has been hiding it from me.' I grimaced at the rush of words, and received a similar reaction from Varqel.

'Well, that's a lot to unpack.'

Understatement of the century. I groaned. 'Try living in my head right now. It's a *lot* of fun.'

V's lips twitched at my retort. 'Is it the King of Marlyst?'

'Goddess, somehow it sounds worse when it's spoken into existence,' I moaned dramatically, knocking my head on the table and staring at the floorboards in the hopes I would morph into a puddle and seep through the cracks, never to be seen again. Hearing Varqel guess what I suspected was just not fun.

Varqel's laughter cut through the room. It was the kind of laugh that came deep from within his belly, filling the entire space.

'Please, floor, please make me a part of you. I promise I'm a good person,' I whispered, refusing to look at him as my comment sent him into another round of laughter. This was not the reaction I had expected.

'Why are you so annoyed by this? I overheard you telling Lyz how attractive you thought he was when you were picking up your contraceptive remedy.'

I looked up to see a cheeky smile. 'That was a private conversation. Girl talk. Not to be overheard,' I defended, and he rolled his eyes.

'Well, Meredith was in on the chat too. You know nothing is private with that girl around.' He wasn't wrong. Meredith likes to gossip. Unless, of course, she was keeping a secret for me.

'Like I said, girl talk.'

He let it drop, circling back to my prior ramblings. 'Your lover isn't treating you well? Has that been going on for a while?'

I winced, not really having meant for that to come out, but I nodded as I stood up and started pacing. I couldn't remain seated while I admitted to V what had been going on. 'Pretty much since I married Eliasson. He wanted the assassination over and done with months ago. But what was I supposed to do? Marry Eliasson and kill him within a month? Forgive me for not wanting to implicate myself. No one would've believed it wasn't me. He's become worse with the assassination coming closer. And now that I've met Xylan, it doesn't feel right to continue it.'

'It won't feel right with Xylan in the picture, if you're fated to be together. Even if that is simply a friendship,' his face screamed his doubt, 'you won't want to be with anyone else. Which is an interesting concept for a physical mage to understand, considering the usual preference for more than one partner. But the True Infinite attraction will always trump those needs. Every single time.'

He's not telling me anything I wasn't already feeling myself. Eliasson was great in bed and everything, but maintaining that act was becoming a struggle now I had had a taste of Xylan, even without the guilt eating at me.

'Speaking of True Infinites,' Varqel segued. 'The Ophiscair Prophecy in its entirety, what are your thoughts?'

I gnawed my lip. 'Well, admitting I have a True Infinite is a start,' I replied reluctantly. 'Some of it I don't understand. Like moon phases? Knowledge finds those who are meant to see?'

Varqel cocked his head, refusing to buy into my efforts to avoid addressing his real question.

I sighed. 'I think it is ridiculous that a simple mention of an eye colour automatically means I'm a part of this bigger plan for Fyriane. However,' I hesitated. 'I have recently discovered some information about Wystia and Merlot. The fact they were the King and Queen of Fyriane, once upon a time. And that her eyes were the exact colour as mine. It's weird.'

Varqel nodded.

'It's just hard, you know?' The words tumbled out of my mouth, unable to be stopped. 'I go from flying under the radar being the third heir to the Salistyan throne, to receiving my powers by myself and have my eyes change so everyone looks at me differently. I fall in love. Then, I'm shipped off to marry a King, earn his and his country's trust, learn their culture, eventually assassinate him, and then rule the Kingdom I've only begun to properly feel connected to. Before I can do that, though, I meet a man who is apparently my True Infinite and the other half of a prophecy I have blissfully ignored since I was sixteen. And now? Now there's apparently an expectation that I'm supposed to unite Fyriane with him. A guy that, in the grand scheme of things, I know nothing about. Not to mention, he's been keeping important information to himself. I'd be lying if I didn't say it hurts and it's overwhelming.'

Varqel reached his hand towards mine, squeezing it tight, offering comfort. 'Little One.'

'When do I catch a break, V?' My voice cracked. 'When will it be my time to decide what I want, who I want to be again? I can't stand the feeling that I don't have a say in the trajectory of my life. That because there's a prophecy out there, my fate is signed, sealed, and delivered.'

And that was truly the crux of the matter. The reason I had denied the prophecy all these years. Sure, I put on a good front. Charging ahead with the complete alteration of my life plans, with the mission, my role as a queen, the natural leader of my Sol. But at the heart of it all? I wanted to have a choice. To choose my own path. And if that path was in line with the prophecy? So be it. But

I wanted to trudge down that path because *I* chose to.

Varqel stood from his chair, rounded the table, and engulfed me in a hug. I returned the gesture, sinking my head into his chest.

'Can I provide some words of advice?' he spoke, his words muffled with how I had pressed my face into him.

I waited, my response not required. We both knew he'd say it anyway. He'd clearly read it in my body language as he pulled away to place his hands on my shoulders.

'Get rid of your lover, but tread carefully, especially at this point in time. Do what you have to do with Eliasson. But remember, it is *your choice* whether you accept the prophecy and your role in it.' He paused, staring into my lime green eyes. 'If you do, then you're destined to be the Queen of Fyriane. Destined for more than just a Dom's queen. So, if you do accept it, you need to start acting like Fyriane's ruler. But you can do it on your own terms. You can choose how you navigate it. The ball's in your court. When you make your decision though, if you *do* decide that's the path you'll take, consider if you really want Eliasson's death on your hands, or if you want to outplay your sister and have someone who knows Arlom intimately and will be on your side when you properly take Fyriane's throne.

'Have a good long think on it before you make any rash decisions. And that goes for your True Infinite as well. Maybe it's worth asking him why he kept information from you before jumping to any conclusions.'

CHAPTER 24

M y eyes rapidly darted between Eliasson and Xylan. They were throwing words back and forth, and I was struggling to keep up. And that was without mentioning that I was completely shocked at their behaviour.

I had thought after a few days rest from meetings some of the tensions would lift. But I was wrong. They'd been simmering away and were now being brought to a thunderous boil right before my eyes.

Eliasson's hand slapped the table so hard it made me flinch. I'd never seen him lose his temper like this before. 'What do you mean there's no more farming equipment being made for the next quarter?' Eliasson roared.

Xylan glared icily at him, and asked, 'Do you require a translation using hand signs?' He didn't wait for a reply, mockingly acting out a sign for 'no', 'equipment' and put up three fingers to signal the quarter.

I bit my lip to stop myself from laughing.

'Hey!' I shouted at Eliasson as he suddenly grabbed my coffee mug and launched it straight at Xylan's face. Xylan ducked his head to the side and the cup crashed into the wall. The resulting splash would be hard to remove.

The King of Marlyst had murder in his eyes as he stood up. Orlandia's hand launched out to grab her brother, shoving him back into his seat.

'Rule number five of the housekeeping list: no throwing things. Rule number seven: no fights,' she said in a detached manner. If I didn't know better, I'd think she was rather enjoying this spectacle. Her comment served to bring the tension back down to a simmer.

My husband let out a huge breath and cracked his neck, regaining control of his emotions. 'That was out of line. I apologise,' he said.

Xylan waved off the apology. 'I provoked you. I'm partly to blame.'

His response had everyone raising their eyebrows in shock, including Slaviya.

'What?' Xylan grumbled, reading the room. 'I can admit when I've gone a bit far. You've got to admit though, my hand signs were spot on.'

This time, I couldn't hold back on the giggle that escaped my lips.

Eliasson looked at me with disapproval. 'Hey, remember whose side you're on,' he berated, agitated.

'Yes, Valare, remember whose side you're on,' Xylan parroted, eyes twinkling, no doubt thinking of the kiss we shared and the fact we were True Infinites.

'What the fuck is that supposed to mean?' Eliasson growled, looking between Xylan and me. Apparently, he'd also picked up on the underlying hint.

I kept my mouth shut as eyes fell on me, waiting for a response. Well, they could wait all they liked. No good could come out of my responding.

'I think they're just jealous of our little secret, young Queen,' Ramone fake whispered, clearly knowing there was more going on and taking the bullet for me. Bless this man.

'What secret?' Both Kings spoke accusingly at the same time. Oh my Goddess. They were both acting like jealous overprotective boyfriends.

'Nothing. I am merely a note-taker in this meeting. I apologise for adding my coppers worth in, I will return to my task. Where was I?' He tapped the pen on his chin, feigning deep thought. He raised the pen as his eyes lit up and returned to writing, 'Oh. Right. The King of Marlyst used his hands to signal 'no' and 'equipment' before –'

'That section won't be required in the meeting notes,' Xylan winced, cutting off Ramone.

'Then how do you suggest I explain King Eliasson throwing a coffee cup at your head and missing?' Ramone blinked innocently.

'It'll simply look as though he's very passionate about pitchforks. That, or he's psychotic. Both options are correct.' Xylan shrugged, deliberately setting things off again.

As Eliasson launched into another heated exchange with Xylan, I made eye contact with Ramone. He threw me an amused grin and a wink. Mission to divert the attention off Valare: successful. I loved this man. Maybe I could convince Qynthia to let him join the Arloman ranks as our scribe. The Goddess knows I needed more allies.

'Back to the matter at hand,' Eliasson's voice boomed. 'Presuming the vote is in favour of cross-collaboration, the equipment supply situation will become even more of an issue. How do you suggest resolving this?'

'This is a business transaction, Eliasson. I provide you with equipment if it's available. Currently, there's a shortage of materials. If it's not available, that's on you to figure out how your Dom will proceed.'

Coming from anyone else, Xylan's statement would be just that, a statement. But from him, right now? There was a challenge in those words. Like he was assessing how Eliasson would bounce back.

The room looked on silently, waiting to see how Eliasson would counter Xylan's challenge. Would he simply take his word for it? Or fight back? Either way, I was staying out of it. My gut was telling me I was the last person who should interfere here.

'We have a fair bit of equipment currently out of service that our people don't have the skills to fix. With a bit of work, we should be able to have them reinstated to their former glory,' Eliasson thought out loud, arms crossed. 'I could organise for them to be delivered to the blacksmith villages in the south of your Dom.'

Approval flashed across Xylan's eyes before he again donned his mask of indifference. 'It'll cost you.'

Eliasson scoffed. 'It'll cost *me*? Last I checked, it's your Dom's responsibility to ensure mine have the tools to provide food for the rest of the continent.'

'That is correct. However, you didn't hear me complaining when you informed us that our wine shipments would be halted for the next week or so,' Xylan countered, raising an unimpressed brow.

'You can't compare the two!' Eliasson spluttered. 'Wine is a luxury, farming equipment is essential.'

'Speak for yourself. After this Forum, wine is a pre-requisite for keeping my sanity in check,' Xylan remarked. This man was outrageous.

Orlandia and the Nyarelleans chuckled. I pursed my lips, suppressing my own giggle, conscious of Eliasson and Slaviya's eyes burning holes through me.

After it was apparent Eliasson would not gift him a response to his dramatic comments, Xylan relented. 'Fine, I'll take a personal delivery of your next batch of wine in exchange for my blacksmith's services.'

Eliasson rolled his eyes. 'Consider it done. I'll deliver it personally.'

'Dashing as you are, Eliasson, I'm not interested in a personal delivery from you.'

'Who, then?' Eliasson demanded.

I felt my cheeks heat as Xylan focused his attention on me.

'Be reasonable,' Eliasson growled, perfectly reading what he was alluding to. He placed a possessive arm over my shoulders, pulling me tight against his side. I suppressed a surprised noise at his overt claim. What had gotten into him?

'I'm nothing if not reasonable.' Xylan purposefully drew out the moment.

I scowled, folding my arms as I shrugged Eliasson's arm off me. I wasn't impressed with either of them right now. I wasn't a piece of meat to be bartered with. I could almost feel their egos growing as they stared at one another. Testosterone filled the air, making me tempted to react with a dramatic gagging noise. They were being ridiculous.

A grin formed on the King of Marlyst's face as he stared directly at me. 'It will be delivered by your Queen,' he said.

I gaped at him, wondering what he was playing at.

'No,' Eliasson snarled.

Xylan feigned disappointment. 'Are you going back on your word King Eliasson? You've agreed to delivery. I can assure you that your precious wife will be safe in my Dom. It would be an opportunity for her to see part of the Marlyst Kingdom.'

'No,' he said. 'Valare isn't leaving Arlom without me.' His voice rung with finality.

I wanted to scream, to remind them I was right there and capable of making my own decision.

'Oh? Is that so?' Xylan tutted. 'Well, I guess there's no deal then.'

Eliasson released some colourful curse words under his breath as his fists clenched by his sides. I could see him fighting himself, weighing his options. Xylan was being difficult and clearly wasn't willing to compromise with this. And Eliasson knew he had to get this across the line otherwise his farmers would struggle. The question was, would he choose to help his people or choose to keep me in Arlom, away from Xylan.

It didn't surprise me one bit when he chose the former. He always placed the needs of his Dom above his own.

'Fine. Valare will deliver your wine on the condition that you'll be at the border to escort her. I won't compromise on her safety while she's in another Dom,' he responded.

I wanted to tell him that my safety wasn't his concern. Never had been, and never would be. I could take care of myself just fine.

'Of course,' Xylan taunted. 'I'll personally see to her wellbeing.'

Did I want to know what his version of 'seeing to my wellbeing' was? Partly yes. Partly no.

I stood, raising my voice before Eliasson could interject or Xylan poked him further. 'Well, now that you two have talked about me like I'm not here, I'm requesting a break. I need to get away from the insufferable amount of testosterone in the air.'

Laughter filled the room as I took my leave to hide behind a pillar as the others walked out, not wanting them to see where I would go. But Eliasson and Xylan stayed behind.

I caught the eyes of Mer, who was walking past, holding a bundle of linen. I grabbed her, pulling her next to me. Miming for her to keep quiet, I pointed to the room I'd just vacated.

'What the fuck are you playing at Xy?' I heard Eliasson demand. I didn't know they were on a nickname basis.

'I'm not playing. I'm simply claiming what's mine. And simultaneously reminding you what isn't yours,' Xylan replied fiercely before storming out of the room.

Damn. Our jaws dropped, eyes widening in mutual shock.

'What the fuck was that?' Mer mouthed.

What the fuck, indeed.

CHAPTER 25

I knew he would come. I was as certain of it as the next breath I would take. He'd been trying to catch me since the confrontation and before tomorrow's vote but I wasn't having a bar of him. Not after the egotistical display with Eliasson. My mental shields were tightly locked down at all times. I knew they were impenetrable, even to someone with his powers. Which was good because I needed to mask my rage. For now.

'So, this is where you come to escape the politics,' Xylan said as he looked around, taking in the calm waves lapping at the shore. They were a complete juxtaposition to how I was feeling.

'One of many spots, I'll have you know. Can't be too predictable. I do have a reputation to uphold, after all.' I cast a side-eyed glance towards him and got a chuckle in return. It confirmed I had successfully hidden the raging inferno inside of me from him.

'May I?' he gestured to the patch of sand next to me.

'Only if you correctly answer this question.' It took all my self-control to stop my lips from twitching upwards into a smile as I toyed with him, instead pasting on a serious face. I still liked his company, after all. Damn True Infinite bond.

Xylan raised his eyebrow in response. 'Oh?'

'Have an unlimited supply of wine or be able to read *Once Upon a Woods* over and over like you're reading it for the first time?'

Without missing a beat, he scoffed, 'Must one choose?'

'My thoughts exactly. You have permission to sit.'

He held my eyes as he sat down, his face showing delight. But there was also a flicker of hesitation. Was he picking up on my emotions?

'That's a lot of pressure to put on a man, Valare. Are your questions always this intense?' he joked.

I cocked my head to the side, quietly assessing him. 'I don't mess around when it comes to *Once Upon a Woods*, nor do I mess around with who I allow to sit on my private beach. You should know most don't leave unscathed.'

'Well, lucky I like a challenge,' he countered, those pale pink eyes holding me captive. The eyes of a liar. For the first time I wondered how he was masking the true colour of his eyes. 'And what does scathed look like to you?'

'Oh, Pretty Boy, you really don't want to know,' I succumbed, responding to his flirtatious banter.

'Oh, Minx, I really do,' he goaded, desire sparking in his eyes.

'Are you flirting with a kept woman, Your Highness?' Despite my anger, I couldn't deny his eyes admiring my body sent a fit of butterflies south. Damn fucking fate.

'It depends. Is the 'kept' woman in question emotionally, spiritually, and mentally 'kept'? Not just physically?' he challenged. He shot me a knowing look.

I hummed, 'And you say I ask the intense questions.' I lowered myself back down onto my elbows, hands gripping into the sand to stop myself acting on the devil in my head screaming to jump him.

He shrugged, lying down on his side to face me. 'Would we call that intense? Or simply calling it how it is?'

'And how is it, Pretty Boy?' I retorted.

'You don't love Eliasson,' he said simply.

Of course, he would say that, knowing what we both are. Deceitful prick. 'Interesting perspective. You can love someone in myriad ways though.'

'True,' he conceded. 'You may love him as a friend and share a mutual understanding of what it means to be a royal and the obligations that come with it. You may even enjoy his body. But you aren't in love with the man romantically.'

'I thought it was clear that I'm here to escape the politics. I would say trying to drive a wedge between my husband and I isn't exactly leaving politics at the door,' I deflected.

'I think driving a wedge between you two would imply there was something there to start off with and, rest assured, this discussion is the furthest thing from a political move.'

I suppressed a scoff. Furthest? Really? I fucking doubted it.

'What's the Kingdom of Marlyst like?' I questioned, abruptly changing the topic. I was also curious to see how much information he'd provide.

He cocked his head, eyes narrowed in annoyance from the change in subject. 'Smooth, Minx. Real smooth.'

My eyes closed in frustration, and I took a few slow, calming breaths. I enjoyed his persistence when I watched him debate the other royals, especially my sister. But when that focused persistence moved to me? It was half a turn on, and half me wanting to scratch his eyes out. With the current True Infinite situation – a situation he had no idea I was aware of – it was the latter I was leaning towards.

'Marlyst is beautiful. A lot colder than here if you're up in the northern mountain range. My people who live in the south close to the Pass enjoy the heat that the Arloman Kingdom does. Most of them are blacksmiths who can work wherever and choose to be in a warmer climate. The further north in the Kingdom you are, the denser the forest becomes. In fact, most of the land is covered in acres of pine trees in the lead up to the Moondallelle Ranges.'

I opened my eyes to see him dreamily staring out at the ocean. He was clearly very fond of Marlyst.

'And your palace?' I prompted.

He cleared his throat. 'What about it?'

'Where is it in your Kingdom? Is it in a town like Amarald? I don't know anything about it,' I pressed.

'Somewhere between the pine trees and mountains.'

He didn't trust me. Despite what he knew about me. About us. Honestly, the only one who shouldn't trust the other was me. 'What's it called?'

Obviously not seeing the harm in telling me the name, though, he replied, 'Mayurial.'

'Hm, that's pretty.'

His eyes swung around to land on mine, 'Indeed. Very pretty.'

Despite myself, I couldn't help the blush that rose to my cheeks, catching his double meaning.

'What do you do for fun in Mayurial?'

'I'll have to show you one day,' he said.

What game was he playing? He'd already ensured I'd be coming to his Kingdom. Still I shot back, 'Is that an invitation?'

'It is,' he replied sincerely.

'Why?' I was interested to see how he would reply.

'Because friends invite their friends over to one another's houses for play dates all the time,' he said, his dimples pronounced as he smiled.

'Oh please, we've known each other for only a few weeks, I would hardly call us friends at this point. Where are you really going with this?' I asked.

'Why are you being so weird about this? Haven't you heard that if a relationship feels right, you should just flow with it?' he countered teasingly, looking at me. 'Fine,' he conceded, seeing the frustration on my face. 'You're right.'

'Well, yes, I'm usually right about most things but which, in particular, are you referring to right now?'

'It's only polite that if I show you mine, you should show me yours.'

I gritted my teeth. I'm going to kill him and his innuendos. But, yes. It is polite to be transparent. The handsome bastard actually winked at me. And didn't that just do something to the spot between my thighs. It had a mind of its own.

I rolled my eyes, using my years of training to appear unaffected by his words. From the outside, at least. 'You've already seen my home. You're in it right now. Not to mention, you're way too close to my own personal quarters.'

Deciding two could play the game, on those last words, I rolled to face him, my top leg moving slightly forward allowing the slit to fall to the side, revealing more skin. I watched his eyes trail up and down my body, unable to hide his interest.

'Oh, I'm not referring to Amarald, Minx. I'm talking about your real home,' Xylan said knowingly.

'Trust me, the Salistyan Queendom is not worth your time.' Unless you're a fiend for oppressively suffocating environments and toxic masculinity, that is.

'Oh, yes, I only had to engage in a two-minute conversation with your sister to figure out that Salistya is not my idea of a good time,' he said with a grin. 'I was referring to your true home. The Solista Isles.'

My head snapped up to his, trying to gauge his intentions. His face gave nothing away. 'What are you playing at, Marlyst?' I ground out, rising off my elbows to sit up and face him. He knew visits to the Isles were highly coveted and not open to the rest of the continent. And the fact he pegged my feelings on the Isles unnerved me.

He noted the change in my stance. 'I'm not playing at anything, *Solistan*.' He paused when my eyes flashed at his use of the word. 'You want to see my home, which is highly desired to outside eyes. I want the courtesy reciprocated. I don't think that's too much to ask.'

'And why should I trust you?' I said between clenched teeth.

He shrugged, shifting himself to mirror my seated stance. Facing me, our bodies were now less than an arm length away from each other. 'I'll show you something of mine, if you show me something of yours.'

My breath hitched as his arm reached forward to grab a loose lock of hair that had fallen across my eye. He twirled it around his finger before tucking it behind my ear. His fingers landed on my mark, setting off the warm, humming pulse. I loved and hated that it calmed me down.

'Can I check we're still talking about places, here?' I breathed out, momentary distrust forgotten.

'Why should we limit ourselves to one meaning?' he replied, fingers travelling down to massage the junction between my shoulder and neck.

'You're entering dangerous territory, Pretty Boy,' I warned. This wasn't how this conversation was supposed to go down.

'Don't act like you aren't enjoying yourself. I don't see you pulling away.'

I couldn't help the fluttering of my eyes as they closed, whimpering as his fingers held the back of my head. The stroking continued, but this time it felt like it was inside my mind, reminding me of the Lull.

'I'll show you mine, if you show me yours,' he whispered gently, all traces of teasing gone.

I swallowed deeply, letting out a shaky breath as I nodded in agreement, suddenly needing confirmation, to see his eyes. His *true* eyes. He better let me see them, otherwise I'll throttle him.

Xylan closed his eyes, breathing deeply in and out for what felt like millennia. Just when I was starting to worry, a shimmering pulse surrounded us for a moment. He opened his eyes.

Where they once had been pale, the real, fuchsia eyes of my True Infinite stared back at me.

CHAPTER 26

Seconds went by, then minutes. The growing silence said more about this moment than any words could express. I felt my mental barrier drop.

A caress in my mind drew my attention back to those fuchsia eyes.

You know, some would think your lack of response quite rude. He smiled tentatively, trying to gauge my reaction.

Some would think entering my mind without permission is quite rude, I thought.

Xylan laughed. 'Trust me, Valare. If you didn't want me in your head, I wouldn't be in there.'

He wasn't wrong.

'So, what is it that you're doing, exactly?' I asked. I was hungry for answers and wanted to give him a chance to explain.

He shook his head. 'I showed you mine, it's time to show me yours. Questions can wait.'

His answer disappointed me. I didn't know why I thought he was going to act differently once it was partly in the open, but his response bolstered the little self-control I had. I raised my mental shields, blocking him from my thoughts. Looks like it was time to show my upper hand.

'No, I don't think they can wait, *True Infinite*,' I said, putting every ounce of my disdain into the words, pulling away from him.

He visibly flinched, his expression paling. 'You worked it out.'

I barked a disbelieving laugh. 'Of course I worked it out. The Lull? The book? The Prophecy? Quite frankly I'm offended you think I wouldn't have. And more than that, I'm furious that you didn't tell me. Instead, you've allowed me to stew over the pull I have towards you, rather than telling me the truth. This is my life too, Xylan.' The more I spoke, the louder my voice became until I was basically screaming at him.

And he took it. He took every word I said and simply nodded. His lack of reaction or any form of reply set the impulsive physical mage in me off.

Without thinking of the ramifications, I teleported the small distance between us, my knees landing on either side of him, straddling him. His hands moved to my hips, holding me there while my hand launched to clutch his throat. A feeling of masculine desire instantly hit me, warming up my whole body. His desire. He didn't deserve a similar reaction from me, and he wasn't going to get it.

'I think you can do better than that, Green Eyes,' he whispered in challenge, his lips so close that I could feel his breath on mine. He was provoking me, imploring me to unleash the pent-up anger inside.

I took the bait. Flicking my wrist, his hands swiftly moved above his head, arms pressing into one another as a vine tied them together. I found myself staring at him, trying to pinpoint any imperfections that needed fixing. And there were none, which was beyond frustrating.

Using my magic, I pushed his chest backwards until he was lying on the ground, arms still stretched above his head. I called some ocean water towards me. Once in my hand, I manipulated the water into a whirling ball, readying to throw it at Xylan. 'Consider this payback from withholding your true identity from me,' I said.

His eyes were filled with primal hunger, his hardening cock in between my thighs showing his complete lack of fear over my ability to physically control him. This wasn't the reaction I was hoping for. I wanted to see him angry. See the fire in his eyes like I felt it in my veins. 'Have you finished playing, Minx?'

'I'm only just getting started, Pretty Boy,' I shot back at him.

My ball of water moved less than an inch towards Xylan before a resounding command rang out in my head. Before I could blink, my hand was over my head, releasing the ball of water. At the same time the vine snapped and Xylan sat up, freed hands grabbing mine, pushing them behind my back, jutting out my now drenched chest. My white dress was now completely see-through, revealing my firm nipples.

'You're not the only one with a few tricks up their sleeves, Queen,' Xylan drawled, his chest pressing against mine, lips an inch away.

'I have questions, mage. And I'm furious with you.'

'And you'll have answers. When you're ready for them,' he responded, not the least bit affected that I knew he was a mage.

'Do you really think you have a leg to stand on right now? *You* lied to *me*. If you think I'm going to let you get away with –'

He cut me off, closing the distance between us, his mouth pressing firmly on mine. Sparks flew as my whole body was set alight with the movement of his lips. A nibble of his teeth on my lower lip asked permission, and I opened my lips on a deep moan. His tongue took advantage of the entrance and twirled around mine. Our tongues fell into a familiar dance as though we'd done this a million times before. I felt his hands move so one held onto both of mine, while the other slid across my stomach, up across my waist and landed on one of my nipples.

A groan rumbled from deep in his chest, eliciting a sharp inhale from me as his fingers started to twist and rub the peaks. This sent jolts of pleasure straight down into my core. His fingers kept going, alternating between each bud, all the while our tongues still danced. We couldn't get enough of each other.

Let my hands go, I demanded, dropping my mental barriers.

He granted my request. Not a second later I leant over him, pushing him into the sand. My hands grabbed his head and shifted it to the side, exposing his neck. I dove to the spot under his ear where his mark was. In one slow lick, I covered it with my tongue. With a loud groan and an uncontrolled thrust of his hips, he let out a string of curse words.

I chuckled darkly, continuing down his neck and across to the other side. I lunged for his throat, biting it hard, my intent to cause pain.

'*Fuck.*' He released a harsh breath. 'Let it out, Valare. All your frustrations and anger. Give me all you've got. I can take it.'

And I did. I grasped his hair, taking his lips once again, dominating the kiss. He submitted, letting me lead as I poured my feelings into him. I bit down on his lower lip, drawing blood, while he moaned. His hips thrust forward again, searching for my body.

This felt so good. So *right*. But then I remembered his actions, his lies. It successfully brought me out of my lust-fuelled haze. I pulled away before he could make further contact, teleporting to land a couple of steps away from him.

We stayed like that for some time, both our chests rising and falling. Behind my rage I felt nothing but disappointment, hurt and betrayal. I let him see and feel the emotions roll out of me. Let him understand how much he'd royally fucked this up.

Based on the way he was holding himself, the message was received loud and clear.

'What does a True Infinite mean to you? What does that make us, Xylan?' I asked, wanting to hear the words from his mouth.

'A True Infinite is your perfect match, soulmate, true love. Whatever you call it, the pairing is destiny. Our pairing is different, our eyes and power are a gift from Wystia and Merlot. We're fated to follow in their footsteps and unite the Doms. To lead and protect Fyriane.'

'How long have you known I was your True Infinite?' My tone held no room for avoiding the question. I shelved the knowledge about Merlot and Wystia to think about later.

He swallowed deeply and closed his eyes in resignation. 'I felt a shift when you were first born but I was also young at the time. But when you were gifted your magic, that's when I felt the full force of you. I realised that shift I felt in my early years was your soul being brought into this world. My fated.' His tone was full of regret and a deep yearning. His hands clenched as he restrained himself, preparing for my response.

'Four years!' I exclaimed. 'Over four fucking years you've known and you didn't think to try and contact me earlier? To activate the Lull and start feeding me information, rather than getting into this huge, colossal mess? Damn it Xylan, I fell in love with someone I should've never been with.' His jaw clenched at that. 'I was forced to marry a fucking *King*. I've been scrambling to understand how my life has spiralled so out of control. I've been trying to work out how the hell I can get myself out of it, desperately searching for answers. I've wondered how the Solistans could ever see me as their true queen when the reality is I've always felt like I wasn't worthy, like I wasn't good enough. But the worst part of it all? I'm surrounded by people, yet I can count on one hand who I can trust. I feel lonely. *So fucking lonely*.' I brushed at the stray tear that escaped down my cheek, taking a shaky breath.

'And you know what the worst part is, Xylan? You know the environment I grew up in. The oppression and subjugation of women. You would've known how difficult it's been for me. To be different. To have all this unexplained power that no one else could relate to, apart from you. And the person I'm fated to be with didn't once try to help or stop the events that unfolded. You held all the knowledge, keeping it to yourself while I struggled to understand who I was. What I am. Where my place is in all of this. And you didn't think that maybe, just maybe, I would've found comfort in this knowledge? To find comfort from the one person who could make me feel less fucking alone?'

'Valare –' His voice broke. My words had shattered him like his lack of words had shattered me.

I held up my hand, not interested in what he had to say. 'We'll act properly while the Royal Forum is underway, but I don't want you to talk to me or look at me outside of it. I'll come to you when or *if* I'm ready. Until then, do what you've done in the past and stay the fuck away from me.'

As an afterthought I added, 'I hope that's enough communication for you, Pretty Boy. I know your opinion of us psychic mages. What did you say again? Oh yes. I don't communicate like psychic mages, but my body doesn't lie. That's where you'll find my feelings. You might be right, but I'd highly recommend you take my words right now at face value. And don't for one second misconstrue my words with trusting you.'

I turned away from him, but not before I saw the effect of my words. He looked like he'd been sucker punched.

I teleported back to my rooms. Only then did I allow myself to succumb to the thoughts screaming in my head. I'm totally fucked.

'I was wondering when you'd return.' A deep, familiar voice sounded in the corner of my room.

Turning around, I suppressed a groan as I stared at mossy green eyes.

Could this night get any worse?

CHAPTER 27

'How did you get in here?' I swallowed.

His head cocked to the side, eyes narrowed in suspicion. 'The same way you just arrived.'

I suppressed a curse, wishing I'd included him in the wards that I placed around my room to keep undesirable people out.

I casually walked towards the day bed in the corner of my room, intentionally creating space between us. Plopping down, I was careful to come across as nonchalant, as if nothing out of the ordinary had happened. As if my heart hadn't just broken into a thousand different pieces.

'It's a bit risky coming to my quarters like this. Never mind that we have royals here at the moment, trying to listen in on conversations,' I said.

'Please, no one is going to be able to hear us,' he scoffed.

'Not the point. You're letting your emotions get the best of you. You know better than that.'

'A bit rich coming from the girl who reeks of a man who's neither her husband, nor me.'

'I think you need to get your senses checked,' I sniffed.

'Classic Valare, trying to put it on everyone else but herself.'

Was he serious? For over a year he's been telling me everything was my fault, never admitting his own role in this. But I was putting it on everyone else?

I'm done. I'm done with men, with this man. This man was no better than the Salistyan pigs I grew up with, just another pain in my ass, and I wanted out of this situation, consequences be damned.

'That's your opinion, and you're allowed to have it. But I disagree,' I said evenly, despite my emotions.

He shrugged dismissively. 'Of course you disagree. You wouldn't be you if you didn't.'

'I think it's best if we call it quits on you and me,' I stated out, going straight for the jugular.

'Call it quits?' he stuttered, eyes darkening.

I nodded, not trusting myself to hold it together in front of the man who knew how to rile me like no other. Well, until recently. My True Infinite was proving to be the best at that.

'Oh, Valare.' He slowly, threateningly stepped towards me, flickers of fire coming out of his fingertips. 'You don't really mean that, do you, my sweet?'

I simply stared at him, finally seeing the threat for what it was. I let my actions speak for themselves. I pulled in air from the open window and slammed it into him to trap him inside a circular barrier. His flames flickered out.

He laughed darkly. 'His cock must be something else if you've had one fuck with this guy and you're ready to drop me. Really, Valare, I thought you'd be a bit better than this. Maybe you've been playing the Arloman whore too well because you're coming across a little too easy, my sweet. Back in my day, I had to wait a year to get inside that tight pussy. Well, at least it was tight back then,' he sneered.

I lashed out using the nearest plant in the room to create a long branch that wrapped itself tightly around his neck. I watched his eyes light up in glee at my reaction. The sadistic fucker always enjoyed getting a reaction from me.

'Your opinion of me personally is irrelevant, and I'd strongly advise you remember where your loyalties lie,' I said firmly, surprising myself that I kept the shake out of my voice.

'Oh, I do know where my loyalties lie,' he wheezed out. 'With my ruler.'

My hold on the branch loosened a fraction, the only sign that his answer shocked me.

Slaviya. His ruler was Slaviya. He was outright admitting he no longer saw me as his queen.

'What do you think Slaviya would say if she knew you were holding me against my own will right now?' he threatened.

'Oh, darling, I didn't think you were that naïve,' I crooned condescendingly, anger building while I clicked my fingers. Water appeared in front of his cheeks, half an inch above his skin. I made it run up and down his chin, imitating a condescending caress. 'I'm the Queen of Arlom. The most powerful physical mage on Fyriane and the key to getting Slaviya what she wants. Do you really think I'm more indispensable than you?' It brought me great joy to see the sweat trickling down his face, courtesy of the water's proximity to him. The element was suffocating to a fire wielder.

'Who the fuck are you? This isn't you, Valare,' he said softly, dropping his threatening stance to portray himself as a lost, lovesick boy. Pathetic. I saw right through the manipulation. It's funny how the tactics turn when you stand up for yourself and they know they don't have a leg to stand on.

'Oh, that's where you're mistaken. This is me. Just the version you get when you've fucked me over one too many times. I refuse to be beaten down anymore. A word of advice for future relationships. Never, ever push loyalty and never, ever push love. Because if you do, it'll always have a time stamp on it. Now, your time's up, and I no longer give a fuck.'

Standing up, I strolled towards him to slowly circle around the shield. His eyes assessed me and followed my every move until I stood right in front of him.

I allowed the tree branch to loosen on his neck, it's point pressing his chin up, forcing him to meet my gaze.

'So, this is how it's going to work. I'm working with your queen towards a mutually beneficial goal. That means our interests align, and you'll do your part as I'll do mine. Business as usual. But when it's all over? We never see each other again. My name and our history don't come out of your mouth. We'll both move on with our lives. If I hear that you go back on any of this, you'll answer directly to me, my sister be damned. Do we understand one another?' I spat.

'Valare –'

'Do we understand one another?' I pressed.

A slight downwards inclination of his head was the best response I was going to get. I released the shields I'd placed around him, the magic gone as if it had never been there in the first place, and unexpectedly heard the directions of his thoughts as though he had spoken out loud.

Quickly realising I could utilise this, I thought it best to drill into him the enemy he'd created.

'Oh, my sweet, before you go.' My voice sounded sickly sweet.

He stared at me rage sizzling in his eyes, clearly wanting to be anywhere but here.

For the record, I'm not picky, and it isn't hard to make me come. You're just a lazy prick. And no. You wouldn't have kept me if you'd made me orgasm all these years. But you would've had far less time, what did you call it, 'riding my emotional roller coaster'. I sneered in his head.

His eyes bulged, disbelief taking over his face. 'How did you know that was what I was –'

'Looks like a new scent wasn't the only thing I acquired tonight,' I winked, a satisfied smirk lighting up my face. 'You're dismissed, pal.'

If that didn't drive it home that we were done, I don't know what would.

The moment he teleported away, I adjusted my protective wards around the room to keep him out for good.

Confident I wouldn't be disturbed again, my façade dropped at the same time I collapsed on the floor, quivering. I didn't hold back the tears, the crippling anxiety taking over my whole being, swallowing me whole.

What had I done?

I lay there for a long time, until exhaustion won out, pulling me into sleep. For the first time in a long while, the nightmares appeared. But instead of my Father, it was Sir I saw. Hatred swam in his moss green eyes.

CHAPTER 28

I was not in the mood to make decisions or talk to people. Not after this morning, which I'd spent catching Mer up to speed on everything that had happened, including the True Infinite revelations and me dumping our close friend. To say she was shocked would be an understatement. Mer clearly disapproved of my timing in ending the relationship, but equally understood my reasons.

As a result of all of it, I'd concluded that anything to do with people was exhausting and not worth effort, so I'd like a hiatus from everyone.

So, no. I didn't want to be here. I wanted to find a beach in the Isles and be by myself, avoid my problems by hiding my head into a book and emotionally eat a dozen scones until I felt a sense of contentment and a full sickly stomach. I did not want to be surrounded by the other royals in the meeting room, all of us about to vote on a decision that would change the direction of Fyriane. It would cascade down to change my future, and I was not in the mood to deal with another new reality.

I wondered if the others in the room were thinking about the prophecy because that was where my thoughts were directed. The rash part of me selfishly wanted nothing more than to vote 'no' to the proposal. Then, Nyarelle wouldn't become more involved in agricultural activities, Marlyst's workers would stay in their own borders, and Arlom would leave Salistya to defend the coastline from the tidal beasts. If there was a 'no' vote, I could resume my life and prevent the union between Xylan and I and – by default – Fyriane, which was becoming ever more inevitable. Granted, this first step would still see the Doms remaining separate. But I knew this initial step would lead to another. And another. And the prophecy would come to life right before my eyes.

The irony of the whole situation was that my suggestions were the reason for the vote. I had prompted talks of unity. Although I knew it was necessary for the continent, it was now a hard pill to swallow. I couldn't even stand to look at the person the prophecy said I was supposed to lead with.

The person in question had accepted my order to stay away. Xylan didn't look at me. He'd positioned himself as far away from me as possible, and was currently laughing at something Qynthia was saying. I knew I had asked this of him, but the fact he was able to laugh right now was grating on my nerves. Not to anyone's surprise, I hadn't heeded Varqel's initial suggestion to hear him out. Instead, I had let my compounding feelings grow, lashing out at Xylan at the first real opportunity. Don't get me wrong, I didn't regret lashing out. He needed to know how I felt. But I'd be lying if I said I wasn't frustrated that I hadn't pushed more for his explanation. It is what it is. No changing the past now.

I felt a brush against my mind, somehow recognising it as Qynthia. I didn't particularly want to talk to her, but I needed her on my side to gain information. Plus, she had provided vital insight into the history of the True Infinites and the prophecy. Whether I liked the information or not, it made it clear there was no doubt her intentions were pure.

I also really wanted to learn more about this new telepathic ability I'd gained. So, I let her in, curious to see what she had to say.

Are you okay? Concern was thick in her words.

I've seen better days. I let her hear my sigh.

Understanding and empathy washed through the connection. *It's a lot to take in. I don't know what happened with you two, but if it's any consolation, I can feel his sorrow and regret too. He may be hiding it a little better, but he's feeling just as terrible as you. The bond may be strained, but it's not fractured. Remember that.*

I'm beyond furious with him.

And your feelings are warranted. But don't let your emotions override your decision making. You know what needs to be done for your people. You were chosen to rule this continent for a reason. Show us you're worthy of that, my Queen.

She disconnected from my mind before I could respond.

I snuck a glance at Xylan just as he looked at me. I saw a flash of worry in his eyes before he quickly looked away. A wave of despair and anguish surged through me, the longing to touch him growing to be overwhelming. This situation sucked.

Eliasson cleared his throat, bringing my attention back to the room. 'I want to take this opportunity to thank you all for what I believe to be a productive Royal Forum. The level of transparency and integrity each one of you has shown in our dealings is a promising step in the right direction. It's clear we all want to ensure the protection and prosperity of Fyriane as a whole.'

The last week or so had seen an interesting shift with the royals – well, everyone except Slaviya, but there were no surprises there. Previously, the rulers had fought fiercely for control and settled trade agreements in their own best interest. There was some of that energy when Xylan and Slaviya had gone head-to-head, and in whatever that standoff had been between Eliasson and Xylan, but for the most part, the rulers had been amicable and arrived at mutually beneficial solutions.

'As our final meeting for this Royal Forum, the conclusion lies in the need for changing in the way we rule Fyriane. A majority rules vote is required to solidify what has come to be the overarching theme of this Forum, which is that Fyriane needs unity moving forward. Gone are the days where one Dom takes care of feeding the continent and the other supplies weapons. We need to capitalise on one another's strengths, transfer and build knowledge, and look to keep Fyriane safe. It's time for the rulers to vote for or against cross collaboration between the Doms,' Eliasson said.

'Queen Qynthia of the Queendom of Nyarelle. Are you in support of or against these proposed changes?' I asked. There was no Ramone for a serious discussion such as this. Only the five of us were able to be present in the room. And Eliasson and I may or may not have practiced our speeches because of that. We were a little nervous closing out our round of hosting.

Placing a hand over her heart, Qynthia bowed towards us as she said, 'I vote in support of the proposed changes.' I nodded to confirm I'd received her vote and wrote it down.

Directing my gaze towards my sister, I asked, 'Queen Slaviya of the Queendom of Salistya. Do you support or reject these changes?'

True to form, without missing a beat my sister voted no.

There was no way of avoiding looking at my True Infinite. 'King Xylan of the Kingdom of Marlyst. Are you in support of or against the proposed changes?'

His eyes locked on mine. He let me see the emotions cross his face: sorrow, regret, yearning, determination. His attention didn't waver from me as he sat up, lifting his chin and presenting himself as the formidable force that he was. 'For the doers, the defenders, and the dreamers. To the devoted, the divisive and the divine. For the True Infinite and the continent of Fyriane, I am in support of this. Protect our family.' He finished speaking with his fingers to his third eye. I saw a flash of fuchsia in his eyes before they returned to his masked pale pink ones.

At the mention of True Infinite, I snuck a look at Slaviya from the corner of my eye to see her shocked expression. Why would she be shocked? It was clear he'd been in favour from the beginning.

I used the distraction of writing down his vote to gather myself, desperately trying to take control of my trembling fingers with no luck. He really was the king of double meanings. I'd received his message loud and clear. He wasn't running. He wasn't turning away. He would fight for me, and fight for our future.

I swallowed loudly before turning to my husband, the term feeling the most inappropriate and hollow than it had since our wedding day. That said a lot considering I came on a mission to assassinate him, and he was only ever a temporary spouse.

'King Eliasson of the Kingdom of Arlom, do you support or reject the cross collaboration of the Doms of Fyriane?'

He searched my face, looking for any sign I had reconsidered my stance on the matter. When I gave him nothing to indicate there had been a change, he answered clearly, 'Yes, Valare and I am in favour of this motion.'

I nodded. This was not the time to be selfish, however much I might want to be. I couldn't hide away in a corner because I was scared of the destiny the fates had handed me. I had to do the right thing. But I would do it my way. On my terms. Now I just needed to work out the logistics of the Eliasson situation, because the doubts I had long been pushing down were bubbling to the surface.

'That concludes the vote. With a three to one result in favour of the cross collaboration, I hereby enact my rights as the hosting royal of this Forum to conclude the matter.' The pride in Eliasson's voice was palpable and felt throughout the room.

Except for one person, of course.

'This is bullshit,' Slaviya icily muttered.

Seemingly unperturbed by her comment, Eliasson simply shrugged. 'Everyone has the right to their vote, Slaviya. However, none of us are above the outcome of the Forums. The verdict is in. My Dom will assist yours in protecting the frontline, the logistics of which we may discuss later. Same goes with you, Qynthia. Valare and I look forward to working together for a prosperous future for Fyriane.'

I schooled my expression, refusing to let the guilt eat at me when he said the words *Valare and I*.

Eliasson continued, his relief evident that his hosting duties were over. 'On that note, this concludes the negotiations segment of the Forum. The closing ball will be held three nights from now. Please take this time to explore Amarald, continue mingling or sit back and relax before your tiring journeys home. It was a pleasure to host you in our beautiful Kingdom,' he finished, pulling me to stand alongside him. He pressed me into his side, planted a kiss on my forehead and directed me out of the room, a clear purpose in his movements.

Once we had turned the corner, Eliasson picked me up and charged towards our quarters as I squealed for him to put me down.

But he didn't, as I knew he wouldn't. Not until my back landed on the soft sheets of his bed and his form rested on top of mine. I pushed thoughts of Xylan out of my head, leaning into the physical mage in me that craved intimacy as I closed off my mental barrier.

I held onto the relaxed and calming sensations that overtook my body. We succumbed to the heaviness behind our eyes at some point in the evening, but I knew it wouldn't last forever. Nothing peaceful in my life ever did.

CHAPTER 29

An alarm blared throughout the entire palace, no doubt extending to the ears of the civilians throughout Amarald.

Without a second thought, I rushed out of bed, putting on my fighting leathers. I made my way downstairs, heading towards the ocean only to be met by my personal Sol, the Royals and their Seconds.

Eliasson rushed up behind me, dressed in his own fighting leathers as he looked me up and down. 'Fyrel, did you see where the threat is coming from?'

Fyrel didn't need to answer for me to know. I felt their presence in the water, dangerously close to the shore.

My heart dropped.

'The ocean, Your Highness. The beasts are here,' Fyrel gravely confirmed.

I shared a look with Slaviya, both of us knowing what needed to happen but equally hesitant. We knew this would change everything. There was no way of hiding our magic in a battle with the tidal beasts. Her attempts to dissuade Arlom aid, and keep magic hidden for a little longer, would all be for nothing after this. With a nod from my sister, I turned towards my Sol.

'Mer, you take Fyrel and Eliasson. Mazyr, Amire, Rynelle, split yourselves up between the others and meet us there. You know where you're going?' I commanded, receiving nods in return. 'Slaviya and I will go separately. I can't expend any energy carrying them, I'll need every reserve I've got.'

'Wait, what are you doing Valare? We can't split up,' Eliasson argued.

'We aren't splitting up, Eliasson. Can you just trust me? Please?' I stuttered, bracing myself for the feelings of betrayal I knew would ultimately follow.

I could see the scepticism on his face. I noticed he side-eyed Xylan who returned his look with a nod. But he was at a loss for what else to say other than, 'Okay.'

I nodded. 'I promise everything will be okay. I need to focus on saving the Kingdom right now and can't have any distractions. I'll explain everything later but please know that I'm sorry.' I stumbled over the last words.

Before he could respond, I nodded at Slaviya and my Sol. I chose to ignore the knowing eyes of the other royal mages.

Slaviya and I teleported to land on the beach which, prior to tonight, had been my private oasis. The waves were enormous, the wind so fierce that I struggled to stay upright. Despite it being pitch black, my eyes adjusted quickly to the view, almost as if it were daylight, and I could see giant tentacles emerge out of the aggressive waves, before crashing back down into the water.

'Shit. You weren't exaggerating when you said they were getting bigger,' I muttered to Slaviya. I'd never seen tentacles on them before either.

My sister merely snorted, rolling back her shoulders to take a fighting stance. I felt the others arrive.

Rynelle stepped up to my side, using a gust of wind to push back the others. He created a fire from the large torch he was holding.

'What the hell …' I heard Fyrel mutter in disbelief.

'Mazyr, Amire, do you think you can combine your magic to create a shield to hold back these waves? Mer needs to work on bringing the water level down,' I said.

'On it,' Mazyr nodded before grabbing Amire's hand. The spark of their twin magic started as a small ball in their joined hands before growing bigger. The twins worked in sync with one another, raising their free hands to frame a rectangular shape before pushing their magic out and across the length of the strip of beach. We watched as the fifty-metre-high shield shimmered into place, effectively stopping the waves from crashing onto the shore.

As Mer began working on the water levels, I spotted more of the massive beasts. I had never seen anything like it. It was the biggest I had ever seen. It had at least twenty thick tentacles crashing against the waves as it made its way closer to the shield. The dwindling water levels did nothing to stop its pursuit.

I turned to Slaviya, kissing my middle fingers and placing them on my chest, 'For the Goddess Wystia, God Merlot and the continent of Fyriane.' I wasn't ready to throw in the True Infinite part yet. Not until we sorted out our shit.

Her eyes flashed, noting my change of wording. But she didn't do anything other than kiss her own fingers and placed them on her third eye. 'Protect our family.'

With a nod, I latched onto her hand and shot us into the air, flying towards the beast. I reached out my free hand, counteracting the twins magic to create a hole in the shield for us to fly through. As we approached, the purple, scaly creature let out a shriek of rage. Its wide mouth opened to reveal an endlessly dark pit framed by hundreds of sharp teeth. One of its tentacles flicked out in an attempt to strike me just as Slaviya pulled and directed Rynelle's fire to weaken the beast. The hit landed, bringing another shriek as the tentacle burned.

I concentrated on the beast's physical presence, lifting its heavy body out of the water. While Slaviya continued to work with the fire to slow the tentacles down, I grabbed a long dagger sheathed on my thigh. I imbued fire and air into the weapon, creating my own green fire dagger, and flung it at the tentacles. In one clean cut, the tentacles dropped into the water one by one. I commanded my weapon back into my hand only to repeat the process again and again.

As predicted, the lack of water was making it increasingly harder for it to breathe, slowing the beast down. Between Slaviya's fire and my dagger, we made quick work of the tentacles until there was only one left on its body.

A sudden yell to my left pulled my attention. One of the stray tentacles had re-formed to create smaller versions of the beast and it had latched onto Slaviya's leg, pulling us down into its awaiting mouth. More beasts appeared from the tentacles, those on shore moving to intercept them. Shit. I'd never encountered this before.

I ceased using my magic on the larger beast, letting it drop into the water as I called upon my dagger to make quick work of the beast holding onto Slaviya. Whatever was on the tentacles had stopped Slaviya's ability to use her magic. She plummeted towards the crashing waves. I lashed out with my magic to gain a firmer grip on her body as I hauled us higher, creating some distance from the beast before teleporting back to the shore.

'Rynelle, get Lyzia. She needs a healer,' I screamed. I turned back to the beast and readied myself to finish it off. But a thought struck my mind when I saw the Marlysts and Nyarelleans shimmering with gold.

I turned to Xylan. 'Do you think you'd be able to help by controlling the beasts mind? Do you have that kind of power?'

'I've never tried with a beast but it's worth a shot. How many are there now?'

'There's the main creature and the smaller ones from the tentacles.'

'Should be doable, but I'll need to come with you through the shield.'

I nodded, grabbing his hand before he could protest. I ignored the warmth under my ear.

'Don't let go of my hand. If you focus on the main creature, I can take care of the rest,' I shouted, not bothering to pay attention to his response as I flew us over the ocean, back to the beasts.

I threw up my other hand, calling the green fire to my palm as I got to work attacking the smaller tentacles as they rose out of the water. The creatures now were significantly easier to dispose of. I presumed it had something to do with them not being attached to the main creature. That, and my green fireballs were effective.

After making quick work of the regenerated beasts, I turned my attention to their source to come up short. It was laying on the surface in a blissful state, purring its little heart out. I couldn't help but laugh as I turned to Xylan with an inquiring look.

'Turns out it quite enjoys belly rubs. So, I made it think it was in the great depths of the ocean getting them,' he smirked.

I allowed my chuckle to linger before concentrating on the task at hand. I reached for my dagger again and aimed for the middle of its body. Poised for the killing shot, my weapon was stilled as a gold shimmer fell around us, a head bobbing out of the water.

The creature looked human with long white hair, and the same nose and lips, but that's where the similarities ended. Its ears were covered in purple scales and shaped like pectoral fins. Its smile revealed two elongated fangs curving downwards to his chin. But the most startling feature were the eyes – they were crystal clear, like a quartz stone. The pupils were a dark blue slit, mimicking that of a reptile. All in all, the creature was freaky.

'Well, it's not nice to treat my pet like this. Do you Fyrianeans not know how to be hospitable?' the creature, clearly male, taunted, moving towards the beast before laying his human-like torso over its body. A purple, scaly tail flicked behind the creature, curling up on the last tentacle of the beast.

'It's okay baby,' he crooned at the beast, running his hand up and down its belly. 'We'll be gone soon.'

What. The. Fuck.

'Who are you? *What* are you?' I demanded.

'I am Lars. I am a merman,' the creature stated matter-of-factly, like I should already know this.

'Give me one good reason, Lars, that I shouldn't destroy you and that beast right this sec –' I started.

'Now, now, mage. Intruding on someone's mind isn't a great start to building a working relationship, is it?' He cut me off, eyes narrowed in accusation towards Xylan.

My gaze swung to Xylan. His fuchsia eyes flashed in determination as his lips twisted into a sneer. 'Working relationship? I'm thinking I should ruin your mind from the inside out, while my partner ruins you physically. Don't need a working relationship for that.'

Partner? Now that's a new word for what we were.

'Firstly, you wouldn't succeed. My mind is protected against that magic. Stop trying to get in there, I do not particularly enjoy the tickling sensation. Secondly, I am here to deliver a message,' Lars stated.

'A message? And you bringing a deadly beast along with you is the right way to do this?' I scoffed.

'Well, it got the attention of the King and Queen of Fyriane, did it not? Although not the King and Queen I had the pleasure of delivering a message to last time. The Svaxlyn will be very interested to hear this new progression,' he drawled.

'I think you have the wrong people,' I denied.

Lars flashed me a wicked, toothy smile. 'No need to lie to me young Queen, your eyes tell me all I need to know.'

'What's the message?' Xylan demanded, cutting me off before I could continue to argue.

Lars focussed his eerie eyes back on Xylan. 'The Svaxlyn wish to claim their rightful dues in accordance with the Svaxlyn Pact. If the rulers of Fyriane do not heed this message, you should expect to see more of these beasts that are bigger and stronger. They will be tasked with destroying your continent.'

'The Svaxlyn Pact?' I asked, confused.

'Dear, the naïve act is getting very old, very quick,' Lars responded.

'Tell your superiors the rulers of Fyriane don't take kindly to messages of violence. We request a formal meeting to discuss these alleged dues.' The firmness of Xylan's voice shocked me.

The merman's deep belly laugh startled us both. 'Oh, Your Highness, why do you think I am here? They are unable to cross into your lands otherwise they would have already. And the agreement that was made is a thousand years overdue. They aren't particularly inclined to *talk*. May I suggest you try a different message?'

A thousand years … was the merman referring to the Royal Forum with Queen Wystia and King Merlot? If he was, that means it's been an eon since they sat in that room with those other beings.

This wasn't good.

'That's the message. Yours has been received, ours sent in turn. Now be gone from our shores, Merman.' The conviction in Xylan's words would have convinced me of his confidence, except he was squeezing my hand to the point of it being painful.

Lars cocked his head to the side, assessing us. 'As you wish. I suspect this will not be the last time we see each other. Until then,' he nodded. In a moment of hesitation, I saw his eyes darting towards the shore, a flash of longing in his gaze. Before I could ask, he was diving into the ocean, carrying the beast with him.

'What the hell was that?' I blurted out, looking at Xylan.

'We don't speak of this to anyone else until we know what it all means, Valare. Promise me,' he said. His fuchsia eyes were filled with unwavering determination.

'Is that not going to be a problem considering they can see all of this play out from the shore?'

He waved his free hand at me dismissively. 'I put an illusion around us as soon as I felt a presence other than the beasts,' he said. 'From their view, time has stopped, and you were delivering the final blow on the beast. When I release the illusion, teleport us straight to the shore and no one will question it.'

Huh. Neat trick. I made a note to find out more about these psychic mages. I was getting a little over finding things out on the run.

'Now, give me your promise,' he demanded.

'Alright, I promise. The Goddess knows I have enough to deal with when I get back to shore.'

'Ah yes, your magical secrets are no more. That will be a fun conversation with your husband,' he teased. Despite everything we'd just learned, he apparently took our working together as a sign of good faith.

'Don't make me go back on my promise,' I threatened. 'And don't for a second think you're forgiven.'

Eyes twinkling with pleasure, Xylan ignored my words. 'Ready?'

'Ready as I'll ever be.'

CHAPTER 30

After we landed on the shore, I rushed towards where Lyzia was working on Slaviya.

'All clear to drop the shield and cease wielding.' My order came out as a bark and I felt Mer, Mazyr and Amire drop.

'How is she?' I demanded.

'I've sedated her to relax the body and extracted the poison from her. Whatever you were fighting has something in its poison that nullifies magic. Your sister would've been in a lot of pain,' she grimaced. 'I trust you got out of the mess unscathed?'

I nodded in confirmation. 'Did you manage to get a vial of the poison?'

She nodded towards several vials lying on the sand. 'I'll get to testing it as soon as I can. Probably after a couple of hours of sleep.' Lyzia shook her head sheepishly as she looked down at her nightgown.

I softened at her attire, realising she must've been in a deep sleep when she was rushed here. 'Thank you for coming.'

She shrugged nonchalantly. 'It's what I'm here for, not to mention it's my pleasure,' she replied. 'The creature must have bypassed the Isles otherwise Varqel and I would've dealt with it. It's very strange it came to these shores,' she said, her eyes watching for my reaction. I had plenty of theories as to what lured them to Arlom. But I wasn't about to share them.

'Very strange, indeed.' I kept my face blank, determined to keep my promise to Xylan.

Lyz tilted her head, a knowing look on her face, lips thinning as she deliberated on whether to push me. She chose against it, merely calling Rynelle over to escort her back to the Isles.

'She should wake up in a few hours. There are no signs of poison still left in her body. Expect her to wake up a bit groggy and she'll require observation over the next twenty-four hours. If there are any signs that she's not recovering as she should, call for me. Otherwise, if everything goes well, I'll see you soon?' Lyzia asked as she grabbed Rynelle's hand.

I nodded to Lyz, watching them teleport away, taking a moment. I wasn't looking forward to what was coming.

I sighed as I stood up, turning to face the group. My eyes landed on Xylan's. His illusionary pale pink eyes were back. I opened my mouth to thank him for his help but was cut off by Eliasson's arms reaching out to grab onto my shoulders.

'Are you hurt?' he demanded, patting all over my body, looking for any injuries.

'Um,' I cleared my throat in confusion. I had expected him to be angry.

'You don't look hurt, but it's hard to see in this light. Maybe we should get you a healer, have you checked over.' His worried voice rose as he fussed over me.

'I'm okay Eliasson. No injuries,' I placated, placing my hands over his to stop his frantic movements.

'Alright. Okay.' A rush of breath left his mouth as he tried to collect himself. 'In that case, I think you and I need to have a serious discussion.' Anger replaced the concern that had been in his tone.

I winced and nodded in agreement as I stepped to the side to look at the others. 'Mer, Mazyr, Amire, I trust you can assist in taking people back to their respective rooms?'

My Sol nodded in unison.

'Please work out between yourselves rotating watches for Slaviya. Any signs of discomfort or something out of sorts, please report to me immediately,' I directed.

'I can look after her,' Qynthia said, stepping next to Slaviya's sleeping form.

'Are you sure?' I asked sceptically, exchanging wary glances with Mer.

'Yes, it's fine. Our quarters are next to one another, it'll be easy for me to move into hers for the night. I suspect your colleagues will require sleep after their efforts tonight.' She smiled, and flashed them sympathetic looks.

'As long as you're okay with that,' I shrugged, not having it in me to question let alone understand her motive behind taking care of Slaviya. 'In that case, ensure everyone gets back to their quarters and you're dismissed for the night. Good job, you did Fyriane proud.' I nodded at them, letting my gratitude show on my face.

'Always honoured to serve you, Queen,' Amire replied.

'Get some rest if you can, Val. This was a big one,' Mer said gently, sympathy shining in her eyes.

I shot Mer a warning look, earning me a confused one in return. I sighed, dropping my barriers, hoping this would work.

Keep Fyrel distracted, please, I told her.

Mer's eyes bulged. She quickly composed herself, giving me a look that said both 'what the hell bitch, you've been holding out on me' and 'we'll talk about this later', and nodded.

I kissed my three middle fingers and placed them on my chest, bowing my head in gratitude to my Sol before whisking Eliasson and I back to our quarters.

CHAPTER 31

Dropping onto Eliasson's bed, I sighed, preparing myself for the onslaught of questions.

'What the fuck was that?' he demanded, pacing up and down the room in anger.

I rubbed my temples. I fixed my gaze on Eliasson, standing a few steps in front of me with his fists clenched by his side and a death stare to match. I'd never seen him like this. Not towards me at least.

'You may want to sit down for what I'm about to tell you,' I replied gently.

'Start talking Valare,' he snarled, refusing to move. Fine. It wasn't my fault if he crumpled to the floor.

Well, really it was, I was too tired to fight.

'I'm a physical mage.' The words sounded insufficient.

He scoffed and shook his head in disbelief. 'And what exactly is a physical mage, Valare?'

Releasing another heavy breath, I started from the beginning. I told Eliasson about the Temple of Wystia and the reason the Salistyan's are trained on the Isles. I told him about the magic that comes to a mage on their sixteenth birthday, the Sol and the three years spent honing their skills before they're allowed to return to the mainland or stay on the Isles. As expected, about halfway through my explanation, his legs gave out and he found himself on the floor. I saw shock take over his body as I delivered one revelation after another. No doubt his mind was spinning.

I stopped talking, allowing his brain to make sense of the words utterly shattering the foundations of the world he thought he was a part of. A world that he was a ruler in. I had known that if he ever found out, it would be brutal. But watching it happen? It was worse than I ever could've imagined. My heart broke for him, for us, for the friendship we'd built.

My eyes welled tears, and I blinked rapidly to push them down. I felt the mental armour I'd always had up around him start to fall as a traitorous tear rolled down my cheek. I swiped at it, knowing full well he was seeing the wave of emotions play out on my face.

'What can a physical mage do exactly?' he asked, ignoring my tears completely.

I started with the commonalities, reciting the lessons I received in my first year as a trainee on the Isles. 'There are different types, or levels if you will, of mages, but every physical mage can teleport between places. The more powerful a mage is, the further they can teleport, and the more people they can carry.'

'Right, which is what you and your … Sol … did tonight?' he asked, hesitantly stumbling on the word for our group of assassins.

'Yes.' I continued with my explanation. 'Once gifted with our magic, every mage becomes physically a lot stronger and gains heightened senses. Where you would've seen only flickers of what was happening tonight, we were able to see it all as if it was happening in broad daylight. We can sense physical bodies around us within a certain distance, and the more powerful a mage is, the further the distance they can sense. We're also able to hold someone in place, paralysing their body so they're unable to move. Also, we're more … primal when it comes to our sex life. We are sensual by nature and tend to have a higher sex drive, and can be quite demanding in that area.'

I decided to omit that physical mages favour polygamy over monogamous relationships to satiate their desires. Nor did I add in my unique ability to tamper with a person's body. He didn't need to know I'd put him to sleep too many times to count, or that I could end his life by merely cutting off his windpipes.

'Well, I've definitely been on the receiving end of that last part,' he smirked, momentarily forgetting his anger, before shaking himself out of it. 'And the use of elements?'

'Regular mages will show favourability to one of the four elements, water, fire, earth or air. However, they may only use this element when it's within reach. For example, a water mage can't summon water out of thin air, they must have it around them, even if it's as little as a dripping tap. They need something to latch onto.'

'I saw, was it Rynelle?' He looked at me for confirmation before continuing once I nodded, 'Using both fire and air.'

'That's because he's a part of the Sol. The Sol are groups of highly skilled mages who show favourability in two elements. The common pairings are either fire and air, or earth and water. From time to time, a Sol may favour a different combination, but it's unlikely. From my understanding, this has only happened a few times. Slaviya is one of those – she favours earth and fire.'

'So, Meredith is …'

'A member of the Sol. Her affinity lies with water and earth. Today you just saw her water magic.'

'And what about you? I saw fire emerge from your hand. I saw you wield a dagger that came straight back to you once you'd thrown it.' His eyes were imploring, struggling to understand how I fit into all of this.

I released yet another sigh, rolling my neck around in circles to ease it. Here comes the crescendo. 'Yes. Then there's me.'

Eliasson let out a snort as he rolled his eyes incredulously. 'Don't tell me you're the exception to every rule?'

I looked away.

'Oh Goddess. You *are* the exception. What are you Valare?' He leant forward against his now crossed legs.

'I don't know anymore,' I whispered.

'You don't know?' he said, his voice rising in mock disbelief. 'This isn't the time for you to continue lying to me, Valare.'

'There's never been anyone like me. Not for over a thousand years, at least.' My breaths started coming faster as I squeezed my hands tighter in my lap, the enormity of the situation hitting me in a new way.

Realisation dawned on his face. 'Your eyes. They're different, not like the others.'

'The first new moon after my sixteenth birthday, it was a black moon. I arrived at the Temple of Wystia with my teachers and no other trainees. Apparently, I was the only one receiving my gifts, which is unheard of as it usually happens in groups. At the time there was nothing to indicate I may be any different from a regular physical mage, except when my magic was given to me. My whole life I had had the moss-coloured eyes of a Salistyan born. That night they instantly turned lime green. They've never returned to their former colour,' I muttered in disgust, wishing, not for the first time, I could just be normal like everyone else.

'What gifts were you given?' he prompted me softly, my clear contempt for my uniqueness placating his anger.

'As I explored my magic throughout training, everything seemed normal at first. I held all the basic gifts you'd see in a physical mage. Granted I had keener senses, and my strength in other factors were much greater than my counterparts, but that happens at times. It was obvious I would be trained as a Sol and destined to be honed into a lethal assassin, which isn't anything new.

'But it wasn't until six months in when our training turned towards the elements that I realised the colour of my eyes wasn't the only different thing I'd gained. Every Salistyan royal before me favoured two elements. But I have equal strengths in all four of the elements,' I stated. His eyes flashed in awe as he gulped down a big breath.

I continued. 'On top of that, I don't require those elements to be near me. I can summon a ball of fire with just the thought of it, plant a seedling and command a tree to sprout immediately, watch it grow to whatever height and width I desire. If I want a full glass of red wine in my hand, I just have to …' I held out my hand as I thought of said wine and a second later, there it was, '… imagine it and command it,' I finished, offering him the glass, which he took and eagerly gulped down.

'Granted, my energy reserves deplete much faster when I don't have a source near me. If there's a body of water or the rush of wind near, I'll always opt to use that and manipulate it. There's no point in expending more energy than necessary,' I explained frankly.

'And the flying?' he probed.

'Ah yes, levitating and flying. That's also a neat talent I gained. I admit it's probably my favourite. It's a cool trick that no one else can do,' I grinned proudly for a moment. 'And before you ask, I created a hole in the shield Maz and Amire had constructed to get through to the beast. Maz favours water and earth, but Amire favours fire and air. Because they're twins, they can share, transfer and combine their magic to create more power. But because I'm stronger than them, I can counteract their magic. It's not an easy feat, but we've had a lot of practise over the years.' I shrugged.

He stared at me in wonder for a good minute before asking, 'So, what does that make you?'

'I honestly don't know. I wasn't lying to you. I'm still trying to figure out what it all means and how I fit. But in its simplest form it means I'm the most powerful physical mage on the Fyriane continent.' My mind flickered to the book of Wystia and Merlot and I added, 'That we know of, at least.'

'Shit,' he breathed. 'I'm married to the most powerful physical mage. Isn't that something.'

I couldn't help the exhausted giggle that left my mouth at the blatant awe in his voice.

Apparently, that giggle snapped him out of his contemplation. 'So, the Arlom teens in the Solista Isles, are they receiving this magic?'

I gulped, knowing this was the moment that everything turned south. 'They are.'

Understanding flashed in his eyes before they settled on rage. 'So, if Arlomans can receive their magic, why does my Kingdom not know about this? Why am I not a physical mage?'

'I can't tell you what I don't know. I know some things, but not all of them, and that's what I've been trying to work out – you're not the only one who has been kept in the dark. What I do know, and can tell you, is my own experience.' I took a deep breath before diving in again, figuring I may as well reveal what I'd found out.

'From what I can gather, long ago the Fyriane continent was united and ruled by King Merlot and Queen Wystia. How they came to be, I still have no idea. I've recently discovered, the king was what they refer to as a psychic mage, whilst the queen was a physical mage. Wystia's magic source came to be captured in the place we now know of as the Temple of Wystia. Merlot's magic source, I believe, has been locked in a place near the Nyarelle and Marlyst Doms. If I were to guess, it's somewhere in the desert far away from our lands, much like the Isles. The royal couple had four children. Each of the Doms we have today are named after them. Salistya and Arlom were physical mages while Nyarelle and Marlyst were psychic mages. I'm assuming upon the disappearance of their parents, the siblings decided to break up the Fyriane continent and took a piece of their own land, starting their own Dom.'

I took a deep breath and continued, needing to give him more information before I explained the Isles.

'Growing up in the Queendom of Salistya was, to put it short, awful. The Queendom is a stifling environment. Even as the third in line for the throne, I was treated like just another Salistyan woman. Born to eventually give birth to as many children as possible who would then become weapons to serve in the army. However, as the army was the number one priority for Salistyans, female teens are granted a reprieve, and can leave the Queendom for five years to learn how to be a weapon. Only those who showed strengths in more than one element were deemed an appropriate fit for the army. There was still an expectation for those women to procreate, but at least they were able to fight alongside the men. But those who only showed strengths in one element?' I shuddered in disgust. 'They were immediately brought back and became part of the breeding program to get the population up. The sires of their children were all Sol selectively picked to enhance the possibility of their children favouring two elements.

'We were raised to think the Arlom Kingdom was weak and didn't deserve to know or be gifted with physical magic. The Queendom fiercely protected the Isles as they knew this was where the source of their power came from. If they didn't have this, what would stop any of the Doms from infiltrating their lands? The land is not ideal for agriculture, nor does it have materials to make weapons. They have nothing, only their army and the physical magic of the Isles. The Queendom has never played nice with the others, as you're aware. We saw it time and time again in the meetings with Slaviya. They stick to themselves and don't offer more information than required. I'm not sure when or how it happened, but somehow somewhere along the line, Salistya was able to hide the true purpose of the Solista Isles and the physical mages of Arlom ceased to exist.'

Eliasson got up and started pacing again in obvious agitation. 'So, what changed?' he challenged.

'What you need to understand, Eliasson, is that my father was a cold-hearted and calculating man who ruled with an iron fist. I was in the Solista Isles enjoying my respite from being under his thumb, totally oblivious to the growing political frictions between Arlom and Salistya. They didn't know about my powers, as my mentor had made sure to hide it from them. He knew I would be subjected to whatever awful training or experiments my father would want me to be involved with otherwise. My family sent word that Slaviya was to marry you and unite our Doms. As you can imagine from what I'd been fed from such a young age, I was shocked. Why would the Queendom agree to this? I knew that your Kingdom wanted to be able to protect themselves and not rely on Salistya as much. Part of that was having access to the Solista Isles.'

'Yes. We knew your army was trained there. We figured that if we were to strengthen our own army, we would need the Isles to do so,' he agreed. 'The betrothal made sense for us to gain access to the Isles, but why would the Queendom agree to it if they wanted us to be shielded from the knowledge of magic?'

'You heard Slaviya. The tidal beasts are becoming more aggressive and making their way down to Arlom's territory,' I said, trying to deflect from the real reason for the union.

'Yes, but that still doesn't make sense. They could've simply brought this up at the Forum, requesting us to allow their army access. Why now? Why marry me?' He was spiralling. I could see it in his actions, in his facial features. My betrayal was starting to dawn on him as I saw him make the logical leap.

'Because the plan was to never keep me as the ruler, was it? Salistya didn't want a union, they wanted to take over Arlom and the first step would be to marry into the royal family …' He trailed off. Eliasson's eyes teared up as he breathed out, 'My life is in danger, isn't it?'

I grew increasingly uncomfortable, avoiding his eyes. I'd arrived at the inevitable fork in the road. I'd known it was coming the minute my magic was revealed. As far as I saw it, I had two choices: lie to Eliasson and save him the anguish, or be truthful about my purpose there, and, from now on, follow my own path.

'I think you're going to want Fyrel for this part,' I whispered.

'Valare, you're splitting my heart in two,' Eliasson cried, tears pouring down his face.

The tears I was keeping at bay were released as I sobbed, 'Please, go get Fyrel. If he's with Meredith, bring her too.'

'How can I trust anything that's coming out of your mouth? How do I know that the minute I leave, I'm not going to be killed instantly? I *loved* you Valare. I wanted to have *children* with you.

Create a life together. The person I'm looking at – my wife – who I've loved for the past year is a stranger. I don't even know you,' he said, pointing at me.

He wasn't to know that he was splitting my heart in two as well. I may not love him as a romantic partner, but I had come to love him as a friend, to see him as my family. It wasn't only his future that was changing with every minute that passed.

'You do know me. I may have held things back from you, Eliasson. The purpose of my being here may be a lie, but the person you've come to know in the last year is still me. I don't expect you to trust me, or to even like me, but I'm begging you. Please. Fyrel needs to know this, and you deserve to have a choice as to how this will go down,' I pleaded.

'You're coming with me. I'll be damned if you go missing before I get back and I sure as hell need your protection to ensure I keep my bloody head on my body,' he said gruffly, fury infusing his movements as he grabbed my arm and pulled us out of the quarters towards Fyrel's rooms.

I let him drag me across the palace, attempting and failing to hold in my tears. When we arrived at Fyrel's rooms, he banged on the door and barged in. He paid no attention to what was very obviously Meredith and Fyrel having heated sex fuelled by, undoubtedly, a healthy dose of anger. She would've had to reveal some secrets to him as well.

Eliasson stomped over, pulling Fyrel off Meredith as she scrambled from all fours to dive under the cover to hide her naked body.

'Get changed, you're both coming with us,' Eliasson demanded, crossing his arms over his chest and staring down at the couple expectantly.

They rushed to get changed before looking between us. Eliasson's stance was full of anger while I was trying to stop the tears falling down my cheeks.

'Teleport us back to my room,' he ordered. I grabbed Fyrel and Eliasson's hands and nodded to Meredith before whisking us away. Meredith landed behind us a second later, rushing towards me and placing a supportive arm around my waist.

'Where were we, Valare?' Eliasson pretended. 'Ah, that's right. You were up to the part where my life was in danger.'

'What —' Fyrel swivelled to face me, bloody murder emanating from every pore in his body.

'Shit,' Meredith whispered.

'You know about this?' Fyrel sneered at Mer. She swallowed loudly, refusing to answer and instead looked to me for guidance.

I took a step back, dragging Meredith with me, to create some distance between the raging Arlomans. 'Eliasson's life is in danger,' I confirmed as I looked at Fyrel. I could feel the tears still drying on my face. 'I wanted you to hear it from me firsthand. I know we don't deserve your grace, but I ask that you remain calm while I explain what's happening.'

Fyrel looked at Eliasson with dread. They had both seen what I was capable of at the beach and knew they had no real leg to stand on. My diplomacy of not reminding them of it was my own form of grace.

'I take it you've caught Fyrel up on what it means to be a physical mage and the gifts of the Isles?' I asked Mer.

She sheepishly nodded, casting her head down as tears began to fall down her face.

'It's okay, Mer. I know this has been hard for you to keep from him,' I soothed, rubbing her arm up and down. 'For what it's worth Fyrel, she really does love you. Please remember that this is out of her control. As you should understand being in your position, she's duty bound to her Queendom.' I saw Fyrel soften. He too had tears in his eyes as he nodded in understanding, his gaze unwaveringly fixed on Meredith.

'I've come to understand that my father agreed to a union between our Doms to train more physical mages and create a bigger army. Despite what Slaviya says, the breeding programs are not as fruitful as she would lead you to believe. The army is suffering, and the beasts are growing in strength and size. They're becoming a formidable force that the Salistyan army alone clearly can't conquer. Granting Arlomans access to the Isles allows for more physical mages and thus a stronger front on our coastal lands. However,' I cleared my throat, 'It was never my father's intention to have an Arloman rule over a Kingdom which held physical mages. They'd always planned for you to be assassinated, Eliasson. This would lead my sister – now me – to be the ruler of Arlom. It would also create a strong force against Marlyst and Nyarelle, who we all know hold a strong alliance.'

Fyrel moved to place himself protectively in front of Eliasson.

'I'm not going to hurt him, Fyrel. If I was going to, I would've done it well and truly before now. Be thankful it was me that married your king and not my sister. If it were Slaviya, Eliasson would have died a year ago, consequences and implications be damned.'

'What changed your mind?' Eliasson asked, stepping to Fyrel's side to look at me.

'When my parents and brother died and Slaviya became Queen, I naturally became heir. I knew how much she detested my father's plans to marry her off, so I naively thought she would put a stop to talks of marriage. I hoped that Slaviya, as a female ruler of a Queendom that had oppressed women for as long as it has stood, would change our Dom for the better. But she hasn't. I've come to see the same cunning look in her eyes as I did my father's. When I found out that I was to be married and the plans I was expected to carry on, I was furious. But I also had no way to stop it from happening. I was a Salistyan and required to be loyal to my queen, even as the next in line for the throne. I was bound by duty.'

'Arlom is a lot like Solista. People are free. Happy. Alive. It amazes me to this day that the Solistans are under Salistyan rule. In all honesty, it would be more fitting that they were under Arloman rule.' I shook my head.

'Living in the Isles opened my eyes to a different way of life. In truth, I wanted nothing to do with Salistya. And then I was sent on this mission.' I took a deep breath. 'Living in Arlom, getting to know you, your people, the culture. It wasn't what I was expecting. It made me second guess whether seeing the mission through was the right thing to do. I stalled, made up a plethora of excuses to Slaviya to get her off my back while I sifted through my thoughts. It took me a while to realise that I'm no longer under my sister's reign. I married an Arloman and that made me loyal to the Arlom Kingdom. I realised I don't have to be a pawn in all of this. I don't have to assassinate a king who is so loved by his people and rules with his heart on his sleeve. And I also don't have to play into whatever it is my sister is planning after you're supposed to be dead, Eliasson. I never really trusted her, even when we were younger, but now I absolutely don't trust her motives. We don't trust her motives.' I looked at Mer as she nodded in agreement, standing in solidarity with me. 'Fyriane was once a united continent under one ruling couple. I fear she's trying to rule Fyriane alone and taking it by force. Arlom and your assassination, Eliasson, are the first pieces of the puzzle.'

The men digested my words.

'So why are you here, Mer?' Fyrel asked softly, love and understanding shining in his eyes.

I nudged Mer, giving her permission to answer freely.

'I'm a part of Valare's Sol. I'm a trained assassin along with Amire, Mazyr and Rynelle. We've trained together since we were gifted our magic. As a group, along with Valare, we assist in assassination missions. This was, or is, our first mission together. We're under strict orders by our queen.' She swallowed nervously and added, 'Slaviya, that is.'

'So …' Eliasson started. 'If you're not going to kill me. What's the plan?'

Mer and I smiled at one another. We didn't need words to reach an understanding of what needed to be done, having already had some pieces in place.

'I'd like to just point out that I still hate you Valare, and neither Eliasson nor I forgive you for this. Despite saving his life,' Fyrel jumped in. The lovesick puppy was gone, and he was back to the insufferable bastard I was used to. It felt good, normal. I could deal with this.

'Oh, I know, sweetheart,' I crooned, falling back into the role of annoying wife of his best friend. 'But looks like you're going to have to play along with me to ensure your safety, aren't you?'

I turned back to business. 'This is what we're going to do.'

Hours later, when we'd finally come to an agreement, I was able to leave Eliasson's room. Understandably, he wanted space. But at least he agreed to be somewhat polite to me in public, so that was a win.

Heading into my room, I closed the door and stared at my bed longingly, wishing I could dive under the covers. Unfortunately, I was making my own path, and I needed to tick all the boxes before resting.

Teleporting out, I landed in the room I'd been craving to visit and avoiding every night since the Forum had started. Making my way over to Xylan's sleeping form, I couldn't help notice he was nude under the covers. Dismissing that thought, I lightly tickled his arm, startling him awake.

'Minx?' he slurred, half asleep. 'What are you doing here?'

I released a massive breath and pushed down my hatred for the words that were about to come out my mouth. The reality was I had to trust this man and extend an olive branch before I was ready to. I focused on those sleepy, beautiful fuchsia eyes which spurred me on despite my discomfort.

'I need your help.'

CHAPTER 32

The days leading up to the ball were beyond painful. I tried my best to maintain my composure in public, but I was drowning in guilt and sleep deprivation. From time to time, I felt Xylan's warm, comforting caress in my mind as if he were saying 'I'm here for you'. He never tried to communicate with me telepathically. I think we both knew that would push me over the edge. I wouldn't be able to control where I would end up and I couldn't afford that. Not now.

Eliasson, to his credit, did a far better job of being diplomatic than I ever could. However, his distance didn't go unnoticed by the other royals. He only spoke to me when required and there was no physical affection towards me. The minute we entered our quarters, he headed to his room. He never spoke to me and never looked in my direction.

I couldn't blame him. I'd betrayed him. I'd shattered his heart and forced him to act, oblivious to the fact other Doms had been hiding secrets from him. How he was able to look at Slaviya, let alone manage a smile, was beyond me. For all the training I'd undergone throughout the years, I knew in my bones I'd never be as brave as him.

Word spread swiftly through the Kingdom about their queen being a witch who could wield magic and fly. Apparently when the sirens began, many townsfolk had run to the foreshore. With all the fire being thrown around, civilians caught sight of Slaviya and I hovering over the middle of the ocean fighting a giant beast. The response to the news was mixed. There were many who were angered by my deceit and demanded answers, while others were simply in awe and afraid. Both weren't great. But had I ever thought this would go down well? I hadn't planned how I was going to break it to the Kingdom, too focused on understanding the Arloman culture, gaining their trust, and, of course, the assassination.

Perhaps the Arlomans seeing it in the flesh would acclimate them. Maybe I was in denial but that's what I decided to tell myself. I couldn't handle another thing being added onto my list of worries or to the overwhelming anxiety of these last few days. It was hard enough to swallow that things hadn't gone to plan with Sir or Eliasson. Tonight, however, had to go to plan. There was no other option.

I stared out at the ocean from the slice of beach I'd come to adore. The currents were calm today, waves lapping gently onto the shore. It was a complete contrast to the war zone from a few nights ago.

I felt the presence of my sister as she landed a couple of metres away. The morning after the attack I'd gone to see how she was recovering. I'd walked in on Qynthia holding Slaviya's hand as she lay there in bed, clearly feeling sorry for herself. Had it been anyone other than the outrageously affectionate Qynthia holding her hand, I would've raised an eyebrow.

We'd discussed the events of the previous night, that Eliasson knew about physical mages, and that news about my gifts would have spread to the wider Kingdom. There was a part of me hoping Slaviya would help me figure out how I should navigate this moving forward, considering it was both a Salistya and Arlom problem. After all, Salistya was the Queendom to deceive Arlom in the first place. But I shouldn't have been surprised when she merely shook her head, snorted, and said, 'That sounds like a you issue, sister,' throwing my words back at me.

I left the room before I could give in to my impulse and give her injuries far worse than the ones she was nursing. We hadn't talked since.

I kept my eyes fixed on the ocean. 'What do you want?'

'I expect everything will unfold as per the plan.' A statement, not a question.

Selfish, hateful bitch. 'Nothing has changed.'

'Good.'

I snapped. 'Aren't you going to ask how I am? If I need anything? You put me in this position, and I feel like I'm the one fucking dying,' I shouted, unable to hold it back anymore. Tears desperately wanted to fall, I was sick and tired of crying.

She crossed her arms over her chest, her cold stare chilling me to the very bone. 'No, Valare. You put yourself in this position.'

I barked out a laugh in disbelief. 'I'm going to bite because I don't know how your delusional fucking mind even came to that conclusion. How have I put myself in this position, sister?' I couldn't help sneering the word sister.

'Vulnerability is a sign of weakness. If you'd heeded the words of our father, you wouldn't be feeling like this right now. You'd be acting as a trained assassin. All head, no heart. So no, Valare. It's not my fault you're in this position. Maybe this will teach you how to rule as a true queen moving forward.'

'Fuck you Slaviya,' I said, a sob escaping. I drew up my knees and burrowed my head between them. Her words cut far deeper than those of our father.

'I'm willing to let you see this plan through, Valare. But I warn you, if you try to be the saviour in this, I'll make your best friend finish the job for you,' she threatened. 'I'm her Queen, and she's under oath to serve the Salistyan Queendom. Choose your path wisely.'

Before I could lash out at her for threatening me with Meredith, she teleported away.

I should've let her die the night she was poisoned, left her body to rot away and rid this world of her. But I couldn't. She was my sister. But more than that, I refused to pull Dwyla into this mess. My freedom had been stripped away, and I'd be damned if I stole hers.

CHAPTER 33

I stare at myself in the mirror as Meredith placed the final clip into my hair. She stepped away triumphantly, evidently pleased with the final product.

Tonight, I will make a statement. Tonight, I won't be wearing teal, the symbol of the union between Arlom and Salistya. Tonight, I was wearing a beautiful cerulean gown to represent the Arloman people. It was a blatant fuck you to Slaviya, who I knew would get the intended message. I may have little control here right now, but what I did have I would use to my advantage.

The A-line gown sat snug against my chest, exposing my shoulders, the sleeves falling loosely down my arms. It was cinched at the waist, outlining my hourglass figure. The material dropped freely from my waistline, landing in a beautiful puddle around the floor. True to my style, the dress had a slit that ran daringly high.

Meredith had worked wonders on my face. She managed to hide the bags under my eyes I'd had since that awful night by giving me a smoky eye that made my not-so-subtle eyes pop even more. A touch of blush and a smear of a natural-looking pink lipstick finished the look. I had insisted on a low bun that sat loosely at the nape of my neck, not wanting an extravagant hairstyle to draw away from the gold crown that sat atop my head. The crown had three spikes at the front, the middle one bigger than the others and holding a large aquamarine stone.

'You look beautiful, Val,' Meredith said as she squeezed my shoulders.

'This is all you, Mer. Who would've thought you'd turn out to be such a good maid?' I attempted to joke, but the half smile I managed to muster wasn't fooling anyone.

'It's going to be okay. It'll all work out the way it needs to. We have our plan, we just need to stick to it.'

'What if something goes wrong.' My lips quivered, a tell-tale sign tears were inevitable.

'Shhh, don't put those ideas into your head. They don't serve anyone,' she admonished, turning me around to face her directly. 'There's a time and place for self-doubt, Valare, and this isn't one of them. You need to remember that you're the most powerful physical mage in Fyriane and you get to choose your own path. People like Slaviya act the way they do because they have little power and are fighting for control. Often they are so insecure in themselves that they deflect their issues onto others. You can't let people like that have power over you. Your mind is the most powerful tool you have, and you must protect it at all costs.'

She was right. Why did I allow people like her and Sir to have power over me? Spontaneously, I vowed to myself that, from here on out, they wouldn't have my mind, nor my power.

'You're right,' I cleared my throat. 'I love you Mer. Thank you for always being there. We'll get through this.'

'Go protect our family, Valare,' Meredith whispered.

She hustled me across the room and all but shoved me into the dining area where Eliasson stood. He was dressed in a beautiful azure suit and a crown to match mine. I slowly walked towards him, holding the gaze of his ocean-coloured eyes. They were swimming with too many emotions to count.

'Are you ready King Eliasson of Arlom?' I asked.

'Are you ready Queen Valare of Arlom?' he parroted in return, holding his arm out for me to take.

I smiled at him hoping he could see my gratitude as I slipped my arm into his and walked towards the ball to face our fate.

As was tradition for the hosting royal couple, we entered the ballroom last. Food and drinks were being served by attendants. As my guest, Meredith had slipped into the room before us and made a beeline to Fyrel. She clearly wanted to spend a last night of bliss with him before everything changed.

I caught the eyes of Rynelle, who immediately produced two glasses of wine for Eliasson and I. He swiftly moved away as we nodded our thanks. Looking around the room, I couldn't help but smile as I saw Mazyr and Amire in attendants' outfits as they handed out food. The former was having a hard time keeping his tray straight, while the latter rolled her eyes at him before moving away to leave him to his own devices.

I took a sip of the wine, a fruity aftertaste sitting on my tongue. I calmed seeing my fellow Sol, knowing the key players were in place. So far so good.

The room was filled with Arlom nobility wearing their finest gowns and suits. As always with these events, the nobility was thirsty for gossip. No doubt the rumour mill will run wild after tonight.

'Valare, Eliasson!' Qynthia squealed in excitement before pulling us into a group hug. 'You both look stunning.'

'Thank you, Qynthia. As always, so do you,' I said sincerely. She did look beautiful. Her long wavy hair was unrestrained and fell down her back. The burnt orange dress she wore accentuated her body in all the right places and complemented her silver crown.

Slaviya nodded at us as she came up on Qynthia's right.

'Slaviya,' Eliasson and I responded stiffly. I didn't bother looking at her, not after the way she spoke to me. No, my eyes were firmly fixed on the man who'd appeared next to Qynthia. The man who's eyes I'd felt on me the moment I'd walked through the door.

Xylan had opted for a tailored black suit that fit his luscious body like a glove. Underneath, he wore a plain white shirt and a black bow tie. He'd shaved the five o'clock shadow I was intimately familiar with, showing his sharp jawline. As I met his pink eyes, he didn't try to hide the compassion that lay in them, nor his hunger as he looked me up and down.

'Eliasson.' He nodded at my husband, shaking Eliasson's hand before turning back to me with his arm still extended. I placed my hand in his, gulping down the shiver that arose when he kissed my knuckles. Unlike the first time where he held onto me for an inappropriate amount of time, he let go quickly and stepped away, eyes never leaving mine. I felt him knock on my mind, asking to drop my shield, which I did.

You look breathtaking, Minx, he told me with adoration.

I could say the same to you. Are you trying to make this night more difficult than it already is? I couldn't resist falling into the flirty nature of our relationship – if you could even call it a relationship at this point.

I felt his chuckle all through my body. *I'll always be here for you. I'm sorry for the way I've conducted myself. I hope in time you will forgive me. But tonight isn't the night for this conversation. I want you to know that you're a strong and capable woman, Valare, and an excellent queen. Whatever happens tonight, always remember that.*

I subtly nodded in his direction, breaking his stare as I closed my mental shield. I didn't trust myself to not crumple in a heap after those tender words.

'Shall we have our first dance, darling?' I asked Eliasson. He nodded and directed us towards the dance floor.

We fell into a graceful dance, matching our steps with the beautiful music of the string quartet. Eliasson twirled me around like a professional, working every corner of the room.

Are we clear on what you need to do? I said to him through our mind link. I didn't dare say the words out loud to Eliasson from fear a physical mage may hear. I'd theorised my telepathic abilities had something to do with Xylan and I being True Infinites, but had yet to confirm it. Nonetheless, I was going to use every tool at my disposal.

I'll accidentally run into an attendant holding drinks and need to excuse myself to go to the bathroom. He thought and nodded, as he pulled me into a dip as the song ended.

'Thank you. For everything.' I swallowed deeply, chastely kissing his cheek.

As he pulled me back to a standing position, he merely nodded as an Arloman noble asked for my hand in the next dance. Eliasson graciously stepped aside and was whisked into a dance with a woman I didn't know.

The rest of the night went much the same way. I danced until my feet hurt, graciously accepting the hands of various Arloman nobles as I was pulled into one dance after another. All the while I kept a keen eye on Eliasson, waiting for the signal. But the signal never came. Despite seeing him leave the room multiple times, he never made his way to the bathroom. It was strange, and I couldn't help my growing sense of dread.

I decided to take a break. I slowly made my way off the dance floor, only to be stopped by a familiar presence behind me.

'Surely you're not leaving the dance floor before I've had my turn with you?' Xylan said. I could hear the smile in his voice. He knew it would be impolite for me to refuse.

I spun on my heels taking his outstretched hand as he pulled me close. There was no space between our torsos. I could feel his muscles moving as he spun me around the room, swaying our hips in a sensual dance. The pulse under my right ear grew strong the longer we held each other.

'Do you feel it, too? Your mark pulsing? It feels like it's calling to me. Every time we touch,' I whispered quietly.

'Hmm,' he hummed, and nodded in confirmation. 'It's beckoning me to follow this feeling. The urge is becoming stronger. The urge to return home.' He squeezed my hand, as he tightened his grip around me to pull me impossibly closer.

'I don't know if I can do this,' I whispered sadly. I was still so angry with him, the sense of betrayal running too deep. I didn't know if I could forgive him, or what a path to forgiveness would even look like.

'Do what?'

'This. Us. Whatever this is. I'm angry with you and I feel too guilty. With Eliasson and my ex –' I couldn't finish the sentence.

'You don't have to do anything. I'm not forcing you, Valare. I'll never do that. Let's just get through tonight and go from there. At the very least I want to see you again. We have a deal for you to deliver goods to the south of Marlyst remember. Can you do that? For me? Please?' He stumbled through his words, trying to discern what the right thing was to say in this moment.

Could I still find time to see Xylan? Deep down I knew I wanted to. Goddess, I wanted to. But the guilt and the pain I felt. All the expectations placed on me right now were just too much.

You can't let people like that have power over you. Meredith's words rang in my mind.

I opened my mouth to answer when a crash behind us made me spin around so fast I nearly hit Xylan. He grabbed my hips to hold me steady.

Eliasson had finally done it, a mess of red wine spilled down his front as he'd executed the first part of our plan. He'd taken a single step towards the door before he was paralysed, frozen in place. A figure teleported behind him, grabbed him in a headlock and pointed a knife at his throat.

'NO!' I screamed. My mind scrambled to understand what was happening.

Moss green eyes under a dark fringe stared at me as silence and shock fell around the room. The guests slowly moved away from the man holding a knife to the King of Arlom's throat.

'No, Rynelle! Don't do this. Please, don't do this,' I cried out in anguish. I called forth my magic to push him away from Eliasson. But I felt nothing. I tried again with the same result. My eyes widened, heart rate picking up as I stole a glance at Xylan. His brows were furrowed and I realised he was having the same problem. Something had stopped us from using our magic.

'The wine,' I gasped, recalling the fruity aftertaste. I realised it shouldn't have been there. Whatever it was, it was stopping our powers. I made to step forward, but my body didn't move, paralysed in place. No. This wasn't supposed to happen. This was all wrong.

'What happened to calling me, Sir?' he mocked, pushing the blade towards Eliasson's throat. 'You should have known better, sweetheart. You picked your side, I've picked mine, and clearly only one of us chose correctly.'

His voice was cold. So cold. For all the love we'd shared, the ups and downs of our relationship, I'd never heard him talk quite like this. He had finally revealed the side everyone had warned me about, and I didn't recognise him.

'Why? Why do this?' Tears streamed down my face, betrayal taking over my body. Xylan's hands tightened on me.

'You think I'd allow him to have you? You think you're allowed to belong to anyone else? You were promised to me,' he spat out. His laugh was harsh. 'If I don't get you, nobody does,' he said possessively, his eyes firing with rage, a twinkle of emerald in those depths.

Before I could blink, he slit Eliasson's throat.

I could do nothing but stand there, magicless, paralysed in place. Forced to watch Eliasson's lifeless body drop to the ground.

EPILOGUE – XYLAN

TWO WEEKS EARLIER

Nervous anticipation. That's what I was feeling loud and clear as I closed my mental shields to everyone but her.

Her emotions were so strong it was hard to discern my own, the waves slamming into my very being. Was she nervous to meet me? Or did she simply hate these Royal Forums as much as I did?

Well. Hate may be a strong word for it. There was no avoiding them. Especially the previous one, made even more interesting with Valare in attendance with Eliasson. *Her husband*. I forced down the usual nausea at the thought of my True Infinite married to someone else. Being in someone else's bed. I shuddered.

Her marrying Eliasson was a necessary evil. It had gotten her out from under the thumb of the Salistyan Queendom and set her on her true path. But it still sucked from where I stood.

'Woah, Xy. Are you okay? There's a lot of passion coming off you right now.' Qynthia shivered with the influx of my emotions.

Oops. 'Sorry Qynth. Why don't you have your shields up?' I asked.

'You know as well as I do your power is too great to shut it down completely. Plus, I wanted to gauge a certain someone's reactions as we approached. Can you do me a favour and lock yourself up a bit tighter? And, why the foul mood suddenly? You're meeting her. Finally. Is this not supposed to be the best day of your life?' she asked. Those last words left her mouth on a dreamy sigh. She always was a hopeless romantic, and the idea of True Infinites was the pinnacle for her.

As the most powerful psychic mage of the age, my magic trumped any other mage's. If I wanted my emotions felt, I simply broke down their shield and made them feel it. My power was both a blessing and a curse. A blessing because, let's be honest, who didn't want to be the strongest and most skilled psychic mage? But when my emotions became turbulent like this, my control tended to slip, accidentally breaking through mental shields. It didn't happen often. But I had a feeling it would become more common while I was acquainting myself with Valare.

I cleared my throat as I tightened my shields. 'I'll try. But these next couple of weeks may be testing. I apologise in advance now. One has their first meeting with their True Infinite only once. And I've no idea how this is going to go down.' I didn't count the last Forum as meeting her, where I had to cast spells to remain invisible, unable to do anything as my father shamed Marlyst, putting a target on our backs. Nor did I count seeing her corporeal form in the Lull as a first meeting.

I nudged the horse into a faster pace as we rode along the last bit of the winding path before it straightened out. The Amarald Palace was straight ahead, three figures in the distance.

'We've got your back, bro,' Orlandia said from her horse, keeping pace with us. 'I, for one, can't wait to meet my future sister-in-law. Well, officially that is.' She threw me a rueful grin as I shook my head. She was a busy body who couldn't keep her nose out of my business. Though she always had the right intentions, her delivery was often questionable.

My arms wound around Qynthia, taking comfort in the familiarity of having my best friend next to me through this.

'Do you think it's a good look to be so close to me right now? I'm not sure it is a good first impression,' she murmured, turning her head to give me a knowing look.

My mouth twitched, fighting a smile. 'I want to see her reaction.'

'Evoking jealousy so early on, Your Highness?' Ramone teased.

'Some may say evoking jealousy, I say testing the waters. If what I've read about the True Infinite is correct, she should feel a pull almost instantly. Let's see how the pull fares when she sees me holding your Queen,' I said.

I wasn't sorry. I needed to gauge her power. She might be a physical mage, but her psychic magic would be brimming under the surface, waiting to escape. Just like my physical magic searched for its key,

As we approached the palace, I shifted my eyes to reflect those of a regular Marlyst. Only those in Marlyst and Nyarelle knew of my fuchsia eyes. I would keep it that way. For now.

'Ramone, are we clear on what needs to happen?' I asked.

As he nodded, a sense of foreboding fell on our group. 'I'm aware, Xy. Qynthia has briefed me on her vision. I'll do my part, as discussed.'

'Thank you,' I said. I couldn't manage more than that. The weight he had to carry in this was too much to ask of him. Yet he would do it with a smile on his face. He was a loyal man, always willing to fight in a cause bigger than himself.

'No need, Xy. It's a pleasure to serve Fyriane,' he said warmly. The sincerity in his voice brought a tear to my eye that I quickly pushed away. There would be time to cry. Today was not the day.

We approached the steps. Ramone and Orlandia dismounted their horses before handing them off to the stable hands.

Wanting Valare's first glimpse to be of me by myself, I stayed hidden behind Qynthia. I might be prodding the bear holding Qynthia, but I wasn't selfish enough to take this moment from her.

Sliding down the horse, I reached back, offering my hand to Qynthia as a wave of emotion pulsed from Valare. Desire. Intrigue. A flash of jealousy.

Qynthia's eyes sparkled with mischief as she murmured quietly, 'Want to bet five gold on her giving in to the attraction in the first seventy-two hours?' I burst out laughing. I kind of hoped it would be only seventy-two hours. She grinned as she took my hand, landing beside me.

As we started walking up the stairs, I allowed myself a quick glance at her as my eyes swept past the other royals. Good God she was beautiful. I groaned, leaning into Qynthia's side as I whispered into her ear, 'I bet ten gold that I'll give in to the attraction within the first twenty-four hours.' This brought a giggle out of Qynthia.

I felt jealousy and had to smother a delighted smile. Oh my, she didn't like that. Not one bit.

PAWNS OF SALISTYA

Her jealousy rivals yours, Qynthia's amused voice sounded in my head. Apparently, I'd lost control of my shields. Again.

'Qynthia, a pleasure as always,' said Eliasson as he kissed her cheek, stepping back and holding his hand out to me. 'King Xylan, it's a pleasure to finally meet you in person. Welcome to Arlom, I hope your travels were not too strenuous.' I had to give it to him, the guy was a good actor.

I took his hand, giving it a nice tight shake. 'The pleasure is all mine, King Eliasson. Thank you for graciously welcoming us to your Kingdom. Your land is a delight to be seen. I have a newfound appreciation for the delightful food that I enjoy courtesy of your farmers,' I replied smoothly, knowing that complimenting another ruler on their Dom was always the right move.

Desire reached me. Fuck. Apparently complimenting a Dom that wasn't her own was also the right move with Valare. Noted.

My eyes shifted to Valare as her sister stepped into view, cutting off Eliasson from introducing her. 'King Xylan, Queen Slaviya of Salistya. Pleasure to meet you.' I looked Valare's sister up and down, rudely shaking her outstretched hand. God, I hated this bitch. I stepped away. No way was she getting my lips on her knuckles, especially not after ruining my first look of her sister.

I turned back to look at the star of the show – in my eyes at least – and she was remarkable. The short teal dress she wore did nothing to hide her hardened nipples. They were begging me to clasp onto them, suck them until I had her quivering in my arms. She clearly wasn't a fan of underwear. I wasn't a fan of them on her either. Unless they were lacy. And it was the only thing she was wearing.

God I need to get it together. First impressions count. If I just looked at her face, it would be considered acceptable, right?

Her striking eyes contrasted beautifully with her olive skin. And that cute nose? It was asking for me to nip at it. I was screwed. I didn't even realise I thought noses were cute.

When those lime-coloured eyes finally met mine directly, a flash of familiarity raced through them. Good. The bond was there.

I stepped forward. 'You must be Valare?' I asked. It came out a bit huskier than intended, but it was worth it to see her cheeks redden as she grappled with the waves of longing I could feel.

'I am. It's very nice to meet you, King Xylan. Welcome to our home.'

Oh yes, I had expected that. She was fighting the pull alright.

Before I could control myself, I grabbed her hand and pressed it to my lips. The mark under my ear buzzed with delight and sent that feeling straight downstairs. 'Please, call me Xylan,' I insisted. No need for this King business. Unless she wanted to roleplay in the bedroom. Then maybe I could make an exception.

Her gasp broke me out of my dirty thoughts as our bodies broke physical contact. Damn. I was hungry for more. Desperate for it. I never wanted to let her go. Apparently Eliasson didn't either. His hand secured itself more firmly around her.

'Alright, Xylan.' She cleared her throat. I enjoyed that I made her nervous. 'Congratulations on, ah, the recent promotion. Sorry to hear about your father,' she rushed out. A look of regret and unease came over her immediately.

That made me laugh. So tactfulness wasn't her strong suite. 'Thank you, it's a pleasure to rule my Kingdom. And no need to be sorry, the God Merlot knows you're probably the only person in Fyriane to have thought his lack of presence a loss.' If her responding smile was anything to go by, I'd managed to put her at ease.

Bless Qynthia and her interjection as she did the rounds introducing herself and Ramone. I needed a moment to collect myself. As much as I'd planned and prepared myself for meeting her, I realised now that nothing would ever have fully prepared me for this. It was intense.

I appreciated her warmth when she responded to Ramone. She was relatable. No snobby queen here, not like her sister.

'And this is my sister Orlandia. Orlandia, this is Queen Slaviya, King Eliasson, and his wife Queen Valare,' I said as I waved my hand across the group in front of us nonchalantly. But really, I wanted to scream to the rooftops this was my True Infinite, and she would always be introduced first and not last. But I couldn't do that. Not yet anyway.

I didn't miss the suspicious look she threw at my sister. Nor did I miss the challenging expression Orlandia wore. God Merlot, help me. I didn't want to regret sending Orlandia to her earlier.

You need to calm down. Breathe. It'll all be okay, Qynthia said to me. She looped her arms through Valare's and Slaviya's, directing them toward the palace.

I followed suit as Eliasson stepped into line beside me, walking through the doors. 'Everything set on your end? Anything I need to be made aware of?' I asked.

'All good. Everything has gone to plan as per Qynthia's vision. I just need to ride it out at this point and put on the show of my life over the coming weeks,' he replied. He had a good poker face, but I wasn't buying it. Dropping down my shield, I felt his influx of feelings.

Nervousness. Excitement. Betrayal. Longing. Love.

Well, looks like some of it he wasn't acting. He loved her. Interesting.

The her in question I found myself staring at. Her body was toned to perfection, the hours training in the Isles showing. And that ass? I suppressed a groan. The way it moved as she took each step nearly did me in. This woman was a gift from the Gods. I was sure of it.

Her head swung around, her eyes pinned on mine. The physical mage in her probably felt me gawking at her like a pubescent teen. Well, I may as well own it. Can't blame me for appreciating the gorgeous sight in front of my eyes.

I threw her a wink, amused to see her stumble before she regained her composure, turning to face away from me.

Eliasson groaned next to me, rearranging his pants to hide his desire. 'That woman is going to be the fucking death of me.'

You and me both, buddy.

ACKNOWLEDGEMENTS

To Nathanael, thank you for pushing me to pursue my dream. Thank you for your unwavering support, love and being my cheerleader every step of the way. Without you, this book would not exist.

To Mum and Dad, the excitement and enthusiasm I received when I first discussed with you the world I wanted to create, prompted me to follow my gut and do this. Thank you.

To my dear friend Hannah, thank you for riding this crazy journey with me, for editing *Pawns of Salistya* in its early stages. Thank you for the laughs and putting up with my excited phone calls while I discussed plot lines, character development and everything Fyriane.

To Monique, for being the best friend a girl could ask for. Thank you for reading *Pawns of Salistya* throughout all its stages, for the hundreds of voice message updates as you were reading; you kept my spirits high and motivated me to continue. But above all, thank you for telling me to 'never stop writing', these words ring in my head more times than you will ever know.

To Kristina, where do I begin? Thank you for your support in the lead up to Pawns of Salistya's release. For staying up all hours of the night to not only help with line edits, but also teaching me along the way. For making me laugh when this publishing journey was so, so close to breaking me. For making my book 'shine'. I can't wait for the day when we are on the same continent, at the same author events, signing our books together. You are amazing.

To Eleanor, thank you for supporting me throughout this journey. You were the first friend to read my book in its entirety. I will forever be grateful for you.

To my editor Charlotte, thank you for your hard work, for helping me to view areas of this book in a different light. Your expertise and explanations have undoubtedly helped me grow as a writer. Thank you for helping me take *Pawns of Salistya* to the next level.

To Kev, Les and the team at Busybird Publishing, thank you for your patience and expertise in guiding me through the publishing process. Thank you for supporting indie authors in bringing their dreams to life.

To Erin, thank you for creating the map of Fyriane and the page break. You are one talented artist, my friend, and I am so thankful for the time you spent bringing my vision to life.

To Josh, thank you for creating the amazing cover for *Pawns of Salistya*.

To my family and friends, your support and help with promoting my book will forever be appreciated.

And to you, the reader, for picking up this book and taking a chance on me. There isn't an accurate word to describe the level of gratitude I have for you. None of this is possible without your support.

ABOUT THE AUTHOR

Hannah has been obsessed with fantasy romance books for as long as she can remember. In her early twenties, she was camping on the sunshine coast in beautiful British Columbia when she turned to her friend and said, 'I would love to write a book, I feel there is so much going on in my head and there are stories that need to be told.' Fast forward a handful of years, Hannah resides in her hometown of Perth, WA, with her partner, and fur babies Walter, Loki and Ridley. She finally watered the seed she planted all those years ago, and her imagination bloomed.

#Fyrianebookhunt

LET'S KEEP IN TOUCH!

To stay up-to-date on new releases, receive bonus chapters and upcoming event dates, sign up to my newsletter at my website:

www.hjbogue.com.au

@hjbogue

@hjbogue

Printed in Australia
Ingram Content Group Australia Pty Ltd
AUHW022334131024
401182AU00002B/5

9 781923 216204